The
WAGES
of
VIRTUE

by
PERCIVAL
CHRISTOPHER
WREN

HARLEQUIN BOOKS
TORONTO · WINNIPEG

THIS HARLEQUIN BOOK

edition is published by arrangement with

JOHN MURRAY (PUBLISHERS) LTD. London, England

Harlequin Edition Published

March, 1953

Printed in Canada

PROLOGUE

LORD HUNTINGTEN EMERGED FROM his little green tent, and strolled over to where Captain Strong, of the Queen's African Rifles sat, in the "drawing-room." The drawing-room was the space under a cedar fir and was furnished with four Roorkee chairs of green canvas and white wood, and a waterproof ground-sheet.

"I do wish the Merlines would roll up," he said. "I want my dinner."

"Not dinner time yet," remarked Captain Strong. "Hungry?"

"No," answered Lord Huntingten almost snappishly. Captain Strong smiled. How old Reggie Huntingten always gave himself away! It was the safe return of Lady Merline that he wanted.

Captain Strong, although a soldier, the conditions of whose life were almost those of perpetual Active Service, was a student—and particularly a student of human nature. Throughout a life of great activity he found, and made, much opportunity for sitting in the stalls of the Theatre of Life and enjoying the Human Comedy. This East African shooting-trip with Lord Huntingten, Sir Montague, and Lady Merline, was affording him great entertainment, inasmuch as Huntingten had fallen in love with Lady Merline and did not know it. Lady Merline was falling in love with Huntingten and knew it only too well, and Merline loved them both. That there would be no sort or kind of "dénouement," in the vulgar sense, Captain Strong was well and gladly aware—for Huntingten was as honourable a man as ever lived, and Lady Merline just as admirable. No saner, wiser, nor better woman had Strong ever met, nor any as well balanced.

"Merline shouldn't keep her out after dusk like this," continued Lord Huntingten. "After all, Africa's Africa and a woman's a woman."

"And Merline's Merline," added Strong with a faint hint of reproof. Lord Huntingten grunted, arose, and strode up and down. A fine upstanding figure of a man in the exceedingly becoming garb of khaki cord riding-breeches, well-cut high boots, brown flannel shirt and broad-brimmed felt hat. Although his hands were small, the arms exposed by the rolled-up shirt-sleeves were those of a navvy, or a black-smith. The face, though tanned and wrinkled, was finely cut and undeniably handsome, with its high-bridged nose, piercing blue eyes, fair silky moustache and prominent chin. Captain Strong, watching him with malicious affection, was reminded of a petulant baby and again of a big naughty boy who, having been stood in the corner for half an hour, firmly believes that the half-hour has long ago expired. What would Huntingten do when he realised his condition and position? Run for his life, or grin and bear it? If the former, where would he go? If, living in Mayfair and falling in love with your neighbour's wife, the correct thing is to go and shoot lions in East Africa, is it, conversely, the correct thing to go and live in Mayfair if, shooting lions in East Africa, you fall in love with your neighbour's wife? Captain Strong smiled at his whimsicality, and show-ed his interesting face at its best.

A huge Swahili orderly of the Queen's African Rifles, clad in a tall yellow tarboosh, a very long blue jersey, khaki shorts, blue puttees and hobnail boots, approached Captain Strong and saluted. He announced that Merline *Bwana* was approaching, and, on Strong's replying that such things did happen, and even with sufficient frequency to render the widest publication of the fact unnecessary, the man informed him that the *macouba Bwana Simba* (the big Lion Master) had given his bearer orders to have the approach of Merline *Bwana* signalled and announced.

Turning to Huntingten, Strong bade that agitated noble-man to be of good cheer, for Merline was safe—his *askaris* were safe—his pony was safe, and it was even reported that all the dogs were safe.

"Three loud cheers," observed his lordship, as his face beamed ruddily, "but, to tell you the truth, it was of *Lady* Merline I was thinking. . . . You never know in Africa, you know. . . ."

Captain Strong smiled.

Sir Montague and Lady Merline rode into camp on their Arab ponies a few minutes later, and there was a bustle of Indian and Swahili "boys" and bearers, about the unlacing of tents, preparing of hot baths, the taking of ponies and guns, and the hurrying up of dinner.

While Sir Montague gave orders concerning the *enyama*[1] for the *safari* servants and porters, whose virtue had merited this addition to their *posho*,[2] Lady Merline entered the "drawing-room," and once again gladdened the heart of Lord Huntingten with her grace and beauty. He struck an attitude, laid his hand upon his heart, and swept the ground with his slouch hat in a most gracefully executed bow. Lady Merline, albeit clad in brief khaki shooting-costume, puttees, tiny hobnail boots, and brown pith helmet, returned the compliment with a Court curtsey.

Their verbal greeting hardly sustained the dignity of the preliminaries.

"How's Bill the Lamb?" quoth the lady.

"How's Margarine?" was the reply.

Sir Montague Merline joined the group.

"Hallo, Bill! Hallo, Strong!" he remarked. "I say, Strong, what's *marodi*, and what's *gisi* in Somali?"

"Same as *tembo* and *mbogo* in Swahili," was the reply.

"Oh! Elephant and buffalo. Well, that one-eyed Somali blighter with the corrugated forehead, whom Abdul brought in, says there are both—close to Bamania over there—about thirteen miles you know."

"He's a liar then," replied Captain Strong.

"Swears the elephants went on the tiles all night in a *shamba*[3] there, the day before yesterday."

"Might go that way, anyhow," put in Lord Huntingten. "Take him with us, and rub his nose in it if there's nothing."

"*You're* nothing if not lucid, Bill," said Lady Merline. "I'm off to change," and added as she turned away, "I vote we go to Bamania anyhow. There may be lemons, or mangoes, or bananas or something in the *shamba*, if there are no elephants or buffaloes."

"Dinner in twenty minutes, Monty," said Captain Strong to Sir Montague Merline and departed to his tent.

"I say, Old Thing, dear," observed Lord Huntingten to the same gentleman, as, with the tip of his little finger, he "wangled' a soda-water bottle with a view of concocting a whisky-and-soda. "We won't let Marguerite have anything to do with elephant or buffalo, will we?"

---

[1] Meat. [2] Food. [3] Garden. Cultivation.

"Good Lord, no!" was the reply. "We've promised her one pot at a lion if we can possibly oblige, but that will have to be her limit, and, what's more, you and I will be one each side of her when she does it."

"Yes," agreed the other, and added, "Except I shall know what nerves are, when it comes off, too."

"Fancy 'nerves' and the *Bwana Simba*," laughed Sir Montague Merline as he held out his glass for the soda. . . . "Here's to Marguerite's first lion," he continued, and the two men solemnly drank the toast.

Sir Montague Merline struck a match for his pipe, the light illuminating his face in the darkness which had fallen in the last few minutes. The first impression one gathered from the face of Captain Sir Montague Merline, of the Queen's African Rifles, was one of unusual gentleness and kindliness. Without being in a way a weak face, it was an essentially friendly and amiable one—a soldierly face without any hint of that fierce harsh and ruthless expression which is apparently cultivated as part of their stock-in trade by the professional soldiers of militarist nations. A physiognomist, observing him, would not be surprised to learn of quixotic actions and a reputation for being "such an awful good chap—one of the best-hearted fellers that ever helped a lame dog over a stile." So far as such a thing can be said of any strong and honest man who does his duty, it could be said of Sir Montague Merline that he had no enemies. Contrary to the dictum that "He who has no enemies has no friends" was the fact that Sir Montague Merline's friends were all who knew him. Of these, his best and closest friend was his wife, and it had been reserved for Lord Huntingten unconsciously to appraise her of the fact that she was this and nothing more. Until he had left his yacht at Mombasa a few weeks before, on the invitation of Captain Strong (issued with their cordial consent) to join their projected shooting trip, Lady Merline had fondly imagined that she knew what love was, and had thought herself a thoroughly happy and contented woman. In a few days after his joining the party it seemed that she must have loved him all her life, and that there could not possibly be a gulf of some fifteen years between then and the childish days when he was "Bill the Lamb" and she the unconsidered adjunct of the nursery and schoolroom, generally addressed as "Margerine." Why had he gone wandering about the world all these years? Why had their re-discovery of each other had to be postponed until now? Why couldn't he have been at home when Monty came wooing and . . . When Lady Merline's thoughts reached this point she resolutely switched them off. She was doing a considerable amount of switching off, these last few days, and realised that when Lord Huntingten awoke to the fact that he too must practise this exercise, the shooting trip would have come to an untimely end. As she crouched over the tiny candle-lit mirror on the *soi-disant* dressing-table in her tent, while hastily changing for dinner that evening, she even considered plausible ways and possible means of terminating the trip when the inevitable day arrived.

She was saved the trouble.

As they sat at dinner a few minutes later, beneath the diamond-studded velvet of the African sky—an excellent dinner of clear soup, sardines, bustard, venison, and tinned fruit—Strong's orderly again appeared in the near distance, saluting and holding two official letters in his hand. These, it appeared, had just been brought by messenger from the railway-station some nineteen miles distant.

Captain Strong was the first to gather their import, and his feeling of annoyance and disappointment was more due to the fact of the interruption of his interesting little drama than to the cancellation of his leave and return to harness.

"Battle, Murder and Sudden Death!" he murmured. "I wish people wouldn't kill people, and cause other people to interfere with the arrangements of people. . . . Our trip's bust."

"What is it?" asked Lady Merline.

"Mutiny and murder down Uganda way," replied her husband, whose letter was a duplicate. "I'm sorry Hunting-ten, old chap," he added, turning to his friend. "We must get to the railway to-morrow—there will be a train through in the afternoon. . . . Better luck next time."

Lord Huntingten looked at Lady Merline, and Lady Merline looked at her plate.

Down the narrowest of narrow jungle-paths marched a small party of the Queen's African Rifles. They marched, perforce, in single file, and at their head was their white officer. A wiser man would have marched in the middle, for the leading man was inevitably bound to "get it" if they came upon the enemy, and, albeit brave and warlike men, negroes of the Queen's African Rifles (like other troops) fight better when commanded by an officer. A "point" of a sergeant and two or three men, a couple of hundred yards in front, is all very well, but the wily foe in ambush knows quite enough to take, as it were, the cash and let the credit go—to let the "point' march on, and to wait for the main body.

Captain Sir Montague Merline was well aware of the unwisdom and military inadvisability of heading the long file, but did it, nevertheless. If called upon to defend his conduct, he would have said that what was gained by the alleged wiser course was more than lost, inasmuch as the confidence of the men is so discreet a leader would not be, to say the least of it, enhanced. The little column moved silently and slowly through the horrible place, a stinking swamp, the atmosphere almost unbreathable, the narrow winding track almost untreadable, the enclosing walls of densest jungle utterly impenetrable—a singularly undesirable spot in which to be attacked by a cunning and blood-thirsty foe of whom this was the "native heath."

Captain Merline put his hand to the breast pocket of his khaki flannel shirt for his whistle, with a faint short blast on which he would signal to his "point" to halt. The whistle never reached his lips. A sudden ragged crash of musketry rang out from the dense vegetation on either side, and from surrounding trees which commanded and enfiladed the path. More than half the little force fell at the first discharge, for it is hard to miss a man with a Snider or a Martini-Henry rifle at three yards' range. For a moment there was confusion, and more than one of those soldiers of the Queen, it must be admitted, fired off his rifle at nothing in particular. A burly sergeant, bringing up the rear, thrust his way to the front shouting an order, and the survivors of the first murderous burst of fire crouched down on either side of the track and endeavoured to force their way into the jungle, form a line on either side, and fire volleys to their left, front and right. Having made his way to the head of the column, Sergeant Isa ibn Yakub found his officer shot through the head, chest and thigh. . . . A glance was sufficient. With a loud click of his tongue he turned away with a look of murderous hate on his ebony face and the lust of slaughter in his rolling yellow eye. He saw a leafy twip fall from a tree that overhung the path and crouched motionless, staring at the spot. Suddenly he raised his rifle and fired, and gave a hoarse shout of glee as a body fell crashing to the ground. In the same second his tarboosh was spun from his head and the shoulder of his blue jersey torn as by an invisible clay. He too wriggled into the undergrowth and joined the volley-firing, which, sustained long enough and sufficiently generously and impartially distributed, must assuredly damage a neighbouring foe and hinder his approach. Equally assuredly it must, however, lead to exhaustion of ammunition, and when the volley-firing slackened and died away, it was for this reason. Sergeant Isa ibn Yakub was a man of brains and resource, as well as of dash and courage. Since the enemy had fallen silent too, he would emerge with his men and collect the ammunition from their dead and wounded comrades. He blew a number of short shrill blasts on the whistle which, with the stripes upon his arm, was the proudest of his possessions.

The ammunition was quickly collected and the worthy Sergeant possessed himself of his dead officer's revolver and cartridges. . . . The next step? If he attempted to remove his wounded, his whole effective force would become stretcher-bearers and still be inadequate to the task. If he abandoned his wounded, should he advance or retire? He would rather fight a lion or three Masai than have to answer these conundrums and shoulder these responsibilities. . . . He was relieved of all necessity in the matter of deciding, for the brooding silence was again suddenly broken by ear-piercing and blood-curdling howls and a second sudden fusillade, as, at some given signal, the enemy burst into the track both before and behind the column. Obviously they were skilfully handled and by one versed in the art of jungle war. The survivors of the little force were completely surrounded—and the rest was rather a massacre than a fight. Sergeant Isa ibn Yakub did his utmost and fought like the lion-hearted warrior he was. It is some satisfaction to know that the one man who escaped and made his way to the temporary base of the little columns to tell the story of the destruction of this particular force, was Sergeant Isa ibn Yakub.

One month later a Lieutenant was promoted to Captain Sir Montague Merline's post, and, twelve months later, Lord Huntingten married his wife.

Captain Strong of the Queen's African Rifles, home on furlough, was best man at the wedding of the handsome and popular Lord Huntingten with the charming and beautiful Lady Merline.

3

At about the same time as the fashionable London press announced to a more or less interested world the more or less important news that Lady Huntingten had presented her lord and master with a son and heir, a small *safari* swung into a tiny African village and came to a halt. The naked Kavarondo porters flung down their loads with grunts and cluckings, and sat them down a huddled mass of smelly humanity. From a litter borne in the middle of the caravan, stepped the leader of the party, one Doctor John Williams, a great (though unknown) surgeon, a medical missionary who gave his life and unusual talents, skill, and knowledge to the alleviation of the miseries of black humanity.

Doctor John Williams looked around at the village to which Fate brought him for the first time, and beheld the usual scene—a collection of huts built of poles and grass, and a few superior dwelling-places with thatched walls and roofs. A couple of women were pounding grain in a wooden mortar; a small group of others was engaged in a kind of rude basket weaving under the porch of a big hut; a man seated by a small fire had apparently "taken up" poker work, for he was decorating a vase-shaped gourd by means of a red-hot iron; a gang of tiny naked piccaninnies with incredibly distended stomachs, was playing around a . . .

What?

Dr. John Williams strode over to the spot. A white man, or the ruin of a sort of a white man, was seated on a native stool and leaning against the bole of one of the towering palms that embowered, shaded, concealed and enriched the little village. His hair was very long and grey, his beard and moustache were long and grey, his face was burnt and bronzed, his eyes blue and bright. On his head were the deplorable ruins of a khaki helmet, and, for the rest, he wore the rags and remains of a pair of khaki shorts. Dr. John Williams stood and stared at him in open-mouthed astonishment. He arose and advanced with extended hand. The doctor was too astounded to speak, and the other could not, for he was dumb. In a minute it was obvious to the newcomer that he was more—that he was in some way "wanting."

From the headman of the villagers, who quickly gathered round, he learned that the white man had been with them for "many nights and days and seasons," that he was afflicted of the gods, very wise, and as a little child. Why "very wise" Dr. John Williams failed to discover, or anything more of the man's history, save that he had simply walked into the village from nowhere in particular and had sat under that tree, all day, ever since. They had given him a hut, milk, corn, cocoanut, and whatever else they had. Also, in addition to this propitiation, they had made a minor god of him, with worship of the milder sorts. Their wisdom and virtue in this particular had been rewarded by him with a period of marked prosperity; and undoubtedly their crops, their cattle, and their married women had benefited by his benevolent presence. . . .

When Doctor John Williams resumed his journey he took the dumb white man with him, and, in due course, reached his own mission, dispensary and wonderful little hospital a few months later. Had he considered that there was any urgency in the case, and the time-factor of any importance, he would have abandoned his sleeping-sickness tour, and gone direct to the hospital to operate upon the skull of his foundling. For this great (and unknown), surgeon, upon examination, had decided that the removal of a bullet which was lodged beneath the scalp and in the solid bone of the top of the man's head was the first, and

11

probably last, step in the direction of the restoration of speech and understanding. Obviously he was in no pain, and he was not mad, but his brain was that of a child whose age was equal to the time which had elapsed since the wound was caused. Probably this had happened about a couple of years ago, for the brain was equal to that of a two-year-old child.

The first few days after his return to his headquarters were always exceedingly busy ones for the doctor. The number of things able to "go wrong" in his absence was incredible, and, as he was the only white man resident in a district some ten thousand square miles in area, the accumulation of work and trouble was sufficient to appal most people. But work and trouble were what the good doctor sought and throve on. . . . One piece of good news there was, however, in the tale of calamities. A pencilled note, scribbled on a leaf of a military pocket-book, informed him that his old friend Strong, of the Queen's African Rifles, had passed through his village three weeks earlier, and would again pass through, on his return, in a week's time.

Good! A few days of Strong's company would be worth a lot. A visit from any white man was something; from a man of one's own class and kind was a great thing; but from worldly-wise, widely-read, clever old Strong! . . . Excellent!

4

Captain Strong, of the Queen's African Rifles, passed from the strong sunlight into the dark coolness of Doctor John Williams' bungalow side by side with his host, who was still shaking him by the hand, in his joy and affection. Laying his riding-whip and helmet on a table he glanced round, stared, turned as white as a sunburnt man may, ejaculated "Oh, my God!" and seized the doctor's arm. His mouth hung open, his eyes were starting from his head, and it was with shaking hand that he pointed to where, in the doctor's living-room, sat the dumb and weak-witted foundling.

Doctor Williams was astounded and mightily interested. "What's up, Strong?" he asked.

"B—b—b—but he's *dead!*" stammered Strong with a gasp.

"Not a bit of it, man," was the reply, "he's as alive as you or I. He's dumb, and he's dotty, but he's alive all right . . . What's wrong with you? You've got a touch of the sun . . ." and then Captain Strong was himself again. If Captain Montague Merline, late of the Queen's African Rifles, were alive, it would not be Jack Strong who would announce the fact . . .

Strong turned and dragged his host out of the room. "Where's he come from?" he asked quickly. "Who is he?"

"Where he came from last," replied the doctor, "is a village called, I believe, Bwongo, about a hundred and twenty miles south-east of here. How he got there I can't tell you. The natives said he just walked up unaccompanied, unwounded, unpursued. He's got a bullet or something in the top of his head and I'm going to lug it out. And then, my boy, with any luck at all, he'll very soon be able to answer you any question you like to put him. Speech and memory will return at the moment the pressure on the brain ceases."

"Will he remember up to the time the bullet hit him, or since, or both?" asked Strong.

"All his life, up to the moment the bullet him him, certainly," was the reply. "What happened since will, at first, be remembered as a dream, probably. If I had to prophesy I should say he'd take up his life from the second in which the bullet hit him, and think, for the moment, that he is still where it happened. By-and-by, he'll realise that there's a gap somewhere, and gradually he'll be able to fill it in with events which will seem half nightmare, half real."

"Anyhow, he'll be certain of his identity and personal history and so forth?" asked Strong.

"Absolutely," said the surgeon. "It will be precisely as though he awoke from an ordinary night's rest . . . . It'll be awfully interesting to hear him give an account of himself . . . All this, of course, if he doesn't die under the operation."

"I hope he will," said Strong.

"What *do* you mean, my dear chap?"

"I hope he'll die under the operation."

"Why?"

"He'll be better dead. . . . And it will be better for

three other people that he should be dead. . . . Is he likely to die?"

"I should say it's ten to one he'll pull through all right . . . . What's it all about, Strong?"

"Look here, old chap," was the earnest reply. "If it were anybody else but you I shouldn't know what to say or do. As it's *you*, my course is clear, for you're the last thing in discretion, wisdom and understanding. . . But don't ask me his name. . . . I know him. . . . Look here, it's like this. His wife's married again. . . . There's a kid. . . . They're well known in Society. . . . Awful business. . . . Ghastly scandal. . . . Shockin' position." Captain Strong took Doctor John Williams by the arm. "Look here, old chap," he said once again. "Need you do this? It isn't as though he was 'conscious,' so to speak, and in pain."

"Yes, I must do it," replied the doctor without hesitation, as the other paused.

"But why?" urged Strong. "I'm absolutely certain that if M——, er—that is—this chap—could have his faculties for a minute he would tell you not to do it. . . . You'll take him from a sort of negative happiness to the most positive and acute unhappiness, and you'll simply blast the lives of his wife and the most excellent chap she's married. . . . She waited a year after this chap 'died' in—er—that last Polar expedition—as was supposed. . . . Think of the poor little kid too. . . . And there's estates and a ti——so on. . . ."

"No good, Strong. My duty in the matter is perfectly clear, and it is to the sick man, as such."

"Well, you'll do a damned cruel thing . . er—sorry, old chap, I mean *do* think it over a bit and look at it from the point of view of the unfortunate lady, the second husband, and the child. . . . And of the chap himself. . . . By God! He won't thank you."

"I look at it from the point of view of the doctor and I'm not out for thanks," was the reply.

"Is that your last word, Williams?"

"It is. I have here a man mentally maimed, mangled and suffering. My first and only duty is to heal him, and I shall do it."

"Right O!" replied Strong, who knew that further words

would be useless. He knew that his friend's intelligence was clear as crystal and his will as firm, and that he accepted no other guide than his own conscience. . . .

"Yes, I fully understand and I give you my solemn promise, Strong," said the doctor as the two men rose to go in, that night. "The moment the man is sane I will tell him that he is not to tell me his name, nor anything else until he has heard what I have to say. I will then break it to him—using my own discretion as to how and when—that he was reported dead, that his will was proved, that his widow wore mourning for a year and then married again, and had a son a year later. . . . I undertake that he shall not leave this house, *knowing that,* unless he is in the fullest possession of his faculties and able to realize with the utmost clearness *all* the bearings of the case and *all* the consequences following his resumption of identity. And I'll let him hide here for just as long as he cares to conceal himself—if he wishes to remain 'dead' for a time."

"Yes . . . And as I can't possibly stay till he recovers, nor, in fact, over to-morrow without gross dereliction of duty, I will leave a letter for you to give him at the earliest safe moment. . . . I'll tell him that I am the only living soul who knows his name as well as his secret. He'll understand that no one else will know this—from me."

As he sat on the side of his bed that night, Captain Strong remarked unto his soul, "Well—one thing—if I know Monty Merline as well as I think, 'Sir Montague Merline' died two years ago, whatever happens. . . . And yet I can't imagine Monty committing suicide, somehow. He's a chap with a conscience as well as the soul of chivalry. . . . Poor, poor, old Monty Merline! . . ."

CHAPTER ONE

SOAP AND SIR MONTAGUE MERLINE

Sir Montague Merline, second-class private soldier of
the First Battalion of the Foreign Legion of France, paused
to straighten his back, to pass his bronzed forearm across
his white forehead, and to put his scrap of soap into his
mouth—the only safe receptacle for the precious morsel,
the tiny cake issued once a month by Madame la République to the Legionary for all his washing purposes. When
one's income is precisely one halfpenny a day (paid when
it has totalled up to the sum of twopence halfpenny), one
does not waste much, nor risk the loss of valuable property; and to lay a piece of soap upon the concrete of *Le
Cercle d'Enfer* reservoir, is not so much to risk the loss
of it as to lose it, when one is surrounded by gentlemen
of the Foreign Legion. Let me not be misunderstood, nor
supposed to be casting aspersions upon the said gentlemen,
but their need for soap is urgent, their income is one halfpenny a day, and soap is of the things with which one
may "decorate oneself" without contravening the law of
the Legion. To steal is to steal, mark you (and to deserve, and probably to get a bayonet through the offending hand, pinning it to the bench or table), but to borrow certain specified articles permanently and without
permission is merely, in the curious slang of the Legion,
"to decorate oneself."

Contrary to what the uninitiated might suppose, *Le
Cercle d'Enfer*—the Circle of Hell—is not a dry, but a
very wet place, it being, in point of fact, the *lavabo* where
the Legionaries of the French Foreign Legion stationed in
Algeria at Sidi-bel-Abbés, daily wash their white fatigue
uniforms and occasionally their underclothing.

Sir Montague Merline did not put his precious morsel
of soap into his pocket, for the excellent reason that there
was no pocket to the single exiguous garment he was at
the moment wearing—a useful piece of material which in
its time played many parts, and knew the service of duster,
towel, turban, tablecloth, polishing pad, tea-cloth, house-
flannel, apron, handkerchief, neckerchief, curtain, servi-
ette, holder, fly-slayer, water-strainer, punkah, and, at the
moment, nether garment. Having *cached* his soap and

having observed *"Peste!"* as he savoured its flavour, he proceeded to pommel, punch, and slap upon the concrete, the greyish-white tunic and breeches, and the cotton vest and shirt which he had generously soaped before the hungry eyes of numerous soapless but oathful fellow-labourers, who less successfully sought that virtue which, in the Legion, is certainly next to, but far ahead of, mere godliness.

In due course, Sir Montague Merline rinsed his garments in the reservoir, wrung them out, bore them to the nearest clothes-line, hung them out to dry, and sat himself down in their shadow to stare at them unwaveringly until dried by the fierce sun—the ancient enemy, for the moment an unwilling friend. To watch them unwaveringly and intently because he knew that the turning of his head for ten seconds might mean their complete and final disappearance—for, like soap, articles of uniform are on the list of things with which a Legionary may "decorate" himself, if he can, without incurring the odium of public opinion. (He may steal any article of equipment, clothing, kit, accoutrement, or general utility, but his patron saint help him and Le Bon Dieu be merciful to him, if he be caught stealing tobacco, wine, food, or money.)

Becoming aware of the presence of Monsieur le Legionnaire Edouard Malvin, Sir Montague Merline increased the vigilance of his scrutiny of his pendent property, for ce cher Edouard was of pick-pockets the very prince and magician; of those who could steal the teeth from a Jew while he sneezed and would steal the scalp from their grandmamma while she objected.

"Ohé! Jean Boule, lend me thy soap," besought this stout and dapper little Austrian, who for some reason pretended to be a Belgian from the Congo. "This cursed alfa-fibre gets dirtier the more you wash it in this cursed water," and he smiled a greasy and ingratiating grin.

Without for one second averting his steady stare from his clothes, the Englishman slowly removed the soap from his mouth, expectorated, remarked *"Peudezébie,"*[1] and took no further notice of the quaint figure which stood by his side, clad only in an ancient red Zouave breeches and the ingratiating smile.

---

[1] An emphatic negative.

"Name of a Name! Name of the Name of a Pipe! Name of the Name of a Dirty Little Furry Red Monkey!" observed Monsieur le Légionnaire Edouard Malvin as he turned to slouch away, twirling the dripping grey-white tunic.

"Meaning me?" asked Sir Montague, replacing the soap in its safe repository and preparing to rise.

"But no! But not in the least, old cabbage. Thou hast the *cafard*. Mais oui, tu as le cafard," replied the Belgian and quickened his retreat.

No, the grey Jean Boule, so old, so young, doyen of Légionnaires, so quick, strong, skilful and enduring at *la boxe* was not the man to cross at any time, and least of all when he had *le cafard*, that terrible Legion madness that all Legionaries know; the madness that drives them to the cells, to gaol, to the Zephyrs, to the firing-party by the open grave; or to desertion and death in the desert. The grey Jean Boule had been a Zephyr of the Penal Battalions once, already, for killing a man, and Monsieur Malvin, although a Legionary for the Foreign Legion, did not wish to die. No, not while Carmelita and Madame la Cantinière lived and loved and sold the good Algiers wine at three-halfpence a bottle. . . . No, bon sang de sort!

M. le Légionnaire Malvin returned to the dense ring of labouring perspiring washers, and edged in behind a gigantic German and a short, broad, burly Alsatian, capitalists as joint proprietors of a fine cake of soap.

Légionnaire Hans Schnitzel, late of Berlin, rinsed his washing in clean water, wrung it, and took it to the nearest drying line. Légionnaire Alphonse Dupont, late of Alsace, placed his soap in the pocket of the dirty white fatigue-uniform which he wore, and which he would wash as soon as he had finished the present job. Immediately, Légionnaire Edouard Malvin transferred the soap from the side pocket of the tunic of the unconscious Légionnaire Alphonse Dupont to that of his own red breeches, and straightway begged the loan of it.

"*Merde!*" replied Dupont. "Nombril de Belzébuth! I will lend it thee *peaudezébie*. Why should I lend thee soap, *vieux dégoutant?* Go decorate thyself, *sale cochon*. Besides 'tis not mine to lend."

"And that is very true," agreed M. Malvin, and sauntered toward Schnitzel, who stood phlegmatically guarding his drying clothes. In his hand was an object which caused the eyebrows of the good M. Malvin to arch and rise, and his mouth to water—nothing less than an actual, real and genuine scrubbing-brush, beautiful in its bristliness. Then righteous anger filled his soul.

"Saligaud!" he hissed. "These pigs of filthy Germans! Soap and a brush. Sacripants! Ils me dégoutant à la fin."

As he regarded the stolid German with increasing envy, hatred, malice and all uncharitableness, and cast about in his quick and cunning mind for means of relieving him of the coveted brush, a sudden roar of wrath and grief from his Alsatian partner, Dupont, sent Schnitzel running to join that unfortunate man in fierce and impartial denunciations of his left-hand and right-hand neighbours, who were thieves, pigs, brigands, dogs, Arabs, and utterly *merdant* and *merdable*. Bursting into the fray Herr Schnitzel found them, in addition, *bloedsinnig* and *dummkopf* in that they could not produce cakes of soap from empty mouths.

As the rage of the bereaved warriors increased, more and more Pomeranian and Alsatian patois invaded the wonderful Legion-French, a French which is not of Paris, nor of anywhere else in the world save La Légion. As Dupont fell upon a laughing Italian with a cry of "Ah! zut! Sacré grimacier," Schnitzel spluttered and roared at a huge slow-moving American who regarded him with a look of pitying but not unkindly contempt. . . .

"Why do the 'eathen rage furious *together* and *imagine* a vain thing?" he enquired in a slow drawl of the excited "furriner," adding "Ain't yew some *schafs-kopf,* sonny!" and, as the big German began to whirl his arms in the windmill fashion peculiar to the non-boxing foreigner who meditates assault and battery, continued—

"Now yew stop *zanking* and playing *verteckens* with me, yew pie-faced Squarehead, and be *schnell* about it, or yew'll git my goat, see? *Vous obtiendrez mon chèvre,* yew perambulating *prachtvoll bierhalle,*" and he coolly turned his back upon the infuriated German with a polite, if laborious, "Guten tag, mein Freund."

Mr. Hiram Cyrus Milton (late of Texas, California, the Yukon, and the "main drag" generally of the wild and woolly West) was exceeding proud of his linguistic knowledge and skill. It may be remarked, *en passant*, that his friends were even prouder of it.

At this moment, le bon Légionnaire Malvin, hovering for opportunity, with a sudden *coup de savate* struck the so-desirable scrubbing-brush from the hand of Herr Schnitzel with a force that seemed to like to take the arm from the shoulder with it. Leaping round with a yell of pain, the unfortunate German found himself, as Malvin had calculated, face to face with the mighty Luigi Rivoli, to attack whom was to be brought to death's door through that of the hospital.

Snatching up the brush which was behind Schnitzel when he turned to face Rivoli, le bon M. Malvin lightly departed from the vulgar scuffle in the direction of the drying clothes of Herren Schnitzel and Dupont, the latter, last seen clasping, with more enthusiasm than love, a wiry Italian to his bosom. The luck of M. Malvin was distinctly in, for not only had he the soap and a brush for the easy cleansing of his own uniform, but he had within his grasp a fresh uniform to wear, and another to sell; for the clothing of ce bon Dupont would fit him to a marvel, while that of the pig-dog Schnitzel would fetch good money, the equivalent of several litres of the thick, red Algerian wine, from a certain Spanish Jew, old Haroun Mendoza, of the Sidi-bel-Abbès ghetto.

With a purr of pleasure, a positive licking of chops, and a murmur of "Ah! Au tient frais," he deftly whipped the property of the embattled Legionaries from the line, no man saying nay. For it is not the etiquette of the Legion to interfere with one who, in the absence of its owner would "decorate" himself with any of those things with which self-decoration is permissible, if not honourable. Indeed, to Sir Montague Merline, sitting close by, and regarding his proceedings with cold impartial eye, M. Malvin observed— " 'Y a de bon, mon salop! I have heard that le bon Dieu helps those who help themselves. I do but help myself in order to give le bon Dieu the opportunity He doubtless desires. I decorate myself incidentally. Mais oui, and I shall decorate myself this evening with a p'tite ouvrière, and tomorrow with une réputation d'ivrogne," and he turned innocently to saunter with his innocent bundle of washing from the *lavabo*, to his *caserne*. Ere he had taken half a dozen steps the cold and quiet voice of the grey Jean Boule broke in upon the resumed day-dreams of the innocently sauntering M. Malvin.

"Might one aspire to the honour of venturing to detain for a brief interview Monsieur le Légionnaire Edouard Malvin?" said the soft metallic voice.

"But certainly, and without charge, mon gars," replied that gentleman, turning and eyeing the incomprehensible and dangerous Jean Boule, *à coin de l'oeil*.

"You seek soap?"

"I do," replied the Austrian "Belgian" promptly. The possession of one cake of soap makes that of another no less desirable.

"Do you seek sorrow also?"

"But no, dear friend. 'J'ai eu toutes les folies.' In this world I seek but wine, woman, and peace. Let me avoid the 'gros bonnets' and lead my happy humble life in peaceful obscurity."

"Then, cher Malvin, since you seek soap and not sorrow, let not my little cake of soap disappear from beneath the polishing-rags in my sack. The little brown sack at the head of my cot, cher Malvin. Enfin! I appoint you guardian and custodian of my little cake of soap. But in a most evil hour for le bon M. Malvin would it disappear. Guard it then, cher Malvin. Respect it. Watch over it as you value, and would retain, your health and beauty, M. Malvin. And when *I* have avenged *my* little piece of soap, the true history of the last ten minutes will deeply interest those earnest searchers after truth, Legionaries Schnitzel and Dupont. Depart in peace and enter upon your new office of Guardian of my Soap! Vous devez en être joliment fier."

"Quite a speech, in effect mon drôle," replied the stout Austrian as he doubtfully fingered his short beard *au poinçon*, and added uneasily, "I am not the only gentleman who 'decorates' himself with soap."

"No? Nor with uniforms. Go in peace, Protector of my Soap."

Removing his almost dry washing from the line, Sir Montague Merline marched across to his barrack-block, climbed the three flights of stone stairs, traversed the long corridor of his company, and entered the big, light, airy room wherein he and twenty-nine other Legionnaires (one

21

of whom held the very exalted and important rank of *Caporal*) lived and moved and had their monotonous being.

Spreading his tunic and breeches on the end of the long table he proceeded to "iron" them, first with his hand, secondly with a tin plate, and finally with the edge of his "quart," the drinking-mug which hung at the head of his bed ready for the reception of the early morning *jus,* the strong coffee which most effectively rouses the Legionary from somnolence and most ineffectively sustains him until midday.

Anon, having persuaded himself that the result of his labours was satisfactory, and up to Legion standards of smartness—which are as high as those of the ordinary *piou-piou* of the French line are low—he folded his uniform in elbow-to-finger-tip lengths, placed it with the *paquetage* on the shelf above his bed, and began to dress for his evening walk-out. The Legionary's time is, in theory, his own after 5 p.m., and the most sacred plank in the most sacred platform of all his sacred tradition is his right to promenade himself at eventide and listen to the Legion's glorious band in the Place Sadi Carnot.

Having laid his uniform, belt, bayonet, and képi on his cot, he stepped across to the next but one (the name-card at the head of which bore the astonishing legend "Bucking Bronco, No. 11356. Soldat 1*ére Classe*), opened a little sack which hung at the head of it, and took from it the remains of an ancient nailbrush, the joint property of Sir Montague Merline, alias Jean Boule, and Hiram Cyrus Milton, alias Bucking Bronco, late of Texas, California, Yukon, and "the main drag" of the United States of America.

Even as Sir Montague's hand was inserted through the neck of the sack, the huge American (who had been wrongfully accused and rashly attacked by Legionary Hans Schnitzel) entered the barrack-room, caught sight of a figure bending over his rag-sack, and crept on tiptoe towards it, his great gnarled fists clenched, his mouth compressed to a straight line beneath his huge drooping moustache, and his grey eyes ablaze. Luckily Sir Montague heard the sounds of his stealthy approach, and turned just in time. The American dropped his fists and smiled.

"Say," he drawled, "I thought it was some herring-gutted

weevil of a Dago or a Squarehead shenannikin with my precious jools. An' I was jest a'goin' ter plug the skinnamalink some. Say, Johnnie, if yew hadn't swivelled any, I was jest goin' ter plug yew, good an' plenty, behind the yeer'ole."

"Just getting the tooth-nail-button-boot-dandy-brush, Buck," replied Sir Montague. "How are you feeling?"

"I'm feelin' purty mean," was the reply. "A dirty Squarehead of a dod-gasted Dutchy from the Farterland grunted in me eye, an' I thought the shavetail was for rough-housin', an' I slugged him one, jus ter start 'im gwine. The gosh-dinged piker jest curled up. He jest wilted on the floor."

The Bucking Bronco, in high disgust, expectorated and then chid himself for forgetting that he was no longer on the free soil of America, where a gentleman may spit as he likes and be a gentleman for a' that and a' that.

"Cheer up, Buck, we'll all soon be dead," replied his comrade, "and don't *you* go getting cafard," and he looked anxiously at the angry-lugubrious face of his friend. "What's the *ordre du jour* for walking-out dress today?" he added. "Blue tunic and red trousers? Or tunic and white? Or *capote,* or what?"

"It was tunic an' white yesterday," replied the American, "an' I guess it is to-day too."

"It's my night to howl, he added cryptically. "Let's go an' pow-wow Carmelita ef thet fresh gorilla Loojey Rivoli ain't got 'er in 'is pocket. I'll shoot 'im up some day, sure. . . ."

A sudden shouting, tumult, and running below, and cries of "Les bleus! Les bleus!" interrupted the Bronco's monologue and drew the two old soldiers to a window that overlooked the vast, neat, gravelled barrack-square, clean, naked, and bleak to the eye as an ice-floe.

"Strike me peculiar," remarked the Bucking Bronco, "It's another big gang of tenderfeet."

"A draft of rookies! Come on—they'll all be for our Company in place of those *poumpists,*[1] and there may be something Anglo-Saxon among them," said Legionary John Bull, and the two men hastily flung their capotes over their

---

[1] Deserters.

sketchy attire and hurried from the room, buttoning them as they went.

Like Charity, the Legionary's overcoat covers a multitude of sins—chiefly of ommission—and is a most useful garment. It protects him from the cold dawn wind, and keeps him warm by night; it protects him from the cruel African sun, and keeps him cool by day, or at least, if not cool, in the frying-pan degree of heat, which is better than that of the fire. He marches in it without a tunic, and relies upon it to conceal the fact when he has failed to "decorate" himself with underclothing. Its skirts, buttoned back, hamper not his legs, and its capacious pockets have many uses. Its one drawback is that, being double-breasted, it buttons up on either side, a fact which has brought the grey hairs of many an honest Legionary in sorrow to the *Cellules,* and given many a brutal and vindictive Sergeant the chance of that cruelty in which his little tyrant soul so revels. For, incredible as it may seem to the lay mind, the ingenious devil whose military mind concocts the *ordres du jour,* changes, by solemn decree, and almost daily, the side upon which the overcoat is to be buttoned up.

In the incredibly maddeningly dull life of the Legion in peace time, the slightest diversion is a god-send and even the arrival of a batch of recruits a most welcome event. To all, it is a distraction; to some, the hope of the arrival of a fellow-countryman (especially to the few English, Americans, Danes, Greeks, Russians, Norwegians, Swedes, and Poles whom cruel Fate has sent to La Légion). To some, a chance of passing on a part of the brutality and tyranny which they themselves suffer; to some, a chance of getting civilian clothes in which to desert; to others, an opportunity of selling knowledge of the ropes, for litres of canteen wine; to many, a hope of working a successful trick on a bewildered recruit—the time-honoured villainy of stealing his new uniform and pretending to buy him another *sub rosa* from the dishonest quartermaster, whereupon the recruit buys back his own original uniform at the cost of his little all (for invariably the alleged substitute uniform costs just that sum of money which the poor wretch has brought with him and augmented by the compulsory sale of his civilian kit to the clothes-dealing harpies and thieves who infest the barrack-gates on the arrival of each draft).

24

As the tiny portal beside the huge barrack-gate was closed and fastened by the Corporal in charge of the squad of "blues" (as the French army calls its recruits[1]), the single file of derelicts halted at the order of the Sergeant of the Guard, who, more in sorrow than in anger, weighed them and found them wanting.

"Sweepings," he summed them up in passing judgment. "Foundlings. Droppings. Crumbs. Tripe. Accidents. Abortions. Cripples. Left by the tide. Blown in by the wind. Born *pékins*.[2] Only one man among them, and he a pig of a Prussian—or perhaps an Englishman. Let us hope he's an Englishman. . . ."

In speaking thus, the worthy Sergeant was behaving with impropriety and contrary to the law and tradition of the Legion. What nouns and adjectives a non-commissioned officer may use wherewith to stigmatise a Legionary, depend wholly and solely upon his taste, fluency and vocabulary. But it is not etiquette to reproach a man with his nationality, however much a matter for reproach that nationality may be.

"Are you an Englishman, most miserable *bleu*?" he suddenly asked of a tall, slim, fair youth, dressed in tweed Norfolk-jacket, and grey flannel trousers, and bearing in every line of feature and form, and in the cut and set of his expensive clothing, the stamp of the man of breeding, birth and position.

"By the special mercy and grace of God, I am an Englishman, Sergeant, thank you," he replied coolly in good, if slow and careful French.

"*Slava Bogu!*" he roared. "Vile *bleu!* And now by the especial mercy and grace of the Devil you are a Légionnaire—or will be, if you survive the making . . ." and added *sotto voce*, "Are you a degraded dog or a broken officer? If so, you can claim to be appointed to the *élèves caporaux* as a non-commissioned officer on probation, if you have a photo of yourself in officer's uniform. Thus you will escape all recruit-drill and live in hope to become,

---

[1] In the days of the high, tight stock and cravat, the recruit was supposed to be livid and blue in the face until he grew accustomed to them.

[2] Civilians.

some day, Sergeant, even as I," and the (for a Sergeant of the Legion) decent-hearted fellow smote his vast chest.

"I thank you, Sergeant," was the drawled reply. "You really dazzle me—but *I* am not a degraded dog of a broken officer.

"Gospodi pomilui!" roared the incensed Sergeant. "Ne me donnez de la gabatine, pratique!" and, for a second, seemed likely to strike the cool and insolent recruit who dared to bandy words with a sergeant of the Legion. His eyes bulged, his moustache bristled, and his scarlet face turned purple as he literally showed his teeth.

"Go easy, old chap," spoke a quiet voice, in English, close beside the Englishman. "That fellow can do you to death if you offend him," and the recruit, turning, beheld a grey-moustached, white-haired elderly man, bronzed, lined, and worn-looking—a typical French army *vielle moustache* —an "old sweat" from whose lips the accents of a refined English gentleman came with the utmost incongruity.

"Good egg," quoth he, extending a hand behind him for a surreptitious shake. "See you anon, what?"

"Yes, you'll all come to the Seventh Company. We are below strength," said Legionary John Bull, in whose weary eyes had shown a new light of interest since they fell upon this compatriot of his own caste and kidney.

"Now what'n hell is he doin' in thet bum outfit?" querried the Bucking Bronco of his friend John Bull, who kept as near as possible to the Englishman whom he had warned against ill-timed causticity of humour.

"I can't place him Buck," replied the puzzled John Bull, his quiet voice rendered almost inaudible by the shouts, howls, yells and cries of the seething mob of Legionaries who swarmed around the line of recruits, assailing their bewildered ears in all the tongues of Europe, and some of those of Asia and Africa.

"He doesn't look hungry, and he doesn't look hunted. I suppose he is one of the few who don't come here to escape either starvation, creditors, or the Law. And he doesn't look desperate like the average turned-down lover, ruined gambler, deserted husband, or busted bankrupt. . . . Wonder if he's come here in search of 'Romance'?"

"Wal, ef he's come hyar for his health an' amoosement he'd go to Hell to cool himself, or ter the den of a grizzly b'ar for gentle stimoolation and recreation. Gee whiz! Didn't he fair git ole Bluebottle's goat? He sure did git next him."

"Bit of a contrast to the rest of the gang, what?" remarked John Bull, and indeed the truth of his remark was very obvious.

"Ain't they a outfit o' dodgasted hoboes an' bindlestiffs!" agreed his friend.

Straight as a lance, thin, very broad in the shoulders and narrow of waist and hip; apparently as clean and unruffled as when leaving his golf-club pavilion for a round on the links; cool, self-possessed, haughty, aristocratic and clean-cut of feature, this Englishman among the other recruits looked like a Derby winner among a string of equine ruins in a knacker's yard; like a panther among bears— a detached and separated creature, something of different flesh and blood. Breed is a very remarkable thing, even more distinctive than race, and in this little band of derelicts was another Englishman, a Cockney youth who had passed from street-arab and gutter-snipe, *via* Reformatory, to hooligan, coster and soldier. No man in that collection of wreckage from Germany, Spain, Italy, France, and the four corners of Europe looked less like the tall recruit than did this brother Englishman.

"There's blood there," he murmured to himself.

"His shoulders hev bin drilled somewhere's, although he's British," added the Bucking one. "Yep. He's one o' the flat-backed push."

"I wonder if he can be a cashiered officer. He's drilled as you say. . . . If he has been broke for something it hasn't marked him much. Nothing hang-dog there," mused Legionary John Bull.

"Nope. He's a blowed-in-the-glass British aristocrat," agreed the large-minded Hiram Cyrus, "and I opine an ex-member of the commishunned ranks o' the British Constitootional Army. He ain't never bin batterin' the main-stem for light-pieces like them other hoodlums an' toughs an' smoudges. Nope. He ain't never throwed his feet for a two-bit poke-out. . . . Look at that road-kid next 'im! Ain't he a peach? I should smile! Wonder the medicine-man didn't turn down some o' them chechaquos. . . ."

And, truly, the draft contained some very queer odd lots.

27

By the side of the English gentleman stood a big fat German boy in knicker-bockers and jersey, bare-legged and wearing a pair of button-boots that had belonged to a woman in the days when they still possessed toe-caps. Pale face, pale hair, and pale eyes, conspired to give him an air of terror—the first seeming to have the hue of fright, the second to stand *en brosse* with fear, and the last to bulge like those of a hunted animal.

Presumably M. le Médicin-Major must have been satisfied that the boy was eighteen years of age, but, though tall and robust, he looked nearer fifteen—an illusion strengthened, doubtless, by the knickerbockers, bare calves, and button-boots.

Next to him stood a gnarled and knotted Spaniard, whose face appeared to be carven from his native mahogany, and whose ragged clothing—grimy, oily, blackened—proclaimed him wharfside coal-heaver, dock-rat, and longshoreman. What did he among the Legion's blues? Was it lack of work, was it slow starvation? Or excess of temper and a quick blow with a coal-shovel upon the head of an enemy in some Marseilles coal-barge—that had brought him to Sidi-bel-Abbès in the sands of Africa?

By his side slouched a dark-faced, blunt-featured Austrian youth, whose evil-looking mouth was unfortunately in no wise concealed by a sparse and straggling moustache, laboriously pinched into two gummed spikes, and whose close-set eyes were not in harmony of focus. His dress appeared to be that of a lower-class clerk, ill-fitting black cloth of lamentable cut, the type of suit that, in its thousands, renders day horrible in European and American cities, and is, alas, spreading to many Asiatic. His linen was filthy, his crinkly hair full of dust, his boots cracked and shapeless. He looked what he was—an absconding Viennese tout who had had a very poor time of it. He proved to be a highly objectionable and despicable scoundrel.

His left-hand neighbour was a weedy, olive-faced youth, wearing a velvet tam-o'-shanter cap, and a brown corduroy suit, of which the baggy, peg-top trousers fitted tightly at the ankles over pearl-buttoned spring-side patent boots. He had long fluffy brown hair, long fluffy brown beard, whiskers, and moustache, long filthy finger nails, and no linen. Apparently a French student from the Sorbonne, or artist from The Quarter, overwhelmed by some terrible cataclysm, some *affaire* of the heart, the pocket, or *l'honneur*.

Beside this gentleman, whose whole appearance was highly offensive to the prejudiced insular eye of the Englishman, stood a typical *Apache*—a horrible-looking creature whose appalling face showed the cunning of the fox, the ferocity of the panther, the cruelty of the wolf the treachery of the bear, the hate of the serpent, and the rage of the boar.

Beside him, and evidently eyeing him askance, stood two youths as extraordinarily similar as were ever twins in this world. Dark, slightly "rat-faced," slender, but decidedly athletic looking.

"Cheer up, *golubtchik!* If one cannot get *vodka* one must drink *kvass*," whispered one.

"All right, Fedia," replied the other. "But I am so hungry and tired. What wouldn't I give for some good hot tea and *blinni!*"

"We're bound to get something of some sort before long —though it won't be *zakuska*. Don't give way on the very threshold now. It is our one chance, or I would not have brought you here, Olichka."

"Ssh!" whispered back the other. "Don't call me that here, Feodor."

"Of course not, Mikhail, stout fellow," replied Feodor, and smote his companion on the back.

Regarding them, sharp-eyed, stood the Cockney, an undersized, narrow-chested, but wiry-looking person—a typical East End sparrow; impudent, assertive, thoroughly self-reliant, tenacious, and courageous; of the class that produces admirable specimens of the genus "Tommy."

In curious contrast to his look of *gamin* alertness was that of his neighbour, a most stolid, dull and heavy-looking Dutchman, whose sole conversational effort was the grunt *"Verstaan nie,"* whenever addressed. Like every other member of the draft he appeared "to feel his position" keenly, and distinctly to deplore it. Such expression as his bovine face possessed, suggested that Algerian sun and sands compared unfavourably with Dutch mists and polders, and the barrack-square of the Legion with the fat and comfortable stern of a Scheldt canal boat.

Square-headed, flat-faced Germans gesticulating Alsatians and Lorraines, fair Swiss, and Belgians, with a sprinkling of Italians, swarthy Spaniards, Austrians and French, made up the remainder of the party, men whose status, age, appearance, bearing and origins were as diverse as their nationalities, levelled by a common desperate need (of food, or sanctuary, or a fresh start in life), and united by a common filthiness, squalor, and dejection—a gang powerless in the bonds of hunger and fear, delivered bound into the relentless, grinding mills of the Legion.

And thus, distinguished and apart, though in their midst, stood the well-dressed Englishman, apparently calm, incurious, with equal mind; his linen fresh, his face shaven, his clothing uncreased, his air rather that of one who awaits the result of the footman's enquiry as to whether Her Ladyship is "at home" to him.

"Any 'Murricans thar?" suddenly bawled the Bucking Bronco.

"Nao," replied the Cockney youth, craning forward. "But I'm Henglish—which is better any d'y in the week, ain't it?"

The eye of the large American travelled slowly and deliberately from the crown of the head to the tip of the toe of the Cockney, and back. He then said nothing—with some eloquence.

"Say, ma honey, yew talk U.S. any?" queried a gigantic Negro, in the uniform of the Legion (presumably recruited in France as a free American citizen of Anglo-Saxon speech), addressing himself to the tall Englishman. "Youse aint Dago, nor Dutchie, nor French. Cough it up, Bo, right hyar ef youse U.S."

The eyes of the young Englishman narrowed slightly, and his naturally haughty expression appeared to deepen toward one of contempt and disgust. Otherwise he took no notice of the Negro, nor of his question.

Remarking, "Some poah white trash," the Nego turned to the next man with the same query.

Cries in various tongues, such as "Anybody from Spain?" "Anyone from Vienna?" "Any Switzers about?" and similar attempts by the crowding, jostling Legionaries to discover a compatriot, and possibly a "towny" evoked gleams and glances of interest from the haggard, wretched

30

eyes of the "blues," and, occasionally, answering cries from their grim and grimy lips.

A swaggering, strutting Sergeant emerged from the neighbouring regimental offices, roared *"Garde à vous,"* brought the recruits to attention, and called the roll. As prophesied by Legionary John Bull, the whole draft was assigned to the Seventh Company, recently depleted by the desertion, en mass, of a *cafard*-smitten German *escouade,* or section, who had gone "on pump," merely to die in the desert at the hands of the Arabs—several horribly tortured, all horribly mangled.

Having called the roll, this Sergeant, not strictly follow-ing the example of the Sergeant of the Guard, looked the draft over more in anger than in sorrow.

"Oh, Name of the Name of Beautiful Beelzebub," bawled he, "but what have we here? To *drill* such worm-casts! Quel métier! Quel chien d'un métier! Stand up, stand up, oh sons of Arab mothers and pariah dogs," and then, feigning sudden and unconquerable sickness, he turned upon the Corporal in charge with a roar of—

"March these sacred pigs to their accursed sties."

As the heterogeneous gangs stepped off at the word of command, *"En avant. Marche!"* toward the Quarter-master's store of the Seventh Company, it was clear to the experienced eye that the great majority were "Back to the army again," and were either deserters, or men who had already put in their military service in the armies of their own countries.

In the store-room they were endowed by the *Fourier-Sergeant,* to the accompaniment of torrential profanity, with white fatigue-uniforms, night-caps, rough shirts, harsh towels, and scraps of soap. From the store-room the squad was "personally conducted" by another, and even more terrible. Sergeant to a washing-shed beyond the drill-ground, and bidden to soap and scour itself, and then stand beneath the primitive shower-baths until purged and clean as never before in its unspeakable life.

As they neared the washing-shed, the bare idea of ablutions, or the idea of bare ablutions, appeared to strike consternation, if not positive terror, into the heart of at least one member of the squad, for the young Russian who had been addressed by his twin as Mikhail suddenly

31

seized the other's arm and said with a gasp——

"Oh, Fedichka, how can I? Oh, Fedia, Fedia, what shall I do?"

"We must trust in God, and use our wits, Olusha I will . . ."

But a roar of "Silence, Oh Son of Seven Pigs," from the Sergeant, cut him short as they reached the shed.

"Now strip and scrub your mangy skins, you dogs. Scrape your crawling hides until the floor is thick in hog-bristles and earth, oh Great-grandsons of Sacred Swine," he further adjudged the wretched "blues," with horrible threats and fearful oaths.

"Wash, you mud-caked vermin, wash, for the carcase of the Legionary must be spotless as the Fame of the Legion, or the honour of its smartest Sergeant—Sergeant Legros," and he tapped his bulging chest lest any Bœotian present should be ignorant of the identity of Sergeant Legros of the Legion.

Walking up and down before the doorless stalls in which the naked recruits washed, Sergeant Legros hurled taunts, gibes, insults, and curses at his charges, stopping from time to time to give special attention to anyone who had the misfortune to acquire his particular regard. Pausing to stare at the tall Englishman in affected disgust at the condition of his brilliant and glowing skin, he inquired——

"Is that a vest, disclosed by scrubbing and the action of water? Or is it your hide, pig?" And was somewhat taken aback by the cool and pleasant reply.

"No, that is not a new, pink silk vest that you see, Sergeant, it really is my own skin—but many thanks for the kind compliment, none the less."

Sergeant Legros eyed the recruit with something dimly and distantly akin to pity. Mad as a March hare, poor wretch, of course—it could not be intentional impudence —and the Sergeant smiled austerely—he would probably die in the cells ere long, if *le cafard* did not send him to the Zephys, the firing-platoon, or the Arabs. Mad to begin with! Ho! Ho! What a jest!—and the Sergeant chuckled.

But what was this? Did the good Sergeant's eyes deceive him? Or was there, in the next compartment, a louzy, lazy "blue" pretending to cleanse his foul and sinful carcase without completely stripping? The young

Russian, Mikhail, standing with his back to the doorway, was unenthusiastically, washing the upper part of his body.

Sergeant Legros stiffened like a pointer, at the sight. Rank disobedience! Flagrant defiance of orders, coupled with the laziest and filthiest indifference to cleanliness! This vile "blue" would put the Legion's clean shirt and canvas fatigue-suit on an indifferently washen body, would he? Let him wait until he was a Legionary, and no longer a recruit—and he should learn something of the powers of the Sergeant Legros.

"Off with those trousers, thou mud-caked flea-bitten scum," he thundered, and then received perhaps the greatest surprise of a surprising life. Fore, ere the offending recruit could turn, or obey, there danced forth from the next cubicle, with a wild whoop, his exact double, who, naked as he was born, turned agile somersaults and catherine-wheels past the astounded Sergeant, down the front of the bathing-shed, and round the corner.

"Sacré Nom de Nom de Bon Dieu-de-Dieu!" ejaculated Sergeant Legros, and rubbed his eyes. He then displayed a sample of the mental quickness of the trained Legionary in darting to the neighbouring corner of the building instead of running down the entire front in the wake of the vanished acrobat.

Dashing along the short sidewalk, Sergeant Legros turned the corner and beheld the errant lunatic approaching in the same literally revolutionary manner.

On catching sight of the Sergeant, the naked recruit halted, and broke into song and dance, the latter being of that peculiarly violent Cossack variety which constrains the performer to crouch low to earth and fling out his legs, alternately, straight before him.

For the first time in his life, words failed Sergeant Legros. For some moments he could but stand over the dancer and gesticulate and stutter. Rising to his feet with an engaging smile——

"Ca va mieux, mon père?" observed the latter amiably.

Seizing him by arm and neck, the apoplectic Sergeant Legros conducted this weird disciple of Terpsichore back to his cubicle, while his mazed mind fumbled in the treasure-house of his vocabulary, and the armoury of his weapons of punishment.

Apparently there was method, however, in the madness of Feodor Kyrilovitch Malekov, for a distinct look of relief and satisfaction crossed his face as, in the midst of a little crowd of open-mouthed, and half-clothed recruits, he caught sight of his brother in complete fatigue-uniform.

Gradually, and very perceptibly the condition of Sergeant Legros improved. His halting recriminations and imprecations became a steady trickle, the trickle a flow, the flow a torrent, and the torrent an overwhelming deluge. By the time he had almost exhausted his vocabulary and himself, he began to see the humorous and interesting aspect of finding two lunatics in one small draft. He would add them to his collection of butts. Possibly, one, or both of them, might even come to equal the Mad Grasshopper in that rôle. Fancy more editions of La Cigale—who had provided him with more amusement and opportunities for brutality than any ten sane Legionaries!

"Now, do great and unmerited honour to your vile, low carcases by putting on the fatigue-uniform of the Legion. Gather up your filthy civilian rags, and hasten," he bawled.

And when the, now wonderously metamorphosed, recruits had all dressed in the new canvas uniforms, they were marched to a small side gate in the wall of the barrack-square, and ordered to sell immediately everything they possessed in the shape of civilian clothing, including boots and socks. Civilian clothing is essential to the would-be deserter, and La Légion does not facilitate desertion.

That the unfortunate recruits got the one or two francs they did receive was solely due to the absence of a "combine" among the scoundrelly Arabs, Greeks, Spanish Jews, Negroes, and nondescript rogues who struggled for the cast-off clothing.

When the swindle of the forced sale was complete, and several poor wretches had parted with their all for a few *sous,* the gate was shut and the weary squad marched to the offices of the Seventh Company that each man's name and profession might be entered in the Company's Roll, and that he might receive his *matricule* number, the number which would henceforth hide his identity, and save him the trouble of retaining a personality and a name.

To Colour-Sergeant Blanc, the tall English youth, like most Legionaires, gave a *nom d'emprunt,* two of his own names, Reginald Rupert. He concealed his surname and sullied the crystal truth of fact by stating that his father was the Commander-in-Chief of the Horse Marines of Great Britain and Inspector-General of the Royal Naval Horse Artillery; that he himself was by profession a wild-rabbit-tamer, and by conviction a Plymouth Rock—all of which was duly and solemnly entered in the great tome by M. Blanc, a man taciturn, *très boutonné,* and of no imagination.

Whatever the recruit may choose to say is written down in the Company lists, and should a recruit wax a little humorous, why—the Legion will very soon cure him of any tendency to humour. The Legion asks no questions, answers none, takes the recruit at his own valuation, and quickly readjusts it for him.

Reconducted to the Store-room of the Seventh Company, the batch of recruits, again to the accompaniment of a fussillade of imprecations, and beneath a torrential deluge of insults and oaths, was violently tailored by a number of non-commissioned officers, and a fatigue-party of Légionnaires.

To "Reginald Rupert," at any rate, the badges of rank worn by the non-commissioned officers were mysterious and confusing—as he noted a man with one chevron giving peremptory orders in a loud tone and bullying manner to a man who wore two chevrons. It also puzzled him that the fat man, who was evidently the senior official present, was addressed by the others as *"chef,"* as though he were a cook. By the time he was fitted out with kit and accoutrement, he had decided that the "chef" (who wore two gold chevrons) was a Sergeant-Major, that the men wearing one gold chevron were Sergeants, and that those wearing two red ones were Corporals; and herein he was entirely correct.

Every man had to fit (rather than be fitted with) a red képi having a brass grenade in front; a double-breasted, dark blue tunic with red facings and green-fringed red epaulettes; a big blue greatcoat, or *capote;* baggy red breeches; two pairs of boots; two pairs of linen spats, and a pair of leather gaiters. He also received a long blue woollen cummerbund, a knapsack of the old British pattern, a bag of cleaning materials, belts, straps, cartridge-pouches, haversack, and field flask.

To the fat Sergeant-Major it was a personal insult, and an impudence amounting almost to blasphemy, that a képi, or tunic should not fit the man to whom it was handed. The idea of adapting a ready-made garment to a man appeared less prominent than that of adapting a ready-made man to a garment.

"What!" he roared in Legion French, to the fat German boy who understood not a word of the tirade. "What? Nom d'un pétard! Sacré Dieu! The tunic will not easily button? Then contract thy vile body until it will, thou off-spring of a diseased pig and a dead dog. I will fit thee to that tunic, and none other, within the week. Wait! But wait—till thou has eaten the Breakfast of the Legion once or twice, fat sow. . . ."

A gloomy, sardonic Legionary placed a képi upon the crispy curling hair of Reginald Rupert. It was miles too big—a ludicrous extinguisher. The Englishman removed it, and returned it with the remark, "Ça ne marche pas, mon ami."

"Merde!" ejaculated the liverish-looking soldier, and called Heaven to witness that he was not to blame if the son of a beetle had a walnut for a head.

Throwing the képi back into the big box he fished out another, banged it on Rupert's head, and was about to bring his open hand down on the top of it, when he caught the cold but blazing eye of the recruit, and noticed the clenched fist and lips. Had the Legionary's right hand descended, the recruit's left hand would have risen with promptitude and force.

"If that is too big, let the sun boil thy brains and bloat thy skull till it fits, and if it be too small, sleep in it," he remarked sourly, and added that thrice-accursed "blues" were creatures of the kind that ate their young, encumbered the earth, polluted the air, loved to *faire Suisse,*[1] and troubled Soldiers of the Legion who might otherwise have been in the Canteen, or at Carmelita's—

---

[1] To drink alone; to sulk.

instead of being the valets of sons of frogs, nameless excrescences. . . .

"Too small," replied Rupert coolly, and flung the cap into the box. "Valet? I should condole with a crocodile that had a clumsy and ignorant yokel like you for a valet," he added, in slow and careful French as he tried on a third cap, which he found more to his liking.

The old Legionary gasped.

"Il m'enmerde!" he murmured, and wiped his brow. He, Jules Duplessis, Soldat 1ère Classe, with four years' service and the *médaille militaire,* had been outfaced, browbeaten, insulted by a miserable "blue." What were the World and La Légion coming to? *"Merde!"*

While trying on his tunic, Rupert saw one of the Russians hand to the other the tunic and trousers which he had tried on. Apparently being as alike as two pins in every respect they had adopted the labour-saving device of one "fitting on" for both.

Having put on the képi, Mikhail bundled up the uniform, struck an attitude with arms akimbo, and inquired of the other——

"Do I look *very* awful in this thing, Fedia?"

"Shut up, you little fool," replied Feodor, with a quick frown. "Try and look more like a *mujik* in *maslianitza,*[1] and less like a young student at private theatricals. You're a Legionary now."

When, at length, the recruits had all been fitted into uniforms, and were ready to depart, they were driven forth with the heart-felt curse and comprehensive anathema of the Sergeant-Major—

"Sweep the room clear of this offal, Corporal," quoth he. "And if thou canst make a Légionnaire's little toe out of the whole draft—thou shalt have the Grand Cross of the Legion of Honour—I promise it."

"En avant. Marche!" bawled the Corporal, and the "blues" were led away, up flights of stairs, and along echoing corridors to their future home, their new quarters. A Légionnaire, carrying a huge earthenware jug, encountering them outside the door thereof, gave them their first welcome to the Legion.

---

[1] The week before Lent or "mad week," when all good mujiks get drunk—or used to do.

"Oh thrice-condemned souls, welcome to Hell," he cried genially, and kicking open the door of a huge room, he liberally sprinkled each passing recruit, murmuring as he did so—

"Le diable vous bénisse."

CHAPTER TWO

A BARRACK-ROOM OF THE LEGION

THE ROOM which Reginald Rupert entered, with a dozen of his fellow "blues," was long and lofty, painfully orderly, and spotlessly clean. Fifteen cots were exactly aligned on each long side, and down the middle of the floor ran long wooden tables and benches, scoured and polished to immaculate whiteness. Above each bed was a shelf on which was piled a very neat erection of uniforms and kit. To the eye of Rupert (experienced in barrack-rooms) there was interesting novelty in the absence of clothes-boxes, and the presence of hanging-cupboards suspended over the tables from the ceiling.

Evidently the French authorities excelled the English in the art of economizing space, as nothing was on the floor that could be accommodated above it. In the hanging-cupboards were tin plates and cups and various utensils of the dinner-table.

The Englishman noted that though the Lebel rifles stood in a rack in a corner of the room, the long sword-bayonets hung by the pillows of their owners, each near a tin quart-pot and a small sack.

On their beds, a few Légionnaires lay sleeping, or sat laboriously polishing their leatherwork—the senseless, endless and detested *astiquage* of the Legion—or cleaning their rifles, bayonets, and buttons. Whatever else the Légionnaire is, or is not, he is meticulously clean, neat, and smart, and when his day's work is done (at four or five o'clock) he must start a half-day's work in "making *fantasie*"—in preparation for the day's work of the morrow.

Rising from his bed in the corner as the party entered, Legionary John Bull approached the Corporal in charge of the room and suggested that the English recruit should be alloted the bed between his own and that of Légionnaire Bronco, as he was of the same mother-tongue and would make quicker progress in their hands than in those of foreigners. As the Corporal, agreeing, indicated the second bed from the window, to Rupert, and told him to take possession of it and make his *paquetage* on the shelf above, the Cockney recruit pushed forward:

" 'Ere, I'm Henglish too! I better jine these blokes."

"Qu'est-ce-qu'il dit, Jean Boule?" enquired the Corporal.

On being informed, Corporal Achille Martel allotted the fourth bed, that on the other side of the Bucking Bronco, to Recruit Higgins with an intimation that the sooner he learnt French, and ceased the use of barbarous tongues the better it would be for his welfare. The Corporal then assigned berths to the remaining recruits, each between those of two old soldiers, of whom the right-hand man was to be the new recruit's guide, philosopher and friend, until he, in his turn, became a prideful, full-blown Legionary.

The young Russian, who had given his name Mikhail Kyrilovitch Malekov observed that the card at the head of the cot on his right-hand bore the inscription: "Luigi Rivoli. No. 13874, Soldat 2ième Classe."

As he stood, irresolute, and apparently in great anxiety and perturbation, nervously opening and shutting a cartridge-pouch, his face suddenly brightened as his twin entered the room and intercepted the departing Corporal.

"*Milles pardons,* Monsieur," he said, saluting smartly and respectfully. "But I earnestly and humbly request that you will permit me to inhabit this room in which is my brother. As we reached this door another *sous-officer* took me and the remainder to the next room when twelve had entered here. . . . Alas! My brother was twelfth, and I thirteenth," he added volubly. "Look you, Monsieur, he is my twin, and we have never been separated yet. We shall get on much faster and better, helping each other, and be more credit to you and your room, *petit père.*"

"Sacré Dieu, and Name of a Purple Frog! Is this a scurvy and lousy beggar, whining for alms at a mosque door? And am I a God-forsaken and disgusting *pékin* that you address me as 'Monsieur'? Name of a Pipe! Have I no rank? Address me henceforth as Monsieur le Caporal, thou kopeck-worth of Russian."

"Oui, oui; milles pardons, Monsieur le Caporal. But grant me this favour and I and my brother will be your slaves."

"Va t'en, babillard! Rompez, jaseur!" snarled the Corporal.

But the Russian, true to type, was tenacious. Producing a five-franc piece he scratched his nose therewith, and dropping the wheedling and suppliant tone, asked the testy Corporal if he thought it likely Messieurs les Caporaux of the Seventh Company could possibly be induced to drink the health of so insignificant an object as Recruit Feodor Kyrilovitch Malekov.

"Corporals do not drink with Légionnaires," was the answer, "but doubtless Corporal Gilles of the next room will join me in a drink to the health of a worthy and promising 'blue,'" and, removing his képi, he stretched his gigantic frame and yawned hugely as the Russian dexterously, and apparently unnoticed, slipped the coin into the képi. Having casually examined the lining of his képi, Monsieur le Caporal Martel replaced it on his head, and with astounding suddenness and ferocity pounced upon an ugly, tow-haired German, and with a shout of "Out, pig! Out of my beautiful room! Thy face disfigures it," he hunted him forth and bestowed him upon the neighbouring Corporal, M. Auguste Gilles, together with a promise of ten bottles of Madame la Cantinière's best, out of the thirty-and-five which the Russian's five-franc piece would purchase.

In a moment the Russian had opened negotiations with the Spaniard who had taken the bed next but one to that of Mikhail.

Like all educated Russians, Feodor Kyrilovitch was an accomplished linguist, and, while speaking French and English idiomatically, could get along very comfortably in Spanish, Italian, and German.

A very few minutes enabled him to make it clear to the Spaniard that an exchange of beds would do him no harm, and enrich him by a two-franc piece.

Meanwhile, Reginald Rupert, with soldierly promptitude, lost no time in setting about the brushing and arrangement of his kit, gathering up, as he did so, the pearls of local wisdom that fell from the lips of his kindly mentor, whose name and description he observed to be "Légionnaire John Bull, No. 11867, Soldat 2ième Classe."

Having shown his pupil the best and quickest way of folding his uniform in elbow-to-finger-tip lengths, and so arranging everything that he could find it in the dark, and array himself *en tenue de campagne d'Afrique* in ten minutes without a light, he invited him to try his own hand at the job.

"Now you try and make that '*paquetage* of the Legion,' " observed the instructor, "and the sooner you learn to make it quickly, the better. As you see, you have no chest for your kit as you had in the British Army, and so you keep your uniform on your shelf, *en paquetage,* for tidiness and smartness, without creases. The Légionnaire is as *chic* and particular as the best trooper of the crackest English cavalry-corps. We look down on the *piou-piou* from a fearful height, and swagger against the *Chasseur d'Afrique* himself. I wish to God we had spurs, but there's no cavalry in the Legion—though there are kinds of Mounted-Rifle Companies on mules, down South. I miss spurs damnably, even after fourteen years of foot-slogging in the Legion. You can't really swagger without spurs—not that the women will look at a Legionary in any case, or the men respect him, save as a fighter. But you can't *swing* without spurs."

"No," agreed Rupert, "I was just thinking I should miss them, and it'll take me some time to get used to a night-cap, a neck-curtained képi, a knapsack, and a steel bayonet-scabbard."

"You'll appreciate the first when you sleep out, and the second when you march, down South. The nights are infernally cold, and the days are appallingly hot—and yet sunstroke is unknown in the Legion. Some put it down to wearing the overcoat to march in. The steel scabbard is bad —noisy and heavy. The knapsack is the very devil on the march, but it's the one and only place in the world in which you can keep a photo, letter, book, or scrap of private property, besides spare uniform and small kit. You'll soon learn to pack it, to stow underclothing in the haversack, and to know the place for everything, so that you can get from bed to barrack-square, fully equipped and accoutred in nine minutes from the bugle. . . . And don't, for Heaven's sake, lose anything, for a spiteful N.C.O. can send you to your death in Biribi—that's the Penal Battalion—by running you in two or three times for 'theft of equipment.' "

The disorderly heap of garments having become an exceedingly neat and ingenious little edifice, compact, symmetrical, and stable, Rupert's instructor introduced the subject of that bane of the Legionary's life—the eternal *astiquage,* the senseless and eternal polishing of the black leather straps and large cartridge-pouches.

"This stuff looks as though it had been left here by the Tenth Legion of Julius Cæsar, rather than made for the Foreign Legion," he remarked. "Let's see what we can make of it. Watch me do this belt, and then you can try the cartridge-cases. Don't mind firing off all the questions you've got to ask, meanwhile."

"Thanks. What sort of chaps are they in this room?" asked Rupert, seating himself on the bed beside his friendly preceptor.

"Very mixed," was the reply. "The fellow on the other side of your berth is an American, an *ex*-U.S.A. army man, miner, lumber-jack, tramp, cowboy, bruiser, rifle and re-volver trick-shooter, and my very dear friend, one of the whitest men I ever met, and one of the most amusing. His French conversation keeps me alive by making me laugh, and he's learning Italian from a twopenny dictionary, and a Travellers' Phrase Book, the better to talk to Carmelita. The next but one is a Neapolitan who calls himself Luigi Rivoli. He used to be a champion Strong Man, and music-hall wrestler, acrobat, and juggler. Did a bit of lion-taming too, or, at any rate, went about with a show that had a cageful of mangy performing lions. He is not really very brave though, but he's a most extraordinary strong brute. Quite a millionaire here too, for Carmelita gives him a whole franc every day of his life."

"What made him enlist then?" asked Rupert, carefully watching the curious *astiquage* methods, so different from the pipe-clay to which he was accustomed.

"This same girl, and she's worth a thousand of Rivoli. It seems she pretended to turn him down, and take up with some other chap to punish Rivoli after some lover's quarrel or other, and our Luigi in a fit of jealous madness stabbed the other chap in the back, and then bolted and enlisted in the Legion, partly to pay her out, but chiefly to save himself. He was doing a turn at a *café-chantant* over in Algiers at the time. Of course, Carmelita flung herself in transports of grief, repentance, and self-accusation upon Luigi's enormous bosom, and keeps him in pocket-money while she waits for him. She followed him, and runs a *café* for Légionnaires here in Sidi-bel-Abbès. She gets scores of offers from our Non-coms., and from Frenchmen of the regular army stationed in Sidi, and her *café* is a sort of little Italian club. My friend, the Bucking Bronco, proposes to her once a week, but she remains true to Luigi, whom she intends to marry as soon as he has done his time. The swine's carrying on at the same time with Madame la Cantinière, who is a widow, and whose canteen he would like to marry. Between the two women he has a good time, and, thanks to Carmelita's money, gets all his work done for him. The brute never does a stroke. Pays substitutes for all fatigues and corvées, has his kit and accoutrements polished, and his clothes washed. Spends the balance of Carmelita's money at the Canteen, ingratiating himself with Madame! Keeps up his great strength with extra food too. He *is* a Hercules, and, moreover, seems immune from African fever and *le cafard,* which is probably due to his escaping three-parts of the work done by the average penniless. And he's as nasty as he is strong."

"What's his particular line of nastiness—besides cheating women I mean?" asked Rupert.

"Oh, he's the Ultimate Bounder," replied the other, as he struck a match and began melting a piece of wax with which to rub his leather belt. "He's the Complete Cad, and the Finished Bully. He's absolute monarch of the rank-and-file of the Seventh Company by reason of his vast wealth, and vaster strength. Those he does not bribe he intimidates. Remember that the Wages of Virtue here is one half-penny a day as opposed to the wages of sin which is rather worse than death.

"Think of the position of a man who has the income of all in this room put together, in addition to the run of his best girl's own *café*. What with squaring Non-coms., hiring substitutes, and terrorizing 'fags,' he hasn't done a stroke, outside parades of course, since he joined—except hazing recruits, and breaking up opponents of his rule."

"How does he fight?" asked Rupert.

"Well, wrestling his *forte*—and he can break the back of any man he gets his arms round—and the rest's a mixture of boxing, ju-jitsu, and *la savate,* which, as you know, is kicking. Yes, he's a dirty fighter, though it's precious rarely that it comes to what you could call a fight. What I'm waiting for is the most unholy and colossal turn-up that's due to come between him and Buck sooner or later. It's bound to come, and it'll be a scrap worth seeing.Buck has been a professional glove-man among other things, and he holds less conservative views than I do, as to what is permissable against an opponent who kicks, clinches, and butts.

"How disgustin'!" murmured the young man. "Will this bird trouble me?"

"He will," answered the other, "but I'll take a hand, and then Buck will too. . . . Yes, I dare say Buck and I can put the gentle Neapolitan off between us."

Reginald Rupert stiffened.

"I beg that you will in no way interfere," he observed coldly. "I should most strongly resent it."

The heart of the old soldier warmed to the youth, as he contrasted his slim boyish grace with mighty strength, natural and developed, of the professional Strong Man, Wrestler, and Acrobat—most tricky, cunning, and dangerous of relentless foes.

"You keep clear of Luigi Rivoli as long as you can," he said with a kindly smile. "And at least remember that Buck and I are with you. Personally, I'm no sort of match for our Luigi in a rough-and-tumble nowadays, should he compel one. But he has let me alone since I told him with some definiteness that he would have to defend himself with either lead or steel, if he insisted on trouble between him and I."

"There now," he continued, rising, "now try that for yourself on a cartridge-pouch. . . . First melt the wax a bit with a match—and don't forget that matches are precious in the Legion as they're so damned dear—and rub it on the leather as I did. Then take this flat block of wood and smooth it over until it's all evenly spread. And then rub hard with the coarse rag for an hour or two, then harder with the fine rag for about half an hour. Next polish with your palm, and then with the wool. Buck and I own a scrap of velvet which you can borrow before Inspection Parades, and big shows—but we don't use it extravagantly of course. . . ."

"Well, that's the *astiquage* curse, and the other's washing white kit without soap, and ironing it without an iron. Of course, Madame la République couldn't give us glazed leather, or khaki webbing—nor could she afford to issue one flat-iron to a barrack-room, so that we could iron a white suit in less than a couple of hours. . . . The devil of it is that it's all done in our 'leisure' time when we're supposed to be resting, or recreating. . . . Think of the British 'Tommy' in India with his *dhobi,* his barrack-sweeper, his table-servant, and his *syce*—or his share in them. If we did nothing in the world but our daily polishing, washing and ironing, we should be busy men. However! *'C'est la Legion!'* And one won't live for ever. . . . You won't want any help with the rifle and bayonet, I suppose?"

"No thanks, I've 'had some,' though I haven't handled a Lebel before," and Reginald Rupert settled down to work while Legionary John Bull proceeded with his toilet.

"Anything else you want to know?" enquired the latter, as he put a final polish upon his gleaming sword-bayonet.

"Well, thanks very much; the more you tell me, the better for me, if it's not troubling you, Sir."

John Bull paused and looked at the recruit.

"Why do you call me 'Sir'?" he enquired.

"Why? . . . Because you are senior and a Sahib, I suppose," replied the youth.

"Thanks, my boy, but don't. I am just Légionnaire John Bull 11867, Soldier of the Second Class. You'll be a soldier of the First Class, and my senior in a few months, I hope. . . . I suppose you've assumed a *nom de guerre* too," replied the other.

"Yes, I gave part of my own name; I'm 'Reginald Rupert' now. Didn't see why I should give my own. I've only come to have a look round and learn a bit. Very keen on experiences, especially military ones."

"Merciful God!" ejaculated John Bull softly. "Out for experiences! You'll get 'em here."

"Keen on seein' life, y'know," explained the young man.

"Much more likely to see death," replied the other. "Do you realize that you're in for five years—and that no money, no influence, no diplomatic representations, no extradition can buy, or beg, or drag you out; and that by the end of five years, if alive, you'll be lucky if you're of any use to the Legion, to yourself, or to anyone else? I, personally, have had unusual luck, and am of unusual physique. I re-enlisted twice, partly because at the end of each five years I was turned loose with nothing in the world but a shapeless blue slop suit—partly for other reasons. . . ."

"Oh! I've only come for a year, and shall desert. I told them so plainly at the enlistment bureau, in Paris," was the ingenuous reply.

The old Legionary smiled.

"A good many of our people desert, at least once," he said, "when under the influence of *le cafard*—especially the Germans. Ninety-nine per cent come to one of three ends—death, capture, or surrender. Death with torture at the hands of the Arabs; capture, or ignominious return and surrender after horrible sufferings from thirst, starvation and exposure."

"Yes; I heard the Legion was a grand military school, and a pretty warm thing, and that desertion was a bit of a feat, and no disgrace if you brought it off—so I thought I'd have a year of the one, and then a shot at the other," replied the young man coolly. "Also, I was up against it somewhat, and well—you know—seeking sorrow."

"You've come to the right place for it then," observed Legionary John Bull, sheathing his bayonet with a snap, as the door banged open. . . . "Ah! Enter our friend Luigi," he added as that worthy swaggered into the room with an obsequious retinue, which included le bon Légionnaire Edouard Malvin, looking very smart and dapper in the uniform of Légionnaire Alphonse Dupont of the Eleventh Company."

"Pah! I smell 'blues'! Disgusting! Sickening!" ejaculated Légionnaire Luigi Rivoli in a tremendous voice, and stood staring menacingly from recruit to recruit.

"Corpo di Bacco!" he roared in Italian and Legion French. "The place reeks of the stinking 'blues.' Were it not that I now go *en ville* to dine and drink my Chianti wine (none of your filthy Algerian slops for Luigi Rivoli), and to smoke my *sigaro estero* at my *café*, I would fling them all down three flights of stairs," and, like his companions, he commenced stripping off his white uniform. Having bared his truly magnificent arms and chest, he struck an attitude, ostentatiously contracted his huge right biceps, and smote it a resounding smack with the palm of his left hand.

"Aha!" he roared, as all turned to look at him.

"Disgustin' bounder," remarked Reginald Rupert very distinctly, as, with a second shout of "Aha!" Rivoli did the same with the left biceps and right hand, and then bunched the vast *pectoralis major* muscles of his chest.

"Magnifique!" cried Légionnaire Edouard Malvin, who was laying out his patron's uniform from his *paquetage,* preparatory to helping him to dress.

"As thou sayest, my *gallo,* 'C'est magnifique,' " replied Luigi Rivoli, and for five minutes contracted, flexed, and slapped the great muscles of his arms, shoulders, and chest.

"Come hither—thou little bambino Malvin, thou Bad Wine, thou Cattevo Vino Francese, and stand behind me. . . . What of the back? Canst thou see the 'bull's head' as I set the *trapezius, rhomboideus,* and *latissimus dorsi* muscles?"

"As clearly as I see your own head, Main de Fer," replied the Austrian in affected astonishment and wonder. "'tis the World's Most Wonderful Back! Why, were Maxick and Saldo, Hackenschmidt, the three Saxons, Sandow—yea—Samson and Hercules themselves here, all would be humiliated and envious."

"Aha!" again bawled Rivoli, "thou art right, *picolo porco,"* and, sinking to a squatting position upon his raised heels, he rose and fell like a jack-in-the-box for some time, before rubbing and smiting his huge thighs and calves to the accompaniment of explosive shouts. Thereafter, he fell upon his hands and toes, and raised and lowered his stiffened body a few dozen times.

The display finished, he enquired with lordly boredom:

"And what are the absurd orders for walking-out dress to-night. Is it blue and red, or blue and white, or overcoats buttoned on the left—or what?"

"Tunic and red, Hercule, and all ready, as you see," replied Malvin, and he proceeded to assist at the toilet of the ex-acrobat, the plutocrat and leader of the rank-and-file of the Seventh Company by virtue of his income of a franc a day, and his phenomenal strength and ferocity.

Turning round that Malvin might buckls his belt and straighten his tunic, the great man's foot touched that of Herbert Higgins (late of Hoxton and the Loyal White-chapel Regiment) who had been earnestly endeavouring for the past quarter of an hour to follow the instructions of the Bucking Bronco—instructions given in an almost incomprehensible tongue, of choice American and choicer French compact.

Profound disgust, deepening almost to horror, was depicted on the face of the Italian as he bestowed a vicious, hacking kick upon the shin of the offending "blue."

"Body of Bacchus, what is this?" he cried. "Cannot I move without treading in *vidanges?* Get beneath the bed and out of my sight, *cauchemar!*"

But far from retreating as bidden, the undersized Cockney rose promptly to his feet with a surprised and aggrieved look upon his face, hitherto expressive only of puzzled bewilderment.

" 'Ere! 'Oo yer fink you're a kickin' of?" he enquired, adding with dignity, "I dunno' 'oo yer fink you *are*. I'm 'Erb Iggins, I am, and don't yer fergit it."

That Mr. Herbert Higgins stood rubbing his injured shin instead of flying at the throat of the Italian, was due in no wise to personal fear, but to an utter ignorance of the rank, importance, and powers of this "narsty-lookin' furriner." He might be some sort of an officer, and to "dot 'im one" might mean lingering gaol, or sudden death. Bitterly he regretted his complete ignorance of the French tongue, and the manners and customs of this strange place. Anyhow, he could give the bloke some lip in good old English.

"Bit too 'andy wiv yer feet, ain't yer? Pretty manners, I don't fink! 'Manners none, an' customs narsty's' abart your mark, ain't it?"

But ere he could proceed with further flowers of rhetoric, and rush in ignorance upon his fate, the huge hand of the American fell upon his shoulder from behind and pressed him back upon his cot.

"Hello, Loojey dear! Throwin' bouquets to yerself agin, air yew? Gittin' fresh agin, air yew, yew greasy Eye-talian, orgin-grindin', ice-cream-barrer-pushin', back-stabbin', garlic-eatin', street-corner, pink-spangled-tights ackerobat," he observed in his own inimitable vernacular, as he unwound his long blue sash preparatory to dressing for the evening.

The Italian eyed the American malevolently, and for the thousandth time, measured him, considered him, weighed him as an opponent in a boxing-wrestling-kicking match, remembered his uncanny magic skill with rifle and revolver, and, for the thousandth time, postponed the inevitable settlement, misliking his face, his mouth, his eye, and his general manner, air, and bearing.

"Give some abominable 'bleu' the honour of lacing the boots of Luigi Rivoli," he roared, turning with a contemptuous gesture from the American and the Cockney, to his henchman, Malvin. Fixing his eye upon the swarthy, spike-moustached Austrian, who sat at the foot of the bed opposite his own, he added:

"Here dog, the privilege is thine. *Allez schieblos!*"[1] and thrust out the unlaced boots that Malvin had pulled on to his feet.

The Austrian, squatting dejected, with his head between his fists, affected not to understand, and made no move.

"Quick," hissed the Italian, and pointed to his boots that there might be no mistake.

The Austrian snarled.

"Bring it to me," said the great man, and, in a second, the recruit was run by the collar of his tunic, his ears, his twisted wrists, his woolly hair, and by a dozen willing hands, to the welcoming arms of the bully.

"Oh, thou deserter from the *Straf Bataillon*,"[2] growled the latter. A sudden grab, a swift twist, and the Austrian was on his face, his elbows meeting and overlapping behind his back, and his arms drawn upward and backward. He shrieked.

A quick jerk and he was on his feet, and then swung from the ground face downward, his wrists behind him in one of Rivoli's big hands, his trouser-ends in the other. Placing his foot in the small of the Austrian's back, the Italian appeared to be about to break the spine of his victim, whose screams were horrible to hear. Dashing him violently to the ground, Rivoli re-seated himself, and thrust forward

---

[1] A curious piece of Legion "French" meaning "Be quick."
[2] Penal battalion.

49

his right foot. Groaning and gasping, the cowed Austrian knelt to his task, but fumbling and failing to give satisfaction, received a kick in the face.

Reginald Rupert dropped the cartridge-pouch which he was polishing, and stepped forward, only to find himself thrust back by a sweep of the American's huge arm, which struck him in the chest like an iron bar, and to be seized by Legionnaire John Bull, who quietly remarked:

"Mind your own business, recruit. . . . *C'est la Légion!*"

No one noticed that the Russian, Mikhail, was white and trembling, and that his brother came and led him to the other end of the room.

"Bungler! *Polisson! Coquin!* Lick the soles of my boots and go," cried Rivoli, and, as the lad hesitated, he rose to his feet.

Cringing and shrinking, the wretched "blue" hastened to obey, thrust forth his tongue, and, as the boot was raised, obediently licked the nether surface and the edges of the sole until its owner was satisfied.

"Austria's proper attitude to Italy, growled the bully. "Now lick the other. . . ."

Le Légionnaire Luigi Rivoli might expect prompt obedience henceforth from le Légionnaire Franz Joseph Meyer.

Standing in the ring of amused satellites was the evil-looking *Apache,* a deeply interested spectator of this congenial and enjoyable scene. His hang-dog face caught the eye of the Italian.

"Come hither, thou *blanc-bec,*" quoth he. "Come hither and show this *vaurien* how to lace the boots of a gentleman.

The *Apache* obeyed with alacrity, and, performing the task with rapidity and skill, turned to depart.

"A nimble-fingered sharper," observed the Italian, and, rising swiftly, bestowed a shattering kick upon the retreating Frenchman. Recovering his balance after the sudden forward propulsion, the *Apache* wheeled round like lightning, bent double, and flew at his assailant. Courage was his one virtue, and he was the finest exponent of the art of butting in all the purlieus and environs of Montmartre, and had not only laid out many a good bourgeois, but had overcome many a rival, by this preliminary to five minutes' strenuous kicking with heavy boots.

But if Monsieur Tou-Tou Boil-the-Cat was a *Roi des*

Apaches, Luigi Rivoli was an acrobat and juggler, and, to mighty strength, added marvellous poise, quickness and skill.

"*Ça ne marche pas, gobemouche,*" he remarked, and, at the right moment, his knee shot up with tremendous force and crashed into the face of the butting *Apache.* For the first time the famous and terrible attack of the King of the Paris hooligans had failed. When the unfortunate monarch regained his senses, some minutes later, and took stock of his remaining teeth and features, he registered a mental memorandum to the effect that he would move along the lines of caution, rather than valour, in his future dealings with the Légionnaire Luigi Rivoli—until his time came.

"*Je m'en souviendrai,*" said he.. . . .

An interesting object-lesson in the effect, upon a certain type of mind, of the methods of the Italian was afforded by the conduct of a Greek recruit, named Dimitropoulos. Stepping forward with ingratiating bows and smiles, as the unfortunate M. Tou-Tou was stretched senseless on the floor, he proclaimed himself to be the best of the *lustroi* of the city of Corinth, and begged for the honour and pleasure of cleaning the boots of Il Signor Luigi Rivoli.

Oh, but yes; a *lustros* of the most distinguished, look you, who had polished the most emininent boots in Greece at ten *leptas* a time. Alas! that he had not all his little implements and sponges, his cloth of velvet, his varnish for the heel. Had he but the tools necessary to the true artist in his profession, the boots of Il Illustrissimo Signor should be then and henceforth of a brightness dazzling and remarkable.

As he gabbled, the Greek scrubbed at Rivoli's boots with a rag and the palm of his hand. Evidently the retinue of the great man had been augmented by one who would be faithful and true while his patron's strength and money lasted. As, at the head of his band of henchmen and parasites, the latter hero turned to leave the barrack-room with a shout of "Allons, *mes enfants d'Enfer,*" he bent his lofty brow upon, cocked his ferocious eye at, and turned his haughty regard toward the remaining recruits, finishing with Reginald Rupert:

"I will teach useful tricks to you little dogs later," he promised. "You shall dance me the *rigolboche,* and the *can-can,*" and swaggered out. . . .

"Nice lad," observed Rupert, looking up from his work—and wondered what the morrow might bring forth. There should be a disappointed Luïgi, or a dead Rupert about, if it came to interference and trouble.

"Sure," agreed Légionnaire Bronco, seating himself on the bed beside his beloved John Bull. "He's some stiff, that guy, an' I allow it'll soon be up ter me ter conduct our Loojey to the bone-orchard. He's a plug-ugly. He's a ward-heeler. Land sakes! I wants ter punch our Loojey till Hell pops; an' when it comes ter shootin' I got Loojey skinned a mile—sure thing. *J'ai Loojey écorché un mille.* . . . Nope, there ain't 'nuff real room fer Looje an' me in Algery—not while Carmelita's around. . . .

"Say, John," he continued, turning to his friend, "she up an' axed me la' night ef he ever went ter the Canteen an' ef Madam lar Canteenair didn't ever git amakin' eyes at her beautiful Looje! Yep! It *is* time Loojey kissed hisself good-bye."

"Oh. What did you tell her?" enquired John Bull. "There is no doubt the swine will marry the Canteen if he can. More profitable than poor little Carmelita's show. He *is* a low stinker, and she's one of the best and prettiest and pluckiest little women who ever lived. . . . She's so *débrouillarde.*"

" Wot did I say? Wal, John, wot I ses was— 'Amakin' eyes at yure Loojey, my dear,' I ses, 'Madam lar Canteenair is a woman with horse-sense an' two eyes in 'er 'ead. She wouldn't look twice at a boastin', swankin,' fat-slappin', back-stabbin', dime-show ackerobat,' I ses. 'Yure Loojey flaps 'is mouth too much. *Il frappe sa bouche trop,'* I ses. But I didn't tell her as haow 'e's amakin up ter Madam lar Canteenair all his possible. She wouldn't believe it of 'im. She wouldn't even believe that 'e *goes* ter the Canteen. I only ses: 'Yure Loojey's a leary lipper, so don't say as haow I ain't warned yer, Carmelita honey,' I ses—an' I puts it inter copper-bottomed Frencho langwago also. Yep!"

"What did Carmelita say?" asked John Bull.

"Nix," was the reply. "It passes my comprehension wot she sees in that fat Eye-talian ice-cream trader. Anyhaow, it's up ter Hiram C. Milton ter git upon his hind legs an' ferbid the bangs ef she goes fer ter marry a greasy organ-grinder . . . serposin' he don't git Madam lar Canteenair," and the Bucking Bronco sighed deeply, produced some strong, black Algerian tobacco, and asked High Heaven if he might hope ever again to stuff some real Tareyton Mixture (the best baccy in the world) in to his "guley-brooley" —whereby Legionary John Bull understood him to mean his *brûle-gueule,* or short pipe—and relapsed into lethargic and taciturn apathy.

"How would you like a prowl round?" asked John Bull, of Rupert.

"Nothing better, thank you, if you think I could pass the Sergeant of the Guard before being dismissed recruit-drills."

"Oh, that'll be all right of you are correctly dressed. Hop into the tunic and red breeches and we'll try it.

CHAPTER THREE

CARMELITA ET CIE

"THOSE BOOTS COMFORTABLE?" asked John Bull as they crossed the great parade-ground.

"Wonderfully," replied Rupert. "I could do a march in them straight away. Fine boots too."

"Yes," agreed the other. "That's one thing you can say for the Legion kit, the boots are splendid—probably the best military boots in the world. You'll see why, before long."

"Long marches?"

"Longest done by any unit of human beings. Our ordinary marches would be records for any other infantry, and our forced marches are incredible—absolute world's records. They call us the *'Cavalerie à pied'* in the Service, you know. One of the many ways of killing us is marching us to death, to keep up the impossible standard. Buck, here, is our champion."

"Wal, yew see—I strolled crost Amurrica ten times," apologized the Bronco, "ahittin' the main drag, so I oughter vamoose some. Yep! I can throw me feet considerable."

"I've never been a foot-slogger myself," admitted Rupert, "but I've Mastered a beagle pack, and won a few running pots at school and during my brief 'Varsity career. What are your distances?"

"Our minimum, when marching quietly out of barracks

and back, without a halt is forty kilometres under our present Colonel, who is known in the Legion as The Marching Pig, and we do it three or four times a week. On forced marches we do anything that is to be done, inasmuch as it is unalterable law of the Legion that all forced marches must be done in one march. If the next post were forty miles away or even fifty, and the matter urgent, we should go straight on without a halt, except the usual 'cigarette space,' or five minutes in every hour, until we got there. I assure you I have very often marched as much as six hundred kilometres in fifteen days, and occasionally much more. And we carry the heaviest kit in the world—over a hundred-weight, in full marching order."

"What is a kilometre?" asked the interested Rupert.

"Call it five furlongs."

"Then an ordinary day's march is about thirty miles without a halt, and you may have to do four hundred miles straight off, at the rate of twenty-five consecutive miles a day? Good Lord above us!"

"Yes, my own personal record is five hundred and sixty miles in nineteen days, without a rest day—under the African sun and across sand. . . ."

"I say—what's *this* game?" interrupted Rupert, as the three turned a corner and entered a small square between the rear of the *caserne* of the Fourth Company and the great barrack-wall—a square of which all exits were guarded by sentries with fixed bayonets. Round and round in a ring at a very rapid quick-step ran a dismal procession of suffering men, to the monotonously reiterated order of a Corporal—

"A droit, *droit*. A droit, *droit*. A droit, *droit*."

Their blanched, starved-looking faces, glazed eyes, protruding tongues and doubled-up bodies made them a doleful spectacle. On each man's back was a burden of a hundred pounds of stones. On each man's emaciated face, a look of agony, and on the canvas-clad back of one man, a great stain of wet blood from a raw wound caused by the cutting and rubbing of the stone-laden knapsack. Each man wore a fatigue-uniform, filthy beyond description.

"Why the hell can't they be set ter sutthin' useful—hoein' pertaties, or splittin' rails, or chewin' gum—'stead o' that silly strain-me-heart and break-me-sperrit game on empty stummicks twice a day?'' observed the Bucking Bronco.

Every panting, straining, gasping wretch in that pitiable *peloton des hommes punis* looked as though his next minute must be his last, his next staggering step bring him crashing to the ground. What could the dreadful alternative be, the fear of which kept these suffering, starving wretches on their tottering, failing legs? Why would they *not collapse,* in spite of Nature? Fear of the Legion's prison? No, they were all serving periods in the Legion's prison already, and twice spending three hours of each prison-day in this agony. Fear of the Legion's Hospital? Yes, and of the Penal Battalion afterwards.

"What sort of crimes have they committed?" asked Rupert, as they turned with feelings of personal shame from the sickening sight.

"Oh, all sorts, but I'm afraid a good many of them have earned the enmity of some Non-com. As a rule, a man who wants to, can keep out of that sort of thing, but there's a lot of luck in it. One gets run in for a lost strap, a dull button, a speck of dust on rifle or bayonet, or perhaps for being slow at drill, slack in saluting, being out of bounds, or something of that sort. A Sergeant gives him three days' confinement to barracks, and enters it in the *livre de punitions.*

"Very likely, the Captain, feeling liverish when he examines the book, makes it eight days' imprisonment. That's not so bad, provided the Commander of the Battalion does not think the scoundrel had better have a month—and it. And that again is bearable so long as the Colonel does not think the scoundrel had better have a month—and imprisonment, though only called 'Ordinary Arrest,' carries with it this beastly *peloton de chasse.* Still, as I say, a good man and keen soldier can generally keep fairly clear of *salle de police* and *cellule.*"

"So Non-coms. can punish off their own bat, in the Legion, can they?" enquired Rupert as they strolled toward the main gate.

"Yes. The N.C.O. is an almighty important bird here, and you have to salute him like an officer. They can give extra corvée, confinement to barracks, and up to eight days' *salle de police,* and give you a pretty bad time while you're doing it, too. In peace time, you know, the N.C.O.'s run the Legion absolutely. We hardly see our officers except on marches, or at manœuvres. Splendid soldiers, but they consider their duty is to lead us in battle, not to be bothered with us in peace. The N.C.O.'s can do the bothering for them. Of course, we're pretty frequently either demonstrating, or actually fighting on the Southern, or the Morrocan border, and then an officer's job is no sinecure. They are real soldiers—but the weak spot is that they avoid us like poison, in barracks."

"We're mostly foreigners, of course," he continued, "half German, and not very many French, and there's absolutely none of that mutual liking and understanding which is the strength of the British Army. . . . And naturally, in a corps like this, they've got to be severe and harsh to the point of cruelty. After all, it's not a girls' school, is it? But take my advice, my boy, and leave the Legion's punishment system of starvation, overwork, and solitary confinement outside your 'experiences' as much as possible. . . ."

"I say—what a ghastly, charnel-house stink," remarked the recipient of this good advice, as the trio passed two iron-roofed buildings, one on each side of the closed main entrance of the barracks. "I noticed it when I first came in here, but I was to windward of it I suppose. It's the bally limit. Poo-o-oh!"

"Yes, you live in that charming odour all night, if you get *salle de police* for any offence and all day as well, if you get 'arrest' in the regimental lock-up—except for your two three-hour turns of *peloton des hommes punis*. It's nothing at this distance, but wait until you're on sentry-go in one of those barrack prisons. There's a legend of a runaway pig that took refuge in one, gave a gasp, and fell dead. . . . Make Dante himself envious if he could go inside. The truth of that Inferno is much stranger than the fiction of his."

"Yep," chimed in the American. "But what gits my goat every time is *cellules*. Yew squats on end in a dark cell fer the whole of yure sentence, an' yew don't go outside it from start to finish, an' thet may be thirty days. Yew gits a quarter-ration o' dry bread an' a double ration of almighty odour. 'Nuff ter raise the roof, but it don't do it. No exercise, no readin', no baccy, no suthin'. There yew sits and there yew starves, an' lucky ef yew don't go balmy. . . ."

"I hope we get you past the Sergeant of the Guard," interrupted John Bull. "Swank it thick as we go by."

The cold eye of the Sergeant ran over the three Legionaries as they passed through the little side wicket without blazing into wrath over any lack of smartness and *chic* in their appearance.

"One to you," said John Bull, as they found themselves safe in the shadow of the Spahi's barracks outside. "If you had looked too like a recruit he'd have turned you back, on principle. . . ."

To Reginald Rupert the walk was full of interest, in spite of the fact that the half-vulgar, half-picturesque Western-Eastern appearance of the town was no novelty. He had already seen all that Sidi-bel-Abbès could show, and much more, in Algiers, Tangiers, Cairo, Alexandria, Port Said, and Suez. But, with a curious sense of proprietorship, he enjoyed listening to the distant strains of the band—their "own" band. To see thousands of Legionaries, Spahis, Turcos, Chasseurs d'Agrique, Sapeurs, Tirailleurs, Zouaves, and other French soldiery, from their own level, as one of themselves, was what interested him. Here was a new situation, here were new conditions, necessities, dangers, sufferings, relationships. Here, in short, were entirely new experiences. . . .

"This is the Rue Prudon," observed John Bull. "It separates the Military goats on the west, from the Civil sheep on the east. Not that you'll find them at all 'civil' though. . . . Reminds me of a joke I heard our Captain telling the Colonel at dinner one night when I was a Mess Orderly. A new man had taken over the Grand Hotel, and he wrote to the Mess President to say he made a specialty of dinner-parties for Military and *Civilized* officers! Bit rough on the Military, what?"

Having crossed the Rue Prudon rubicon, and invaded the Place de Quinconces with its Pailais de Justice and prison, the Promenade Publique with its beautiful trees, and the Rue Montagnac with its shops and life and glitter, the three Legionaries quitted the quarter of electric arc-lights, brilliant cafés, shops, hotels, apértif-drinking citi-

zens, promenading Frenchwomen, newspaper kiosks, loit-
ering soldiers, shrill hawkers of the *Echo d'Oran,* white-
burnoused Arabs(who gazed coldly upon the hated Franzwazi, and bowed to officials with stately dignity, arms folded on breast), quick-stepping Chaseurs, scarlet-cloaked
Spahis, and swaggering Turcos, crossed the Place Sadi
Carnot, and made for the maze of alleys, slums, and courts
(the quarter of the Spanish Jews, town Arabs, *hadris,*
adjar-wearing women, Berbers, Negroes, half-castes, semi-
Oriental scum, "white trash," and Legionaries), in one of
which was situated Carmelita's Café de la Légion.

2

La Belle Carmelita, black-haired, red-cheeked, black-
eyed, red-lipped, lithe, swift, and graceful, sat at the re-
ceipt of custom. Carmelita's Café de la Légion was for
the Legion, and had to make its profits out of men whose
pay is one halfpenny a day. It is therefore matter for
little surprise that it compared unfavourably with Voisin's,
the Café de la Paix, the Pré Catalan, Maxim's, the Café
Grossenwahn, the Das Prinzess Café, the restaurants of
the Place Pigalle, Le Rat Mort, or even Les Noctambules,
Le Cabaret de l'Enfer, the Chat Noir, the Elysée Montmartre, and the famous and infamous *caveaux* of Le
Quartier—in the eyes of those Legionaries who had tried
some, or all, of these places.

However, it had four walls, a floor, and a roof; benches
and a large number of tables and chairs, many of which
were quite reliable. It had a bar, it had Algerian wine at
one penny a bottle, it had *vert-vert* and *tord-boyaud* and
bapédi and *shum-shum*. It had really good coffee, and
really bad cigarettes. It had meals also—but above all,
and before all, it had a welcome. A welcome for the
Legionary. The man to whose presence the good people
of Sidi-bel-Abbès (French petty officials, half-castes, Spanish Jews, Arabs, clerks, workmen, shopkeepers, waiters, and
lowest-class bourgeoisie) took exception at the bandstand,
in the Gardens, in the Cafés, in the very streets; the man
from the contamination of whose touch the very cocottes,
the demi-mondaines, the joyless *filles de joie*, even the
daughters of the pavement, drew aside the skirts of their

dingy finery (for though the Wages of Virtue are a half-penny a day for the famous Legion, the Wages of Sin are more for the infamous legion); the man at whom even the Goums, the Arab *gens-d'armes* shouted as at a pariah dog, this man, the Soldier of the Legion, had a welcome in Carmelita's Café. There were two women in all the world who would endure to breathe the same air as the sad Sons of the Legion—Madame la Cantiniére (official *fille du régiment*) and Carmelita. Is it matter for wonder that the Legion's sons loved them—particularly Carmelita, who, unlike Madame, was under no obligation to shed the light of her countenance upon them? Any man in the Legion might speak to Carmelita provided he spoke as a gentleman should speak to a lady—and did not want to be pinned to her bar by the ears, and the bayonets of his indignant brothers-in-arms—any man who might speak to no other woman in the world outside the Legion. (Madame la Cantiniére is inside the Legion, *bien entendu,* and always married to it in the person of one of its sons.) She would meet him as an equal for the sake of her beautiful, wonderful, adored Luigi Rivoli, his brother-in-arms. Perhaps one must be such an outcast that the sight of one causes even painted lips to curl in contemptuous disdain; such a *thing* that one is deterred from entering decent Cafés, decent places of amusement and decent boulevards so low that one is strictly doomed to the environment of one's prison, or the slums, and to the society of one's fellow dregs, before one can appreciate the attitude of the Sons of the Legion to Carmelita. They revered her as they did not revere the Mother of God, and they, broken and crucified wretches, envied Luigi Rivoli as they did not envy the repentant thief absolved by Her Son.

She, Carmelita, welcomed *them,* Legionaries! It is perhaps comprehensible, if not excusable, that the attitude of Madame la Cantiniére was wholly different, that she hated Carmelita as a rival, and with single heart, double venom and treble voice, denounced her, her house, her wine, her coffee, and all those *chenapans* and *sacripants* her clients.

So the Legion loved Carmelita, Madame la Cantiniére hated her, the Bucking Bronco worshipped her, John Bull admired her, le bon M. Edouard Malvin desired her, and

Luigi Rivoli owned her—body, soul and cash-box—what time he sought to do the same for Madame la Cantiniére, whose body and cash-box were as much larger than those of Carmelita as her soul was smaller.

Between two fools one comes to the ground—sometimes —but Luigi intended to come to a bed of roses, and to have a cash-box beneath it. One of the fools should marry and support him, preferably the richer fool, and meantime, on the sublety, the cleverness, the piquancy—of being loved and supported by both while marrying neither! Many a time as he lay on his cot while a henchman polished the great cartridge-pouches (that earned the Legion the sobriquet of "the Leather-Bellies" from the Russians in the Crimea), the belts, the buttons, the boots, and the rifle and bayonet of the noble Luigi, while another washed his fatigue uniforms and underclothing, that honourable man would chuckle aloud as he saw himself frequently cashing a ten-franc piece of Carmelita's at Madame's Canteen, and receiving change for a twenty-franc piece from the fond, yielding Madame. Ten francs too much, a sigh too many, and a kiss too few—for Madame did not kiss, being, contrary to popular belief with regard to vivandiéres in general, and the Legion's vivandiére in particular, of rigid virtue, oh, but yes, of a respectability profound and colossal—during "vacation." Her present vacation had lasted for three months, and Madame felt it was time to replace le pauvre Eitenne Baptiste—cut in small pieces by certain Arab ladies. Madame was a business woman, Madame needed a husband in her business, and Madame had an eye for a fine man. None finer than Luigi Rivoli, and Madame had never tried an Italian. Husbands do not last long in the Legion, and Madame had had three French, one Belgian, and one Swiss (seriatim, *bien entendu*). No, none finer in the whole Legion than Rivoli. None, nom de Dieu! But a foreign husband may be a terrible trial, look you, and an Italian is a foreigner in a sense that a French-speaking Belgian or Swiss is not. No, an Italian is not a Frenchman even though he be a Légionnaire. And there were tales of him and this vile shameless creature from Naples, who decoyed les braves Légionnaires from their true and lawful Canteen to her noisome den in the foul slums, there to spend their hard-earned sous on her poisonous red-ink wine, her muddy-water coffee, and her—worse things. Yes, that cunning little fox le Légionnaire Edouard Malvin had thrown out hints to Madame about this Neapolitan *ragazza*—but then, ce bon M. Malvin was himself a suitor for Madame's hand—as well as a most remarkable liar and rogue.

. . . . And the business soul of scheming, but amorous Madame, much troubled, still halted between two opinions —while the romantic and simple soul of loving little Carmelita remained steadfast, and troubled but little. Just a little, because the fine *gentilhomme,* Légionnaire Jean Boule, and the great, kind Légionnaire Boucking Bronceau, and certain others, seemed somehow to *warn* her against her Luigi; seemed to despise him, and hint at treachery. She did not count the sly Belgian (or Austrian) Edouard Malvin. The big stupid Americano was jealous, of course, but Il Signor Inglese was not and he was—oh, like a Reverend Father—so gentle and honest and good. But no, her Luigi could not be false, and the next Légionnaire who said a word against him should be forbidden Le Café de la Légion, ill as it could afford to lose even halfpenny custom—what with the rent, taxes, *bakshish* to gens-d'armes, service, cooking, lighting, wine, spirits, coffee and Luigi's daily dinner, Chianti and franc pocket-money. . . . If only that franc could be increased —but one must eat, or get so thin—and the great Luigi liked not skinny women. What was a franc a day to such a man as Luigi, her Luigi, strongest, finest hand-somest of men?—and but for her he would never have been in this accursed Legion. Save for her aggravating wickedness, he would never have stabbed poor Guiseppe Longigotto and punished her by enlisting. How great and fine a hero of splendid vengeance! A true Neapolitan, yet how magnanimous when punishment was meted! He had forgiven—and forgotten—the dead Guiseppe, and he had forgiven her, and he accepted her miserable franc, dinner and Chianti wine daily. Also he had allowed her —miserable ingrate that she had been to annoy him and make him jealous—to find the money that had mysteriously but materially assisted in procuring the perpetual late-pass that allowed him to remain with her till two in the morning, long after all the other poor Légionnaires had returned to their dreadful barracks. Noble Luigi! Yet there were people who coupled his name with that of wealthy Madame la Cantiniére in the barrack yonder.

She had overheard Légionnaires doing it, here in her own Café, though they had instantly and stoutly denied it when accused, and had looked furtive and ashamed. Absurd, jealous wretches, whose heads Luigi could knock together as easily as she could click her castanets. . . .

At the age of fifteen, Carmelita, most beautiful of form and coarsely beautiful of face, of perfect health, grace, poise, and carriage, fell desperately in love with the great Signor Carlo Scopinaro, born Luigi Rivoli, a star of her own firmament but of far greater magnitude.

Luigi Rivoli, one of a troupe of acrobats who performed at the Naples Scala, Vesuvie, and Variétés, meditating setting up on his own account as Strong Man, Acrobat, Juggler, Wrestler, Dancer, and Professor of Physical Culture, was, to the humble "tumbler" of the quay, as the be-Knighted Actor-Manager of a West End Theatre to the last joined chorus girl, or walking-lady on his boards. And yet the great Signor Carlo Scopinaro, born Luigi Rivoli, meditating desertion from his troupe and needing an "assistant," deigned to accept the services and whole-souled adoration of the girl who was as much more skilful as she was less powerful than he.

When, in her perfect, ardent, and beautiful love, her reckless and uncounting adoration, she gave herself, mind, body and soul, to her hero and her god, he accepted the little gift "without prejudice"—as the lawyers say. "Without prejudice" to Luigi's future, that is.

During their short engagement at the Scala—terminated by the Troupe's earnest endeavour to assassinate the defaulting and defalcating Luigi, and her family's endeavour to maim Carmelita for setting up on her own account, and deserting her loving "parents"—it was rather the girl whom the public applauded for her wonderful back-somersaults, contortions, hand-walking, catherine-wheels, trapeze-work, and dancing, than the man for his feats with dumb-bells of doubtful solidity, his stereotyped ball-juggling, his chain-breaking, and weight-lifting, his muscle-slapping and *Ha!* shouting, posturing and grimacing, and his issuing of challenges to wrestle any man in the world for any sum he liked to name, and in any style known to science. And, when engagements at the lower-class halls and cafés of Barcelona, Marseilles, Toulon, Genoa, Rome, Brindisi, Venice, Trieste, Corinth, Athens, Constantinople, Port Said, Alexandria, Messina, Valetta, Algiers, Oran, Tangiers, or Casa Blanca were obtained, it was always, and obviously, the girl rather than the man, who decided the proprietor or manager to engage them, and who won the applause of his patrons.

When times were bad, as after Luigi's occasional wrestling defeats and during the bad weeks of Luigi's typhoid, convalescence, and long weakness at Marseilles, it was Carmelita, the humbler and lesser light, who (the Halls being worked out) tried desperately to keep the wolf from the door by returning to the quay-side business, and, for dirty coppers, exhibiting to passengers, coal-trimmers, cargo-workers, porters and loafers, the performances that had been subject of signed contracts and given on fine stages in beautiful music-halls and cafés, to refined and appreciative audiences. Incidentally the girl learned much French (little knowing how useful it was to prove), as well as smatterings of Spanish, Greek, Turkish, English and Arabic.

So Carmelita had "assisted" the great Luigi in the times of his prosperity and had striven to maintain him in eclipse, by quay-side, public-house, workmen's dinner-hour, low café, back-yard, gambling-den, and wine-shop exhibitions of her youthful skill, grace, agility, and beauty— and had failed to make enough by that means. To the end of her life poor Carmelita could never, never forget that terrible time at Marseilles, try as she might to thrust it into the background of her thoughts. For there, ever there, in the background it remained, save when called to cruel prominence by some mischance, or at rare intervals by the noble Luigi himself, when displeased by some failure on the part of Carmelita. A terrible, terrible memory, for Carmelita's nature was essentially virginal, delicate, and of crystal purity. Where she loved she gave all —and Luigi was to Carmelita as much her husband as if they had been married in every church they had passed, in every cathedral they had seen, and by every *padre* they had met. . . .

A terrible, terrible memory. . . . But Luigi's life was at stake, and what true woman, asked Carmelita, would have not taken the last step of all (when every other failed) to raise the money necessary for doctors, medicine, delicacies, food, fuel, and lodging? If, by thrusting her right hand into the fire, Carmelita could have burnt away those haunting and corroding Marseilles memories, then into the fire her right hand would have been thrust. Yet, side by side with the self-horror and self-disgust was no remorse nor repentance. If, tomorrow, Luigi's life could only thus again be saved, thus saved should it be, as when at Marseilles he lay convalescent but dying for lack of the money wherewith to buy the delicacies that would save him. . . . Luigi's life always, and at any time, before Carmelita's scruples and shrinkings.

In return, Luigi had been kind to her and had often spoken of matrimony—some day—in spite of what she had done at Marseilles when he was too ill to look after her, and provide her with all she needed. Once even, when they were on the crest of a great wave of prosperity, Luigi had gone so far as to mention her seventeenth birthday as a possible suitable date for their wedding. That had been a great and glorious time, though all too short, alas!

Later had come a time of poverty, straits, mean shifts and misery, followed by Luigi's job as a "tamer" of tame lions. This post of lion-tamer to a cageful of mangy, weary lions, captive-born, pessimistic, timid and depressed, had been secured by Guiseppe Longigotto, and handed over to Luigi (on its proving safe and satisfactory), in the interests of Guiseppe's adored and hungry Carmelita. Arrayed in the costume worn by all the Best Lion-tamers, Luigi looked a truly noble figure, as, with flashing eyes and gleaming teeth, he cracked the whip and fired the revolver that induced the bored and disgusted lions to amble round the cage, crouching and cringing, in humility and fear. That insignificant little rat, Guiseppe, was far more in the picture, of course, as fiddler to the show, than he was in his original rôle of tamer of the lions. Followed a bad time along the African coast, culminating, at Algiers, in poor Guiseppe's impassioned pleadings that Carmelita would marry him. Luigi's jealousy, his overbearing airs of proprietorship, his drunken cruelty, his presuming on her love and obedience to him until she sought to give him a fright and teach him a lesson, his killing of the poor, pretty musician, and his flight to Sidi-bel-Abbès. . . .

To Sidi-bel-Abbès also fled Carmelita, and, with the proceeds of Guiseppe's dying gift to her, eked out by promises of many things to many people, such as Jew and Arab lessors and landlords, French dealers, Spanish-Jew jobbers and contractors, and Negro labourers, contrived to open La Café de la Légion, to run it with herself as proprietress, manageress, barmaid, musician, singer, actress, and *danseuse,* and to make it pay to the extent of a daily franc, bottle of Chianti, and a macaroni, polenta, or spaghetti meal for Luigi, and a very meagre living for herself.

And by-and-by her splendid and noble Luigi would marry her, and they would go to America—and live happily ever after.

"Ben venuit, Signori!" cried Carmelita on catching sight of Il Signor Jean Boule and the Bucking Bronco. *"Soyez le bien venu, Monsieur Jean Boule et Monsieur Bronco, Che cosa posso offrirvi?"* and, as they seated themselves at a small round table near the bar, hastened to bring the wine favoured by these favoured customers—the so gentle English Signor, *gentilhomme,* (doubtless once a *milord,* a *nobile*), and the so gentle, foolish Americano, so slow and strong, who looked at her with eyes of love, kind eyes, with a good true love. No *milordino* he, no *piccol Signor* (but nevertheless, a good man, a *uomo dabbéne, most certainly . . . .*)

Reginald Rupert was duly presented as Légionnaire Rupert, with all formality and ceremony, to the Madamigella Carmelita, who ran her bright, black eye over him, summed him up as another *gentiluomo,* an obvious *gentilhomme,* pitied him, and wondered what he had "done."

Carmelita loved a "gentleman" in the abstract, although she loved Luigi Rivoli in the concrete; adored aristocrats in general, in spite of the fact that she adored Luigi Rivoli in particular. To her experienced and observant young eye, Légionnaire Jean Boule and this young *bleu* were of the same class, the *aristocratico* class of *Inghilterra;*

birds of a feather, if not of a nest. They might be father and son, so alike were they in their difference from the rest. So different even from the English-speaking Americano, so different from her Luigi.

"Buona sera, Signor," said Carmelita to Rupert. *"Siete venuto per la via di Francie?"* and then, in Legion-French and Italian, proceeded to comment upon the new recruit's appearance, his *capelli riccioluti,* and to enquire whether he used the *calamistro* and *ferro da ricci* to obtain the fine crisp wave in his hair.

Reginald Rupert (to whom love and war were the two things worth living for), on understanding the drift of the lady's remarks, proposed forthwith "to cross the bar" and "put out to see" whether he could not give her a personal demonstration of the art of hair-curling, but—

"Non vi pigliate fastadio," said Carmelita. "Don't trouble yourself, Signor Azzurro—Monsieur Bleu. And if Signor Luigi Rivoli should enter and see the young Signor on my side of the bar—Luigi's side of the bar—why, one look of his eye would so make the young Signor's hair curl that, for the rest of his life, the *calamistro,* the curling-tongs, would be superfluous."

"Yep," chimed in the Bucking Bronco. "I guess as haow it's about time yure Loojey's bright eyes got closed, my dear, an' I'm goin' ter bung 'em both up one o' these fine days, when I got the cafard. Yure Loojey's a great lady-killer an' recruit-killer, we know, an' he can talk a tin ear on a donkey. I say *Il parlerait une oreille d'étain sur un âne.* Yure Loojey'd make a hen-rabbit git mad an' bark. I say *Votre Loojey causerait une lapine devenir fou et écorcer.* I got it in fer yure Loojey. I say *Je l'ai dans pour votre Loojey.* . . . Comprenny? *Intendete quel che dico?"* and the Bucking Bronco drank off a pint of wine, drew his tiny, well-thumbed French dictionary from one pocket and his "Travellers' Italian Phrase-book" from another, cursed the Tower of Babel, and all foreign tongues, and sought words wherewith to say that it was high time for Luigi Rivoli "to quit beefin' aroun' Madam lar Canteenair, to wipe off his chin considerable, to cease being a sticker, a sucker, and a skinamalink girl-sponging meal-and-money cadger; and to quit tellin' stories made out o' whole cloth,[1] that cut no ice with nobody except Carmelita."

This young lady gathered that, as usual, the poor, silly jealous Americano was belittling and insulting her Luigi, if not actually threatening him. *Him,* who could break any Americano across his knee. With a toss of her head and a contemptuous "Invidioso! Scioccone!" for the Bronco, a flick on the nose with the *krenfell* flower from her ear for Rupert, a blown kiss for *Babbo* Jean Boule, Carmelita flitted away, going from table to table to minister to the mental, moral, and physical needs of her other devoted Légionnaires as they arrived—men of strange and dreadful lives who loved her then and there, who remembered her thereafter and elsewhere, and who sent her letters, curios, pressed flowers and strange presents from the ends of the earth where flies the *tricouleur,* and the Flag of the Legion —in Tonkin, Madagascar, Senegal, Morocco, the Sahara— in every Southern Algerian station wherever the men of the Legion tramped to their death to the strains of the regimental march of *"Tiens, voilà du boudin."*

In the extreme corner of the big, badly-lit room a Legionary sat alone, his back to the company, his head upon his folded arms. Passing near, on her tour of ministration, Carmelita's quick eye and ear perceived that the man was sobbing and weeping bitterly. It might be the poor Grasshopper passing through one of his terrible dark hours, and Carmelita's kind heart melted with pity for the poor soul, smartest of soldiers, and maddest of madmen.

Going over to where he sat apart, Carmelita bent over him, placed her arm around his neck, and stroked his glossy dark hair.

"Pourquoi faites-vous Suisse, mon pauvre?" she murmured with a motherly caress. "What is it? Tell Carmelita." The man raised his face from his arms, smiled through his tears and kissed the hand that rested on his shoulder. The handsome and delicate face, the small, well-kept hands, the voice, were those of a man of culture and refinement.

"I ja nai ka!—How delightful!" he said. "You will make things right. I am to be made *machi-bugiyo,* governor of the city to-morrow, and I wish to remain a Japanese lady. I do not want to lay aside the *sumagoto* and *samisen* for the *wakizashi* and the *katana*—the lute for the dagger

---

[1] Untrue.

and sword. I don't want to sit on a *tokonoma* in a *yashiki* surrounded by *karo*. . . ."

"No, no, no, mon cher, you shall not indeed. See, le bon Dieu and Le bon Jean Boule will look after you," said Carmelita, gently stroking his hot forehead and soothing him with little crooning sounds and caresses as though he had really been the child that, in mind and understanding, he was.

John Bull, followed by Rupert, unobtrusively joined Carmelita. Seating himself beside the unhappy man, he took his hands and gazed steadily into his suffused eyes.

"Tell me all about it, Cigale," said he. "You know we can put it right. When has Jean Boule failed to explain and arrange things for you?"

The madman repeated that he dreaded to have to sit on the raised dias of the Palace of a Governor of a City surrounded by officials and advisers.

"I know I should soon be involved in a *kataki-uchi* with a neighbouring clan, and have to commit hara-kiri if I failed to keep the Mikado's peace. It is terrible. You don't know how I long to remain a lady. I want silk and music and cherry-blossom instead of steel and blood," and again he laid his head upon his arms and continued his low hopeless sobbing.

Reginald Rupert's face expressed blank astonishment at the sight of the weeping soldier.

"What's up?" he said.

Légionnaire John Bull tapped his forehead.

"Poor chap will behave *more Japonico* for the rest of the day now. I fancy he's been an attaché in Japan. You don't know Japanese by any chance? I have forgotten the little I knew."

Rupert shook his head.

"Look here, Cigale," said John Bull, raising the afflicted man and again fixing the steady, benign gaze upon his eyes, "why are you making all this trouble for yourself? You know I am the Mikado and All-powerful! You have only to appeal to me and the Shogun must release you. Of course you can remain a Japanese lady—and I'll tell you what, ma chère, ma petite fille Japonaise, not only shall you remain a lady, but a lady of the old school and of the days before the accursed Foreign Devils came in to break down ancient customs. I promise it. To-morrow you shall shave off your eyebrows and paint them in two inches above your eyes. I promise it. More. Your teeth shall be lacquered black. Now cease these ungrateful repinings, and be a happy maiden once again. By order of the Mikado!"

Once again the voice and eye, and the gentle wise sympathy and comprehension of ce bon Jean Boule had succeeded and triumphed. The madman, falling at his feet, knelt and bowed three times, his forehead touching the ground, in approved geisha fashion.

"And now you've got to come and lie down, or you won't be fit for the eye-brow-shaving ceremony to-morrow," said Carmelita, and led him to a broad, low divan, which made a cosy, if dirty, corner remote from the bar.

"That's as extraordinary a case as ever I came across," remarked John Bull to Rupert as they rejoined the Bucking Bronco, who was talking to the Cockney and the Russian twins, "as mad as any lunatic in any asylum in the world, and yet as absolutely competent and correct in every detail of soldiering as any soldier in the Legion. He is the Perfect Private Soldier—and a perfect lunatic. Most of the time, off parade that is, he thinks he's a grasshopper, and the rest of the time he thinks he's of some remarkable foreign nationality, such as a Zulu, an Eskimo, or a Chinaman. I should very much like to know his story, but we don't ask men their 'stories' in the Legion."

Carmelita returned to her high seat by the door of her little room behind the bar—the door upon the outside of which many curious regards had oftentimes been fixed.

Carmelita was troubled. Why did not Luigi come? Were his duties so numerous and onerous nowadays that he had but a bare hour for his late dinner and his bottle of Chianti? Time was, when he arrived as soon after five o'clock as a wash and change of uniform permitted. Time was, when he could spend from early evening to late night in the Café de la Légion, out-staying the latest visitors. And that time was also the time when Madame la Cantinière was not a widow —the days before Madame's husband had been sliced, sawn, snapped, torn, and generally mangled by certain other widows—of certain Arabs—away to the South. This might be coincidence of course, and yet — and yet — several Légionnaires who had no axe to grind and who were not jealous of Luigi's fortune, had undoubtedly coupled his name with that of Madame. . . .

"An' haow did yew find yure little way to our dope-joint hyar?" the Bucking Bronco enquired of Mikhail Kyrilovitch, as he did the honours of Carmelita's "joint" to the three *bleus* who had entered while John Bull was talking to the Grasshopper.

"Well, since you arx, we jest ups an' follers you, old bloke, when yer goes aht wiv these two uvver Henglish coves," replied the Cockney.

"I'm afraid I can't ask yew moojiks ter hev a little caviare an' wodky, becos' Carmelita is out of it. . . . But there's cawfy in the sammy-var I hev no doubt," the American said graciously.

The Russians thanked him, and Feodor pledging him in a glass of absinthe, promised to teach him the art of concocting *lompopo*, while Mikhail quietly sipped his glass of sticky, sweet Algerian wine.

Restless Carmelita joined the group, and her friend Jean Boule introduced the three new patrons.

"Prahd an' honoured, Miss, I'm shore," said the Cockney. " 'Ave a port-an'-lemon or thereabahts?"

But Carmelita was too interested in the startling similarity of the twins to pay attention to the civilities and blandishments of the Cockney, albeit he surreptitiously wetted his fingers with wine and smoothed his smooth and shining "cowlick" or "quiff" (the highly ornamental fringe which, having descended to his eyebrows, turned aspiringly upward).

"*Gemello*," she murmured, turning from Feodor and his cheery greeting to Mikhail, who responded with a graceful little bow, suddenly terminated and changed to a curt nod, like that given by Feodor. As Carmelita continued her direct gaze, a dull flush grew and mantled over his face.

"*Cielo!* But how the boy blushes! Now is it for his own sins, or mine, I wonder?" laughed Carmelita, pointing accusingly at poor Mikhail's suffused face.

"Gawdstreuth! Can't 'e blush," remarked Mr. Higgins.

The dull flush became a vivid, burning blush under Carmelita's pointing finger, and the regard of the amused Legionaries.

"*Corpo di Bacco!*" laughed the teasing girl. "A blushing

Legionary! The dear, sweet, good boy. If only *I* could blush like that. And he brings his blushes to Madame la République's Legion. Well, it is not *porta vasi a Samo!*"[1]

"Never mind, Sonny," said the American soothingly, "there's many a worse stunt than blushin'. I uster use blushes considerable meself—when I was a looker 'bout yure age." He translated.

Carmelita's laughter pealed out again at the idea of the blushing American. Feodor's laughter mingled with Carmelita's, but sounded forced.

"Isn't it funny?" he remarked. "My brother has always been like that, but believe me, Padrona, I could not blush to save my life."

"Si, si," laughed Carmelita. "You have sinned and he has blushed—all your lives, is it not so—le pauvre petit?" and saucily rubbed the side of Mikhail's crimson face with the backs of her fingers—and looked unwontedly thoughtful as he jerked his head away with a look of annoyance.

"La, la, la!" said Carmelita. "Mustn't he be teased then?"

"Come, Signora," broke in Feodor again, "you're making him blush worse than ever. Such kindness is absolutely wasted. Now I . . ."

"No, *you* wouldn't blush with shame and fright, no, nor yet with innocence, would you, Signor Feodor? *E un peccato!*" replied the girl, and lightly brushed his cheek as she spoke.

The good Feodor did not blush, but the look of thoughtfulness deepened on Carmelita's face.

To the finer perceptions of John Bull there seemed to be something strained and discomfortable in the atmosphere. Carmelita had fallen silent, Feodor seemed annoyed and anxious, Mikhail frightened and anxious, and Mr. 'Erb 'Iggins of too gibing a humour.

"You are making me positively jealous, Signora Carmelita, and leaving me thirsty," he said, and with a small repentant squeal Carmelita flitted to the bar.

"Would you like a biscuit too, Signor Jean Boule?" she called, and tossed one across to him as she spoke. John Bull neatly caught the biscuit as it flew somewhat wide. Carmelita, like most women, could not throw straight.

"Tiro maestro," she applauded, and launched another at

---
[1] Lit., "to carry coals to Newcastle."

the unprepared Mikhail with a cry of "Catch, *goffo*." Instinctively he "made a lap" and spread out his hands.

"Esattamente!" commented Carmelita beneath her breath and apparently lost interest in the little group. . . .

A quartet of Legionaries swaggered into the café and approached the bar—Messieurs Malvin, Borges, Bauer and Hirsch henchmen and satellites of Luigi Rivoli—and saluted to Carmelita's greeting of "Buona sera, Signori. . . ."

"Bonsoir, M. Malvin," added she to the dapper, low-bowing Austrian, whose evil face, with its close-set ugly eyes, sharp crooked nose, waxed moustache, and heavy jowl, were familiar to her as those of one of Luigi's more intimate followers. "Where is Signor Luigi Rivoli to-night? He has no guard duty?"

"No, mia signora—er—that is—yes," replied Malvin in affected discomfort. "He is—ah—on duty."

"On duty in the Canteen?" asked Carmelita, flushing.

"What do I know of the comings and goings of the great Luigi Rivoli?" answered Malvin. "Doubtless he will fortify himself with a litre of wine at Madame's bar in the Canteen before walking down here."

"Luigi Rivoli drinks no sticky Algerian wine," said Carmelita angrily and her eyes and teeth flashed dangerously. "He drinks Chianti from Home. He never enters her Canteen."

"Ah! So?" murmured Malvin in a non-committal manner. And then Carmelita's anxiety grew a little greater —greater even than her dislike and distrust of M. Eduard Malvin, and she did what she had never done before. She voiced it to him.

"Look you, Monsieur Malvin, tell me the truth. I will not tell my Luigi that you have accused him to me, or say that you have spoken ill of him behind his back. Tell me the truth. *Is* he in the Canteen? Tell me, cher Monsieur Malvin."

"Have I the double sight, bella Carmelita? How should I know where le Légionnaire Rivoli may be?" fenced the soi-disant Belgian.

"Tell me the truth, cher Monsieur Malvin. Where is my Luigi?" again asked Carmelita pleadingly.

"Donna e Madonna," replied the M. Malvin, with piteous eyes, broken voice, and protecting hand placed

gently over that of Carmelita which lay clenched upon the zinc-covered bar. "What shall I say? Luigi Rivoli is a giant among men—I, a little fat *deboletto*, a *sparutello* whom the great Luigi could kill with one hand. Though I love Carmelita, I fear Luigi. How shall I tell of his doings with that husband-seeking *puttana* of the Canteen; of his serving behind the bar, helping her, taking her money, drinking her wine (wine of Algiers); of his passionate and burning prayers that she will marry him? How can I, his friend, tell of those things? But oh! Carmelita, my poor honest heart is wrung . . ." and le bon Monsieur Malvin paused to hope that his neck also would not be wrung as a result of this moving eloquence.

For a moment Carmelita's eyes blazed and her hands and her little white teeth clenched. Mother of God! if Luigi played her false after all she had done for him, after all she had given him—given *for* him! . . . But no, it was unthinkable. . . . This Malvin was an utter knave and liar, and would fool her for his own ends—the very man *fare un pesce d' Aprile a qualcuno*. He should see how far his tricks succeeded with Carmelita of the Legion, the chosen of Carlo Scopinaro! And yet . . . and yet . . . She would ask Il Signor Jean Boule again. He would never lie. He would neither backbite Luigi Rivoli, nor stand by and see Carmelita deceived. Yes, she would ask Jean Boule, and then if he *too* accused Luigi she would find some means to see and hear for herself. . . . Trust her woman's wit for that. And meantime this serpent of a Malvin . . .

"*Se ne vada!*" she hissed, whirling upon him suddenly, and pointed to the door. Malvin slunk away, by no means anxious to be present at the scene which would certainly follow should Luigi enter before Carmelita's mood had changed. He would endeavour to meet and delay him. . . .

"What do yew say to acontinuin' o' this hyar gin-crawl?" asked the Bucking Bronco of Rupert. "Come and see our other pisen-joint and Madame lar Canten air."

"Anything you like," replied Rupert.

"Let's go out when they do," said Mikhail quickly, in Russian, to Feodor.

"All right, silly Olka," was the whispered reply.

"Silly Fedka, to call me Olka," was the whispered retort.

"You're a pretty *budotchnik*,[1] aren't you?"

As the party filed out of the café, Mikhail Kyrilovitch, who was walking last of the party, felt a hand slip within his arm to detain him. Turning, he beheld Carmelita's earnest little face near his own. In his ear she whispered in French—

"I have your secret, little one—but have no fear. Should anyone discover it, come to Carmelita," and before the astonished Mikhail could reply she was clearing empty glasses and bottles from their table.

CHAPTER FOUR

The Canteen of the Legion

From the Canteen, a building in the corner of the barrack-square, proceeded sounds of revelry by night.

"Blimey! Them furriners are singin' 'Gawd save the Queen' like bloomin' Christians," remarked 'Erb as the little party approached the modest Temple of Bacchus.

"No, they are Germans singing *'Heil dir im Sieges Kranz,'*" replied Feodor Kyrilovitch in English.

"And singing it most uncommonly well," added Legionary John Bull.

"Fancy them 'eathens pinchin' the toon like that," commented 'Erb. "They oughtn't to be allowed. . . . Do they 'old concerts 'ere? I dessay they'd like to 'ear some good Henglish songs. . . ."

Reginald Rupert never forgot his first glimpse of the Canteen of the Legion, though he entered it hundreds of times and spent hundreds of hours beneath its corrugated iron roof. Scores of Legionaries, variously clad in blue and red or white, sat on benches at long tables, or lunged at the long zinc-covered bar, behind which were Madame and hundreds of bottles and large wine-glasses.

Madame had a beady eye a perceptible moustache, a frankly downy chin, two other chins, a more than ample figure, and looked, what she was, a female campsutler. Perhaps Madame appeared more Ouidaesque on the march, wearing her official blue uniform as duly constituted and appointed *fille du régiment*. At present she looked . . . However, the bow of Reginald Rupert, together with his

---

[1] Guardian, watchman.

smile and honeyed words, were those of Mayfair, as he was introduced by Madame's admired friend ce bon Jean Boule, and he stepped straight into Madame's experienced but capacious heart. Nor was the brightness of the image dulled by the ten-franc piece which he tendered with the request that Madame would supply the party with her most blushful Hippocrene. 'Erb, being introduced, struck an attitude, his hand upon his heart. Madame coughed affectedly.

"Makes a noise like a 'igh-class parlour-maid bein' jilted, don' she?" he observed critically.

Having handed a couple of bottles and a large glass to each member of the party, by way of commencement in liquidating the coin, she returned to her confidential whispering with Monsieur le Légionnaire Luigi Rivoli (who lolled, somewhat drunk, in a corner of the bar) as the group seated itself at the end of a long table near the window.

It being "holiday," that is, pay-day, the Canteen was full, and most of its patrons had contrived to emulate it. A very large number had laid out the whole of their *décompte* —every farthing of two-pence halfpenny—on wine. Others, wiser and more continent, had reserved a halfpenny for tobacco. In one corner of the room an impromptu German glee party was singing with such excellence that the majority of the drinkers were listening to them with obvious appreciation. With hardly a break, and with the greatest impartiality they proceeded from part-song to hymn, from hymn to drinking-song, from drinking-song to sentimental love ditty. Finally *Ein feste burg ist unser Gott* being succeeded by *Die Wacht am Rhein* and *Deutschland über Alles,* the French element in the room thought that a little French music would be a pleasing corrective, and with one accord, if not in one key, gave a spirited rendering of the Marseillaise.

"This is really extraordinary good wine," remarked Rupert to John Bull.

"Yes," replied the latter. "It's every bit as good at three-halfpence a bottle as it is at three-and-six in England, and I'd advise you to stick to it and let absinthe alone. It does one no harm, in reason, and is a great comfort. It's our greatest blessing and our greatest curse. Absinthe is pure curse—and inevitably means 'cafard.' "

"What is this same 'cafard' of which one hears so much?" asked Rupert.

"Well, the word itself means 'beetle,' I believe, and sooner or later the man who drinks absinthe in this climate feels the beetle crawling round and round in his brain. He then does the maddest things and ascribes the impulse to the beetle. He finally goes mad and generally commits murder or suicide, or both. That is one form of *cafard*, and other is mere fedupness, a combination of liverish temper, boredom and utter hatred and loathing of the terrible annui of the life."

"Have you had it?" asked the other.

"Everyone has it at times," was the reply, "especially in the tiny desert-stations where the awful heat, monotony, and lack of employment leave one the choice of drink or madness. If you drink you're certain to go mad, if you don't drink you're sure to. Of course, men like ourselves—educated, intelligent, and all that—have more chance than the average 'Tommy' type, but it's very dangerous for the highly strung excitable sort. He's apt to go mad and stay mad. We only get fits of it."

"Don't the authorities do anything to amuse and employ the men in desert stations, like we do in India?" enquired the younger man.

"Asolutely nothing. They prohibit the *Village Négre* in every station, compel men to lie on their cots from eleven till four, and do nothing at all to relieve the maddening monotony of drill, sentry-go and punishment. On the other hand, *cafard* is so recognised an institution that punishments for offences committed under its influence are comparatively light. It takes different people differently, and is sometimes comic—though generally tragic."

"I should think you're bound to get something of the sort wherever men lead a very hard and very monotonous life, in great heat," said Rupert.

"Oh, yes," agreed John Bull. "After all *le cafard* is not the private and peculiar specialty of the Legion. We get a very great deal of madness of course, but I think it's nearly as much due to predisposition as it is to the hard monotonous life. . . . You see we are a unique collection, and a considerable minority of us must be more or less queer in some way, or they wouldn't be here."

Rupert wondered why the speaker was "here" but refrained from asking.

"Can you classify the recruits at all clearly?" he asked.

"Oh, yes," was the reply. "The bulk of them are here simply and solely for a living; hungry men who came here for board and lodging. Thousands of foreigners in France have found themselves down on their uppers, with their last sou gone, fairly on their beam-ends and their room-rent overdue. To such men the Foreign Legion offers a home. Then, again, thousands of soldiers commit some heinous military 'crime' and desert to the Foreign Legion to start afresh. We get most of our Germans and Austrians that way, and not a few French who pretend to be Belgians to avoid awkward questions as to their papers. We get Alsatians by the hundred of course, too. It is their only chance of avoiding service under the hated German. They fight for France, and by their five years' Legion-service earn the right to naturalisation also. There are a good many French, too, who are 'rehabilitating themselves. Men who have come to grief at home and prefer the Legion to prison. Then there is undoubtedly a wanted-by-the-police class of men who have bolted from all parts of Europe and taken sanctuary here. Yes, I should say the out-of-work, deserters, runaways and Alsations make up three parts of the Legion."

"And what is the other part?"

"Oh, keen soldiers who have deliberately chosen the Legion for its splendid military training and constant fighting experience—romantics who have read vain imaginings and figments of the female mind like 'Under Two Flags'; and the queerest of Queer Fish, oddments and remnants from the ends of the earth. . . ." A shout of "Ohé, Grasshopper!" caused him to turn.

In the doorway, crouching on his heels, was the man they had left lying on the settee at Carmelita's. Emitting strange chirruping squeaks, turning his head slowly from left to right, and occasionally brushing it from back to front with the sides of his "forelegs," the Grasshopper approached with long, hopping bounds.

"And that was once an ornament of Chancelleries and Courts," said John Bull, as he rose to his feet. "Poor devil! Got his cafard once and for all at Ain Sefra. There was a big grasshopper or locust in his *gamelle* of soup one day. . . .

I suppose he was on the verge at the moment. Anyhow, he burst into tears and has been a grasshopper ever since, except when he's a Jap or something of that sort. . . . He's a grasshopper when he's 'normal' you might say."

Going over to where the man squatted, the old Legionary took him by the arm. "Come and sit on my blade of grass and drink some dew, Cigale," said he.

Smiling up brightly at the face which he always recognized as that of a sympathetic friend, the Grasshopper arose and accompanied John Bull to the end of the long table at which sat the Englishmen, the Russians, and the American. . . .

As the evening wore on, the heady wine took effect. The fun, which had been fast and furious, grew uproarious. Dozens of different men were singing as many different songs, several were merely howling in sheer joyless glee, many were dancing singly, others in pairs, or in fours; one, endeavouring to clamber on to the bar and execute a *pas seul,* was bodily lifted and thrown half-way down the room by the fighting-drunk Luigi Rivoli. It was noticeable that, as excitement waxed, the use of French waned, as men reverted to their native tongues. It crossed the mind of Rupert that a blindfolded stranger, entering the room, might well imagine himself to be assisting at the building of the Tower of Babel. A neighbouring party of Spaniards dropping their gutteral, sibilant Legion-French (with their *ze* for *je, zamais* for *jamais,* and *zour* for *jour*) with one accord broke into their liquid Spanish and *Nombre de Dios* took the place of *Nom de Dieu,* as their saturnine faces creased into leathery smiles. Evidently the new recruit who sat in their midst was paying his footing with the few francs that he had brought with him, or obtained for his clothes, for each of the party had four bottles in solemn row before him, and it was not with the clearest of utterance that the recruit solemnly and portentously remarked as he drained his last bottle—

"Santissima Maria! Wine is the tomb of memory, but he who sows in sand does not reap fish," the hearing of which moved his neighbour to drop his empty bottles upon the ground with a tear, and a farewell to them—

"Vaya usted con Dios. Adios." He then turned with truculent ferocity and a terrific scowl upon the provider of the feast and growled—*"Sangre de Cristo!* thou peseta-less burro, give me a cigarillo or with the blessing and aid of el Eterno Padre I will cut thy throat with my thumb-nail. Hasten, perro!"

With a grunt of "Cosa d'España," the recruit removed his képi, too a cigarette therefrom and placed it in the steel-trap mouth of his *amigo,* to be rewarded with an incredibly sweet and sunny smile and a "Bueno! Gracias, Senor José. . . ."

Letting his eye roam from this queer band of ex-mule-teers, brigands and smugglers to another party who were wading in the wassail, it needed not the loud "Donner-wetters!" and rambling reminiscent monologue of a fat brush-haired youth (on the unspeakable villainies of der Herr Wacht-meister whose wicked *schadenfreude* had sent good men to this *schweinerei* of a Legion, and who was only fit for the military-train or to be decapitated with his own *pallasch*) to label them Germans enjoying a *kommers.* Their solid, heavy bearing, their business-like and some-what brutish way of drinking in great gulps and draughts—as though a distended stomach rather than tickled palate was the serious business of the evening, if not the end and object of life—together with their upturned moustaches, piggish little eyes, and tow-coloured bristles, proclaimed them sons of Kultur.

Rupert could not forbear a smile at the heavy, philosoph-ical gravity with which the speaker, ceasing his monologue, heaved a deep, deep sigh and delivered the weighty dictum that a *schoppen* of the beer of Munich was worth all the wine of Algiers, and the Hofbrauhaus worth all the vine-yards and canteens of Africa.

It interested him to notice that among all the nationalities represented, the French were by far the gayest (albiet with a humour somewhat *macabre*) and the Germans the most morose and gloomy. He was to learn later that they provid-ed by far the greatest number of deserters, that they were eternally grumbling, notably bitter and resentful, and devoid of the faintest spark of humour.

His attention was diverted from the Germans by a sudden and horrible caterwauling which arose from a band of Frenchmen who suddenly commenced at the tops of their voices to howl that doleful dirge the "Hymne des Pacifiques." Until they had finished conversation was impossible.

"Not all foam neither, Miss, please," murmured the sleeping 'Erb in the comparative silence which followed the ending of this devastating chant.

"What's the penalty here for drunkenness?" asked Rupert of John Bull.

"Depends on what you do," was the reply. "There's no penalty for drunkenness, as such, so long as it leads to no sins of omission nor commission. . . . The danger of getting drunk is that it gives such an opportunity to any Non-com. who has a down on you. When he sees his man drunk, he'll follow him and give him some order, or find him some *corvée,* in the hope that the man will disobey or abuse him —possibly strike him. Then it's Biribi for the man, and a good mark, as well as private vengeance, for the zealous Sergeant, who is again noted as a strong disciplinarian. Our Sergeant-Major, for example, is known as the 'Suicide-maker,' and is said to be very proud of the title. The number of men he has sent to their graves direct, or *via* the Penal Battalions, must be enormous, and, so far as I can see, he has attained his high and exceedingly influential position simply and solely by excelling in the art of inventing crimes and punishing them severely—for he is a dull uneducated peasant without brains or ability. It is this type of Non-com., the monotony, and the poverty, that make the Legion such a hell for anyone who is not dead keen on soldiering for its own sake. . . ."

"I'm very glad you're keen," he added.

"Oh, rather. I'm as keen as mustard," replied Rupert, "and I was utterly fed up with peace-soldiering and poodle-faking. I have done Sandhurst and had a turn as a trooper in a crack cavalry corps. I wanted to have a look-in at the North-west Mounted Police in Canada after this, and then the Cape Mounted Rifles. I shan't mind the hardships and monotony here if I can get some active service, and feel I am learning something. I have a few thousand francs, too, at the *Credit Lyonnais,* so I shan't have to bear the poverty cross."

"A few thousand francs, my dear chap!" observed John Bull, smiling. "Crœsus! A few thousand francs will give you a few hundred fair-weather friends, relief from a few hundred disagreeable corvées, and duties; give you wine, tobacco, food, medicine, books, distractions—almost anything but escape from the Legion's military duties as distinguished from the menial. There is nowhere in the world where money makes so much difference as in the Legion—simply because nowhere is it so rare. If among the blind the one-eyed is king, among Legionaries he who has a franc is a bloated plutocrat. Where else in the world is tenpence the equivalent of the daily wages of twenty men—twenty soldier-labourers? Yes, a few thousand francs will greatly alleviate your lot in the Legion, or expedite your departure when you've had enough—for it's quite hopeless to desert without mufti and money."

"I'll leave some in the bank, then, against the time I feel I've had enough. . . . By the way, if you or your friend—er—Mr. Bronco at any time. . . . If I could be of service . . . financially . . ." and he coloured uncomfortably.

To offer money to this grave, handsome gentleman of refined speech and manners was like tipping an Ambassador, or offering the "price of a pot" to your Colonel, or your Grandfather.

"What do you mean by *corvée* and the Legion's menial duties, and soldier-labourers?" he continued hurriedly to change the subject.

"Yesterday," replied Sir Montague Merline coolly, "I was told off as one of a fatigue-party to clean the congested open sewers of the native gaol of Sidi-bel-Abbés. I reflected on the dignity of labour, and remembered the beautiful words of John Bright, or John Bunyan, or some other johnnie about, 'Who sweeps a room as unto God, makes himself and the action fine.' I certainly made myself very dirty. . . . The Legionaries are the labourers, scavengers, gardeners, builders, road-makers, street-cleaners, and general coolies of any place in which they are stationed. They are drafted to the barracks of the Spahis and Turcos—the Native Cavalry and Infantry—to do jobs that the Spahis and Turcos would rather die than touch; and, of course, they're employed for every kind of work to which Government would never dream of setting French regulars. I have myself worked (for a ha'penny a day) at wheeling clay, breaking stones, sawing logs, digging, carrying bricks, hauling trucks, shovelling sand, felling trees, weeding gardens, sweeping streets, grave-digging, and every kind of unskilled manuel corvée you can think of—in addition, of course, to the daily routine-work and military training of a soldier of the Legion—which is three times as arduous as that of any other soldier in the world."

"Sa—a—ay, John," drawled the Bucking Bronco, rousing himself at last from the deep brooding reverie into which he had plunged in search of mental images and memories of Carmelita, "give yure noo soul-affinity the other side o' the medal likewise, or yew'll push him off the water-waggon into the absinthe-barrel."

"Well," continued John Bull, "you can honestly say you belong to the most famous, most reckless, most courageous regiment in the world; to the regiment that has fought more battles, won more battles, lost more men and gained more honours, than any in the whole history of war. You belong to the Legion that never retreats, that dies—and of whose deaths no record is kept. . . . It is the last of the real Mercenaries, the Soldiers of Fortune, and if France sent it to-morrow to such a task that five thousand men were wastefully and vainly killed, not a question would be asked in the Chamber, nor the Press: nothing would be said, nothing known outside the War Department. We exist to die for France in the desert, the swamp, or the jungle, by bullet or disease—in Algeria, Morocco, Sahara, the Soudan, West Africa, Madagascar, and Cochin China—in doing what her regular French and Native troops neither could nor would do. We are here to die, and it's the duty of our officers to kill us—more or less usefully. To kill us for France, working or fighting. . . ."

"'Ear, 'ear, John!" applauded the Bucking Bronco. "Some orator, ain't he?" he observed with pride, turning to Mikhail who had been following the old Legionary with parted lips and shining eyes. "Guess ol' John's some stump-speecher as well as a looker. . . . Go it, ol' section-boss, git on a char," and he smote his beloved John resoundly upon the back.

John Bull, despite his years and grey hairs, blushed painfully.

"Sorry," he grunted.

"But, indeed, Monsieur speaks most interestingly and

with eloquence. Pray continue," said Mikhail with diffident earnestness.

John Bull looked still more uncomfortable.

"Do go on," said Rupert.

"Oh, that's all," replied John Bull. . . . "But we are the cheapest labourers, the finest soldiers, the most dangerous, reckless devils ever gathered together. . . . The incredible army—and there's anything from eight to twelve thousand of us in Africa and China and nobody but the War Minister knows the real number. You're a ha-penny hero now, my boy, and a ha-penny labourer, and you're not expected to wear out in less than five years—unless you're killed by the enemy, disease, or the Non-coms."

Conversation at this point again became more and more difficult in the increasing din, which was not diminished as 'Erb awoke, yawned, stated that he had a mouth like the bottom of a parrot's cage, that he was thoroughly blighted, and indeed blasted, produced a large mouth-organ, and rendered "Knocked 'em in the Old Kent Road," with enthusiastic soul and vigorous lungs.

Roused to a pinnacle of joyous enthusiasm and yearning for emulation, not only the little Parisian, but the whole party of Frenchmen leapt upon their table with wild whoops and commenced to dance, some the *carmagnole,* some the *can-can,* some the cake-walk, and others the *bamboula,* the *chachuqua,* or the *"singe-sur-poele."* Glasses and bottles crashed to the ground, and Legionaries with them. A form broke.

Above the stamping, howling, smashing, and crashing, Madame's shrill screams rang clear, as she mingled imprecations and commands with lamentations that Luigi Rivoli had departed. Pandemonium increased to *"tohuwabohu."* Louder wailed the mouth-organ, louder bawled the Frenchmen, louder screamed Madame, loudest of all shrilled the "Lights Out" bugle in the barrack-square—and peace reigned. In a minute the room was empty, silent and dark, as the clock struck nine.

2

"You'll be awakened by yells of *'Au jus'* from the garde-chambre at about five to-morrow," said John Bull to Rupert as they undressed. "As soon as you have swallowed

83

the coffee he'll pour into your mug from his jug, hop out and sweep under your bed. The room-orderly has got to sweep out the room and be on parade as soon as the rest, and it's impossible unless everybody sweeps under his own bed and leaves the orderly to do the rest.''

"What about food?" asked the other, who had the healthy appetite of his years and health.

"Oh—plain and sufficient," was the answer. "Good soup and bread; hard biscuit twice a week; and wine every other day—monotonous of course. Meals at eleven o'clock and five o'clock only. . . . By the way, unless your feet are fairly tough, you'd better wear *chaussettes russes* until they harden—strips of greasy linen bound round, you know. The skin will soon toughen if you pour *bapédi,* or any other strong spirit into your boots, and you can tallow your feet before a long march. Having no socks will seem funny at first, but in time you come to hate the idea of them. Much less cleanly really, and the cause of all blisters.''

Rupert looked doubtful, and thought of his silk-sock bills.

"Good night, and Good Luck in the Legion," added John Bull as he lay down.

"Good night—and thanks awfully, sir, for your kindness," replied Rupert, and vainly endeavoured to compose himself to sleep on his bed which consisted of a straw-stuffed mattress, a straw-stuffed pillow, and two thin raspy blankets. . . .

Mikhail Kyrilovitch sat on his bed whispering with his brother, about the medical examination of recruits which would take place on the morrow.

"Well, we can only hope for the best," said Feodor at last, "and they all say the same thing—that it is generally the merest formality. The Médecin-Major looks at your face and teeth and asks if you are healthy. It's not like what Ivan and I went through in Paris. . . . They wouldn't have two searching medical examinations unless there appeared to be signs of weakness, I should think.''

When the room was wrapped in silence and darkness the latter arose.

"Good night, *golubtchik,*" he whispered, "and when your heart fails you, remember Marie Spiridinoff—and be thankful you are here rather than There.''

Mikhail shuddered.

Anon, every soul in the room was awakened by the up-roarious entrance of the great Luigi Rivoli supported by Messieurs Malvin, Borges and Bauer, all very drunk and roaring *"Brigadier vous avez raison,"* a song which tailed off into an inane repetition of—

> "Si le Caporal savait ça
> Il dirait 'nom de Dieu,' "

in the midst of which the great man collapsed upon his bed, while, with much hiccupping laughter and foul jokes, his faithful satellites contrived to remove his boots and leave him to sleep the sleep of the just and the drunken. . . .

Anon the Dutch youth, Hans Djoolte, sat up and looked around. All was quiet and apparently everyone was asleep. The conscience of Hans was pricking him—he had said his prayers lying in bed, and that was not the way in which he had been taught to say them by his good Dutch mother, whose very last words as she died, had been, "Say your prayers each night, my son, wherever you may be."

Hans got out of bed, knelt down, and said his prayers again. Thenceforward, he always did so as soon as he had undressed, regardless of consequences—which at first were serious. But even the good Luigi Rivoli, in time, grew tired of beating him, particularly when the four English-speaking occupants of the *chambrée* intimated their united disapproval of Luigi's interference. The most startling novelty, by repetition, becomes the most familiar common-place, and the day, or rather the night, arrived when Hans Djoolte could pray unmolested. . . . Occupants of less favoured *chambrées* came to see the sight. The *es-couade* indeed became rather proud of having two authen-tic lunatics. . . .

CHAPTER FIVE

THE TRIVIAL ROUND

As JOHN BULL has prophesied, Rupert was awakened by yells of *"Au jus! Au jus! Au jus!"* from the garde-chambre, the room-orderly on duty, as he went from cot to cot with a huge jug.

Each sleepy soul roused himself sufficiently to hold out the tin mug which hung at the head of his bed, and to receive a half-pint or so of the "gravy"—which proved to be really excellent coffee. For his own part, Rupert would have been glad of the addition of a little milk and sugar, but he had swallowed too much milkless and sugarless tea (from a basin) in the British Army, to be concerned about such a trifle. . . .

"Good morning. Put on the white trousers and come downstairs with me," said John Bull, as he also swallowed his coffee. "Be quick, or you won't get a chance at the lavatory. There's washing accommodation for six men when sixty want it. . . . Come on."

As he hurried from the room, Rupert noticed that Corporal Martel lay comfortably in bed while the rest hurriedly dressed. From time to time he mechanically shouted: "Levez-vous, mes enfants. . . ." "Levez-vous, assassins. . . ." "Levez-vous scélérats. . . ."

After each of his shouts came, in antistrophe, the anxious yell of the garde-chambre (who had to sweep the room before parade) of "Balayez au-desous vos lits!"

Returning from his hasty and primitive wash, Rupert noticed that the Austrian recruit was lacing Rivoli's boots, while the Apache, grimacing behind his back, brushed the Neapolitan down, Malvin superintending their labours.

"Shove on the white tunic and blue sash," said John Bull to his protégé—"and you'll want knapsack, cartridge-belt, bayonet and rifle. . . . Bye-bye! I must be off. You'll have recruit-drills separate from us for some time. . . . See you later. . . ."

2

Légionnaire Reginald Rupert soon found that French drill methods of training differed but little from English, though perhaps more thorough and systematically progressive, and undoubtedly better calculated to develop initiative.

It did not take the Corporal-Instructor long to single him out as an unusually keen and intelligent recruit, and Rupert was himself surprised at the pleasure he derived from being placed as Number One of the *escouade* of recruits, after a few days. His knowledge of French helped him considerably, of course, and on that first morning he had obeyed the Corporal's roar of *"Sac à terre," "A gauche," "A droit," "En avant, marche," "Pas gymnastique,"* or *"Formez les fais-ceaux,"* before the majority of the others had translated them. He also excelled in the eating of the "Breakfast of the Legion," which is nothing more nor less than a terribly punishing run, in quick time, round and round the parade-ground. By the time the Corporal called a halt, Rupert, who was a fine runner, in the pink of condition, was beginning to feel that he had about shot his bolt, while, with one or two exceptions, the rest of the squad were in a state of real distress, gasping, groaning, and coughing, with protruding eyeballs and faces white, green, or blue. During the brief "cigarette halt," he gazed round with some amusement at the prostrate forms of his exhausted comrades.

The Russian, Feodor, seemed to be in pretty well as good condition as himself—in striking contrast to Mikhail, whose state was pitiable, as he knelt doubled up, drawing his breath in terrible gasps, and holding his side as though suffering agonies from "stitch."

'Erb was in better case, but he lay panting as though his little chest would burst.

"Gawdstrewth, matey," he grunted to M. Tou-tou Boil-the-Cat, "I ain't run so much since I last see a copper."

The Apache, green-faced and blue-lipped, showed his teeth in a vicious snarl, by way of reply. Absinthe and black cigarettes are a poor training diet.

The fat Dutch lad, Hans Djoolte, appeared to be *in extremis* and likely to disappear in a pool of perspiration. The gnarled-looking Spaniard drew his breath with noisy whoops, and stout Germans, Alsatians, Belgians and Frenchmen gave the impression of persons just rescued from drowning or suffocation by smoke. Having finished his cigarette, the Corporal ran to the far side of the parade-ground, raised his hand with a shout, and cried, *"A moi."*

"Well run, *bleu,"* he observed to Rupert, who arrived first.

Before the "breakfast" half-hour was over, he was thoroughly tired, and more than a little sorry for some of the others. M. Tou-tou Boil-the-Cat was violently sick;

the plump Dutchman was soaked from head to foot; many a good, stout Hans, Fritz and Carl wished they had never been born; and Mikhail Kyrilovitch distinguished himself by falling flat in a dead faint, to the contemptuous and outspoken disgust of the Corporal.

It was indeed a kill-or-cure training, and, in some cases, bade fair to kill before it cured. One drill-manoeuvre interested Rupert by its novelty and yet by its suggestion of the old Roman *testudo*. On the order *"A genoux,"* all had to fall on their knees and every man of the squad, not in the front rank, to thrust his head well under the knapsack of the man in front of him. Since, under service conditions, knapsacks would be stuffed with spare uniforms and underclothing, and covered with tent-canvas, blanket, spare boots, fuel or a cooking-pot, excellent head-cover was thus provided against shrapnel and shell fragments, and from bullets from some of such rifles as are used by the Chinese, African, Madagascan, and Arab foes of the Legion. Interested or not, it was with unfeigned thankfulness that, at about eleven o'clock, Rupert found himself marching back to barracks and heard the *"Rompez"* command of dismissal outside the *caserne* of his Company. Hurrying up to the *chambrée* he put his Lebel in the rack, his knapsack and belts on the shelf above his bed, and lay down to get that amount of rest without which he felt he could not face breakfast.

"Hallo, Rupert! Had a gruelling?" enquired John Bull, entering and throwing off his accoutrements. "They make you earn your little bit of corn, don't they? You feel it less day by day though, and soon find you can do it without turning a hair. Not much chance of a chap with weak lungs or heart surviving the 'Breakfast of the Legion,' for long. You see the point of the training when you begin the desert marches."

"Quite looking forward to it," said Rupert.

"It's better looking back on it, on the whole," rejoined the other grimly. . . . "Feel like breakfast?" he added in French, remembering that the more his young friend spoke in that tongue the better.

"Oh, I'm all right. What'll it be?"

"Well, not *bec-fins* and *pêche Melba* exactly. Say a mug

of bread-soup, containing potato and vegetables and a scrap of meat. Sort of Irish stew."

"*Arlequins* at two sous the plate, first, for me, please," put in M. Tou-tou Boil-the-Cat, whose small compact frame seemed to have recovered its normal elasticity and vigour.

As he spoke, the voice of a kitchen-orderly was raised below in a long-drawn howl of "Soup! A la Soupe!" Turning with one accord to the *gard-chambre* the Legionnaires bawled *"Soupe!"* as one man, and like an arrow from a bow, the room-orderly sped forth, to return a minute later bearing the soup-kettle and a basket of loaves of grey bread. Tin plates and utensils were snatched from the hanging-cupboards, and mugs from their hooks on the wall and the Legionaries seated themselves on the benches that ran down either side of the long table.

" 'Fraid you'll have to stand out, Rupert, being a recruit," said John Bull. "There's only room for twenty at this table."

"Of course. Thanks," was the reply, and the speaker betook himself to his bed, and sat him down with his mug and crust.

With cheerful sociability, 'Erb had already seated himself at table, and was beating a loud tattoo with mug and plate as he awaited the administrations of the soup-laden Ganymede.

Suddenly the expansive and genial smile faded on 'Erb's happy face, as he felt himself seized by the scruff of his neck and the seat of his trousers, and raised four feet in the air. . . . For a second he hovered, descended a foot and was then shot through the air with appalling violence to some distant corner of the earth. Fortunately for 'Erb, that corner contained a bed and he landed fairly on it. . . . The Legionary Herbert Higgins in the innocence of his ignorance had occupied the Seats of the Mighty, had sat down in the place of Luigi Rivoli—and Luigi had removed the insect.

"Gawd love us!" said 'Erb. "Oo'd a' thought it?" as he realized that he was still in barracks and had only travelled from the table to a cot, a distance of some six feet. . . .

Mikhail Kyrilovitch lay stretched on his bed, too exhausted to eat. It interested and rather touched Rupert to see how tenderly the other Russian half raised him from the bed, coaxed him with soup and, failing, produced a bottle of wine from behind the *paquetage* on his shelf, and induced him to drink a little. . . .

"Potato fatigue after this, Rupert," said John Bull as he came over to the recruit, and offered him a cigarette. "Ghastly stuff you'll find this black Algerian tobacco, but one gets used to it. It's funny, but when I get a taste of any of the tobaccos from Home, I find my palate so ruined that I don't enjoy it. Seems acrid and strong though it's infinitely milder. . . ."

The Kitchen-Corporal thrust his head in at the door of the *chambrée,* roared *"Aux patates"* and vanished. Trooping down to the kitchen, the whole Company stood in a ring and solemnly peeled potatoes. Here, at any rate, Mikhail Kyrilovitch distinguished himself among the recruits, for not only was his the first potato to fall peeled into the bucket, but his peel was the thinnest, his output the greatest. Standing next to him, Rupert noticed how tiny were his hands and wrists, and how delicate his nails.

"Apparently this is part of regular routine and not a corvée," he remarked.

"Mais oui, Monsieur," replied Mikhail primly.

"Great tip to get cunning at dodging extra fatigues when you're a soldier," continued Rupert.

"Mais oui, Monsieur," replied Mikhail primly.

"Expect they'll catch us wretched recruits on that lay until we get artful."

"Mais oui, Monsieur," replied Mikhail primly.

What a funny shy lad he was, with his eternal "Mais oui, Monsieur" . . . Perhaps that was all the French he knew! . . .

"Do you think the medical-examination will be very—er—searching, Monsieur?" asked Mikhail.

So he did know French after all. What was he trembling about now?

"Shouldn't think so. Why? You're all right, aren't you? You wouldn't have passed the doctor when you enlisted, otherwise."

"Non, Monsieur."

"Where did you enlist?"

"At Paris, Monsieur."

"So did I; Rue St. Dominique. Little fat cove in red breeches and a white tunic. I suppose you had the same chap?"

"Er—oui, Monsieur."

"I suppose he overhauled you very thoroughly? . . . Wasn't it infernally cold standing stark naked in that beastly room while he punched you about?"

"Oh!—er—oui, Monsieur. Oh, please let us . . . Er—wasn't that running dreadful this morning?" . . .

"I say, Monsieur Rupaire, do you think we shall have the same 'breakfast' every morning?" put in Feodor Kyrilovitch. "It'll be the death of my brother here, if we do. He never was a runner."

" 'Fraid so, during recruits' course," replied Rupert, and added: "I noticed a great difference between you and your brother."

"Oh, it's only just in that respect," was the reply. "I've always been better winded than he. . . . Illness when he was a kid. . . . Lungs not over strong. . . ."

Even as he prophesied, an Orderly-Sergeant swooped down upon them as the potato-fatigue finished and, while the old Legionaries somehow melted into thin air and vanished like the baseless fabric of a vision, the recruits were captured and commandeered for a barrack-scavenging corvée which kept them hard at work until it was time to fall in for "theory."

This Rupert discovered to be instruction in recognition of badges of rank, and, later, in every sort and kind of rule and regulation; in musketry, tactics, training and the principles of theory of drill, entrenchment, scouting, skirmishing, and every other branch of military education.

At two o'clock, drill began again, and lasted until four, at which hour Monsieur le Médicin-Major held the medical examination, the idea of which seemed so disturbing to Mikhail Kyrilovitch. It proved to be the merest formality—a glance, a question, a caution against excess, and the recruits were passed and certified as *bon pour le service* at the rate of twenty to the quarter-hour. They were, moreover, free for the remainder of the day (provided they escaped all victim-hunting Non-coms., in search of corvée-parties) with the exception of such hours as might be necessary for labours of *astiquage* and the *lavabo*.

On returning to the *chambrée,* Rupert found his friend John Bull awaiting him.

"Well, Rupert," he cried cheerily, "what sort of a day have you had? Tired? We'll get 'soupe' again shortly. I'll take you to the *lavabo* afterwards, and show you the ropes. Got to have your white kit, arms and accoutrements all *klim-bim,* as the Germans say, before you dress and go out, or else you'll have to do it in the dark."

"Yes, thanks," replied Rupert. "I'll get straight first. I hate 'spit and polish' after Lights Out. What'll the next meal be?"

"Same as this morning—the eternal 'soupe.' The only variety in food is when dog-biscuit replaces bread. . . . Nothing to grumble at really, except the infernal monotony. Quantity is all right—in fact some fellows save up a lot of bread and biscuit and sell it in the town. (Eight days *salle de police* if you're caught.) But sometimes you feel you could eat anything in the wide world except Legion 'soupe,' bread and biscuit. . . ."

After the second and last meal of the day, at about five o'clock, Rupert was introduced to the *lavabo* and its ways —particularly its ways in the matter of disappearing soap and vanishing "washing"—and, his first essay in laundry-work concluded, returned with Legionary John Bull and the Bucking Bronco for an hour or two of leather-polishing, accoutrement-cleaning and "ironing" without an iron.

The room began to fill and was a scene of more or less silent industry. On his bed, the great Luigi Rivoli lay magnificently asleep while, on neighbouring cots and benches, his weapons, accoutrements, boots and uniform received the attentions of his henchmen.

Anon the great man awoke, yawned cavernously, ejaculated *"Dannazione"* and sat up. One gathered that the condition of his mouth was not all that it might be, and that his head ached. Even he was not exempt from the penalties incurred by lesser men, and even he had to recognize the fact that a next-morning follows an evening-before. Certain denizens of the *chambrée* felt, and looked, uneasy, but were reassured by the reflection that there was still a stock of *bleus* unchastened, and available for the great man's needs and diversion. Rising, he roared *"Oho!"*, smacked and flexed his muscles according to his evening ritual, and announced that a recruit might be permitted to fetch him water.

Feodor Kyrilovitch unobtrusively changed places with his brother Mikhail, whose bed was next to that of the bully.

"Here, dog," roared the Neapolitan, and brought his "quart" down with a right resounding blow upon the bare head of Feodor. Without a word the Russian took the mug and hurried to the nearest lavatory. Returning he handed it respectfully to Rivoli, and pointing into it said in broken Italian—

"There would appear to be a mark on the bottom of the Signor's cup."

The great man looked—and smiled graciously as he recognized a gold twenty-franc piece. "A thoroughly intelligent recruit," he added, turning to Malvin who nodded and smiled drily. It entered the mind of le bon Légionnaire Malvin that his recruit should also give an exhibition of his intelligence to le bon Légionnaire Malvin.

"Where's that fat pig from Olanda who can only whine *'Verstaan nie'* when he is spoken to?" enquired Rivoli, looking round. "Let me see if I can 'Verstaan' him how to put my boots on smartly."

But, fortunately for himself, the Dutch recruit, Hans Djoolte, was not present.

"Not there?" thundered the great man, on being informed. "How dare the fat calf be not there? Let it be known that I desire all the recruits of this room to be on duty from 'Soupe' till six, or later, in case I should want them. Let them all parade before me now."

Some sheepishly grinning, some with looks of alarm, some under strong protest, all the recruits with one exception, "fell in" at the foot of the Italian's bed. Some were dismissed as they came up; the two Russians, as having paid their footing very handsomely; the *Apache,* and Franz Josef Meyer, as having been properly broken to bit and curb; the Greek, as a declared admirer and slave; and one or two others who had already wisely propitiated, or, to their sorrow, encountered less pleasantly, the uncrowned king of the Seventh Company. The remainder received tasks, admonitions and warnings, which were received variously, but without open defiance.

The attitude of le Légionnaire 'Erbiggins was characteristic. Realizing that he had not a ghost of a chance of success against a man twice his weight and thrice his strength, he took the leggings which were given him to clean and returned a stream of nervous English, of which the pungent insults and vile language accorded but ill with the bland innocence of his face, and the deferential acquiescence of his manner.

"Ain't yew goin' ter jine the merry throng?" asked the Bucking Bronco of Reginald Rupert, upon hearing the recruit reply to Malvin's order to join the line, with a recommendation that Malvin should go to the devil.

"I am not," replied Rupert.

"Wal, I guess we'll back yew up, sonny," said the American with an approving smile.

"I shall be glad if you will in no way interfere," returned the Englishman.

"Gee-whillikins!" commented the Bucking Bronco.

John Bull looked anxious. "He's the strongest man I have ever seen," he remarked, "besides being a professional wrestler and acrobat."

Malvin again approached, grinning maliciously.

"Il Signor Luigi Rivoli would be sorry to have to come and fetch you, English pig," said he. "Sorry for you, that is. Do you wish to find yourself *au grabat*,[1] you scurvy, mangy, lousy cur of a recruit? . . . What reply shall I take Il Signor Luigi Rivoli?"

"That!" replied the Englishman, and therewith smote the fat Austrian a most tremendous smack across his heavy blue jowl with the open hand, sending him staggering several yards. Without paying further attention to the great man's ambassador, he strode in the direction of the great man himself, with blazing eyes and clenched jaw.

"You want me, do you?" he shouted at the astonished Luigi, who was rising open-mouthed from his bed; and, putting the whole weight of his body behind the blow, drove most skilfully and scientifically straight at the point of his jaw.

It must be confessed that the Italian was taken unawares,

---

[1] On a sick bed.

and in the very act of getting up, so that his hands were down, and he was neither standing nor sitting.

He was down and out, and lay across his bed stunned and motionless.

But le Légionnaire Jean Boule looked ahead.

"You've made two bad enemies, my boy, I'm afraid. . . . What about when he comes around?"

"I'll give him some more, if I can," replied Rupert. "Don't interfere, anyhow."

"Shake, sonny," said the Bucking Bronco solemnly. "An' look at hyar. Let's interfere, to the extent o' makin' thet cunning coyote fight down in the squar'."

"Thanks," replied the Englishman. "Right-ho! If he won't fight downstairs, tell him he can take the three of us."

"Fower, matey. Us fower Henglishmen agin' 'im an' 'is ole bleedin' gang." put in 'Erb. " 'E's a bloke as wants takin' dahn a peg. . . . Too free wiv' hisself. . . . Chucks is weight abaht too much. . . . An' I'll tell yer wot, Cocky. Keep a heye on that cove as you giv' a smack in the chops."

"Sure thing," agreed the Bucking Bronco, and turning to the Belgian who stood ruefully holding his face and looking as venomous as a broken-backed cobra, added: "Yew look at hyar, Mounseer Malvin, my lad. Don't yew git handlin' yure Rosalie[1] any dark night. Yew try ter *zigouiller*[2] my pal Rupert, an' I'll draw yure innards up through yure mouth till yew look like half a pound of dumplin' on the end of half a yard of macaroni."

Rivoli twitched, stirred, and groaned. It was interesting to note that none of his clients and henchmen offered any assistance.

"Donna e Madonna!" he said. "Corpo di Bacco!" and gazed around. "What has happened? . . ." and then he remembered. "A minute," he said. "Wait but a minute—and then bring him to me."

Obedience and acquiescence awoke in the bosoms of his supporters. The great Luigi was alive on his throne again. The Greek passed him a mug of water.

"Yes, wait but a moment, and then just hand him to me. . . . One of you might go over to the hospital and say

---

[1] Bayonet   [2] To bayonet.

a bed will be wanted shortly," he added. "And another of you might look up old Jules Latour down at the cemetery and tell him to start another grave."

"You're coming to *me,* for a change, Rivoli," cut in Rupert contemptuously. "You're going to fight me down below. There's going to be a ring, and fair play. Will you come now, or will you wait till to-morrow? I can wait if you feel shaken."

"Plug the ugly skunk while he's rattled, Bub," advised the American.

"I will kill him and eat him *now,*" said the Italian rising magnificently. Apparently his splendid constitution and physique had triumphed completely, and it was as though the blow had not been struck.

"Come on, b'ys," yelped the American, "an' ef thet dago don't fight as square as he knows haow, I'll pull his lower jaw off his face."

In a moment the room was empty, except for Mikhail Kyrilovitch, who sat on the edge of his brother's bed and shuddered.

Clattering down the stairs and gathering numbers as it went, the party made for the broad space, or passage, between high walls near the back entrance of the Company's *caserne,* a safe and secluded spot for fights. As they went along, John Bull gave good advice to his young friend.

"Remember he's a wrestler and a *savate man,*" he said, "and that public opinion here recognizes the use of both in a fight—so you can expect him to clinch and kick as well as butt."

"Right-o!" said Rupert.

A large ring was formed by the rapidly growing crowd of spectators, a ring, into the middle of which the Bucking Bronco stepped to declare that he would rearrange the features, as well as the ideas, of any supporter of Luigi Rivoli who in any way interfered with the fight.

The two combatants stripped to the waist and faced each other. It was a pleasant surprise to John Bull to notice that his friend looked bigger "peeled," than he did when dressed. (It is a good test of muscular development.) Obviously the youth was in the pink of condition and had systematically developed his muscles. But for the presence of Rivoli, the arms and torso of the Englishman would have evoked admiring comments. As it was, the gigantic figure of the Italian dwarfed him, for he looked what he was—a professional Strong Man whose stock-in-trade was his enormous muscles and their mighty strength. . . . It was not so much a contrast between David and Goliath as between Apollo and Hercules.

The Italian assumed his favourite wrestling attitude with open hands advanced; the Englishman, the position of boxing.

The two faced each other amidst the perfect silence of the large throng.

Suddenly the Italian swiftly advanced his left foot and made a lightning grab with his left hand at the Englishman's neck. The latter ducked; the great arm swung, harmless, above his head, and two sharp smacks rang out like pistol-shots as the Englishman planted a left and right with terrific force upon the Italian's ribs. Rivoli's gasp was almost as audible as the blows. He sprang back, breathing heavily.

John Bull moistened his lips and thanked God. Rupert circled round his opponent, sparring for an opening. Slowly . . . slowly . . . almost imperceptibly, the Italian's head and shoulders bent further and further back. What the devil was he doing?—wondered the Englishman—getting his head out of danger? Certainly his jaw was handsomely swollen. . . . Anyhow he was exposing his mark, the spot where the ribs divide. If he could get a "right" in there, with all his weight and strength, Il Signor Luigi Rivoli would have to look to himself in the ensuing seconds. Rupert made a spring. As he did so, the Italian's body turned sideways and leant over until almost parallel with the ground, as his right knee drew up to his chest and his right foot shot out with the force of a horse's kick. It caught the advancing Englishman squarely on the mouth, and sent him flying head over heels like a shot rabbit. The Italian darted forward—and so did the Bucking Bronco.

"Assez!" he shouted. "Let him get up." At this point his Legion French failed him, and he added in his own vernacular, "Ef yew think yu're gwine ter kick him while he's down, yew've got another think comin', Loojey Rivoli," and barred his path.

John Bull raised Rupert's head on to his knee. He was senseless and bleeding from mouth and nose.

Pushing his way through the ring, came 'Erb, a mug of water in one hand, a towel in the other. Filling his mouth with water, he ejected a fine spray over Rupert's face and chest, and then, taking the towel by two corners of a long side, flapped it mightily over the prostrate man.

The latter opened his eyes, sat up, and spat out a tooth.

"Damned kicking cad," he remarked, on collecting his scattered wits and faculties.

"No Queensbury rules here, old chap," said John Bull.

"You do the sime fer 'im, matey. Kick 'is bleedin' faice in. . . . W'y carn't 'e fight like a man, the dirty furriner?" and turning from his ministrations to where the great Luigi received the congratulations of his admiring supporters, he bawled with the full strength of his lungs: "Yah! you dirty furriner!" and crowned the taunt by putting his fingers to his nose and emitting a bellowing *Boo-oo-oo!* of incredibly bull-like realism. "If I wasn't yer second, matey, I'd go an' kick 'im in the stummick naow, I would," he muttered, resuming his labour of love.

Rupert struggled to his feet.

"Give me the mug," he said to 'Erb, and washed out his mouth. "How long 'time' is observed on these occasions?" he asked of John Bull.

"Oh, nothing's regular," was the reply. " 'Rounds' end when you fall apart, and 'time' ends when both are ready. . . . You aren't going for him again, are you?"

"I'm going for him as long as I can stand and see," was the answer. 'Erb patted him on the back.

"Blimey! You're a White Man, matey," he commended. "S'welp me, you are!"

"Seconds out of the ring," bawled the Bucking Bronco, and unceremoniously shoved back all who delayed.

A look of incredulity spread over the face of the Italian. Could it be possible that the fool did not know that he was utterly beaten and abolished? . . . He tenderly felt his jaw and aching ribs. . . .

It was true. The Englishman advanced upon him, the

light of battle in his eyes, and fierce determination expressed in the frown upon his white face. His mouth bore no expression—it was merely a mess.

A cheer went up from the spectators.

A recruit asking for it *twice,* from Luigi Rivoli!

That famous man, though by no means anxious, was slightly perplexed. There was something here to which he was not accustomed. It was the first time in his experience that this had happened. Few men had defied and faced him once—none had done it twice. This, in itself was bad, and in the nature of a faint blow to his prestige. . . . He had tried a grapple—with unfortunate results; he had tried a kick—most successfully, and he would try another in a moment. Lest his opponent should be warily expecting it, he would now administer a battering-ram butt. He crouched forward, extending his open hands as though to grapple, and, suddenly ducking his head, flung himself forward, intending to drive the breath from his enemy's body and seize him by the throat ere he recovered.

Lightly and swiftly the Englishman side-stepped and, as he did so, smote the Italian with all his strength full upon the ear—a blow which caused that organ to swell hugely, and to "sing" for hours. Rivoli staggered sideways and fell. The Englishman stood back and waited. Rivoli arose as quickly as he fell, and, with a roar of rage, charged straight at the Englishman, who drove straight at his face, left and right, cutting his knuckles to the bone. Heavy and true as were the blows, they could not avail to stop that twenty-stone projectile, and, in a second, the Italian's arms were round him. One mighty hug and heave, and his whole body, clasped as in a vice to that of the Italian, was bent over backward in a bow.

"That's torn it," groaned the American and dashed his képi upon the ground. "Fer two damns I'd . . ."

John Bull laid a restraining hand upon his arm.

"Go it, Rupert," bawled 'Erb, dancing in a frenzy of excitement. "Git 'is froat. . . . Swing up yer knee. . . . Kick 'im."

"Shut up," snapped John Bull. "He's not a hooligan. . ."

One of Rupert's arms was imprisoned in those of the Italian. True to his training and standards, he played the game as he had learnt it, and kept his free right hand from his opponent's throat. With his failing strength he rained short-arm blows on the Italian's face, until it was turned sideways and crushed against his neck and shoulder.

John Bull mistook the bully's action.

"If you bite his throat, I'll shoot you, Rivoli," he shouted, and applauding cheers followed the threat.

The muscles of Rivoli's back and arms tightened and bunched as he strained with all his strength. Slowly but surely he bent further over, drawing the Englishman's body closer and closer in his embrace.

To John Bull, the seconds seemed years. Complete silence reigned. Rupert's blows weakened and became feeble. They ceased. Rivoli bent over further. As Rupert's right arm fell to his side, the Italian seized it from behind. His victim was now absolutely powerless and motionless. John Bull was reminded of a boa-constrictor which he had once seen crush a deer. Suddenly the Italian's left arm was withdrawn, his right hand retained his grip of the other. Thrusting his left hand beneath the Englishman's chin he put all his colossal strength into one great effort—pushing the head back until it seemed that the neck must break, and at the same time contracting his great right arm and bending himself almost double. He then raised his opponent and dashed him to the ground. . . .

Reginald Rupert recovered consciousness in the Legion's Hospital.

A skilful, if somewhat brutal, surgeon soon decided that his back was not broken but only badly sprained.

On leaving hospital, a fortnight later, he did eight days *salle de police* by way of convalescence.

On return to duty, he found himself something of a hero in the Seventh Company, and decidedly the hero of the recruits of his *chambrée*.

Disregarding the earnest entreaties of John Bull and the reiterated advice of the Bucking Bronco, and of the almost worshipping 'Erb—he awaited Luigi Rivoli on the evening after his release and challenged him to fight.

The great man burst into explosive laughter—laughter almost too explosive to be wholly genuine.

"Fight you, whelp! Fight you, whelp!" he scoffed. "*Why* should I fight you? Pah! Out of my sight—I have something else to do."

"Oh, have you? Well, don't forget that I have nothing else to do, any time you feel like fighting. See?" replied the Englishman.

The Italian again roared with laughter, and Rupert with beating heart and well-concealed sense of mighty relief, returned to his cot to work.

It was noticeable that Il Signor Luigi Rivoli invariably had something else to do, so far as Rupert was concerned, and molested him no more.

CHAPTER SIX

LE CAFARD AND OTHER THINGS

FOR LEGIONNAIRE REGINALD RUPERT the days slipped past with incredible rapidity, and, at the end of six months, this adaptable and exceedingly keen young man felt himself to be an old and seasoned Legionary, for whom the Depôt held little more in the way of instruction and experience.

His thoughts began to turn to Foreign Service. When would he be able to volunteer for a draft going to Tonkin, Madagascar, Senegal, or some other place of scenes and experiences entirely different from those of Algeria? When would he see some active service—that which he had come so far to see, and for which he had undergone these hardships and privations?

Deeply interested as he was in all things military, and anxious as he was to learn and become the Complete Soldier, he found himself beginning to grow very weary of the trivial round, the common task, of life in the Depôt. Once he knew his drill as an Infantryman, he began to feel that the proportion of training and instruction to that of corvée and fatigues was small. He had not travelled all the way to Algiers to handle broom and wheelbarrow, and perform non-military labours at a wage of a halfpenny per day. Of course, one took the rough with the smooth and shrugged one's shoulders with the inevitable "Que voulezous? C'est la Légion," but, none the less, he had had enough, and more than enough, of Depôt life.

Sitting one night on his cot, and talking to the man for whom he now had a very genuine and warm affection, he remarked—

"Don't you get fed up with Depôt life, Bull?"

"I have been fed up with life, Depôt and otherwise, for over twenty years," was the reply. . . . "Don't forget that life here in Sidi is a great deal better than life in a desert-station in the South. It *is* supportable anyhow; there—it simply isn't; and those who don't desert and die, go mad and die. The exceptions, who do neither, deteriorate horribly, and come away very different men. . . . Make the most of Sidi, my boy, while you are here, and remember that foreign service, when in Tonkin, Madagascar, or Western Africa, inevitably means fever and dysentery, and generally broken health for life. . . . Moreover, Algeria is the only part of the French colonial possessions in which the climate lets one enjoy one's pipe."

That very night, shortly after the *caserne* had fallen silent and still, its inmates wrapped in the heavy sleep of the thoroughly weary, an alarm-bugle sounded in the barrack-square, and, a minute later, non-commissioned officers hurried from room to room, bawling, *"Aux armes! Aux armes! Aux armes!"* at the top of their voices.

Rupert sat up in his bed, as Corporal Achille Martel began to shout, *"Levez-vous donc. Levez-vous! Faites le sac! Faites le sac! En tenue de Campagne d'Afrique."*

" 'Ooray!" shrilled 'Erb. "Oo-bloomin'-ray."

"Buck up, Rupert," said John Bull. "We've got to be on the barrack-square in full 'African field equipment' in ten minutes."

The *chambrée* became the scene of feverish activity, as well as of delirious excitement and joy. In spite of it being the small hours of the morning, every man howled or whistled his own favourite song, without a sign of that liverish grumpiness which generally accompanies early-morning effort. The great Luigi's slaves worked at double pressure since they had to equip their lord and master as well as themselves. Feodor Kyrilovitch appeared to pack his own knapsack with one hand and that of Mikhail with the other, while he whispered words of cheer and encouragement. The Dutch boy, Hans Djoolte, having finished his work, knelt down beside his bed and engaged in prayer. Speculation was rife as to whether France had declared war on Morocco, or whether the Arabs were in rebellion

102

for the hundredth time, and lighting the torch of destruction all along the Algerian border.

In ten minutes from the blowing of the alarm-bugle, the Battalion was on parade in the barrack-square, every man fully-equipped and laden like a beast of burden. One thought filled every mind as the ammunition boxes were brought from the magazine and prized open. *What would the cardboard packets contain?* A few seconds after the first packet had been torn open by the first man to whom one was tossed, the news had spread throughout the Battalion.

Ball-Cartridge!

The Deity in that moment received the heartfelt fervid thanks of almost every man in the barrack-square, for ball-cartridge meant active service—in any case, a blessed thing, whatever might result—the blessing of death, of promotion, of decorations, of wounds and discharge from the Legion. The blessing of change to begin with.

There was one exception however. When Caporal Achille Martel "told off" Légionnaire Mikhail Kyrilovitch for orderly-duty to the *Adjudant Vaguemestre*,[1] duty which would keep him behind in barracks, that Legionary certainly contrived to conceal any disappointment that he may have felt.

A few minutes later the Legion's magnificent band struck up the Legion's march of *"Tiens, violà du boudin,"* and the Battalion swung out of the gate, past the barracks of the Spahis, through the quiet sleeping streets into the main road and so out of the town to which many of them never returned.

In the third row of fours of the Seventh Company marched the Bucking Bronco, John Bull, Reginald Rupert, and Herbert Higgins. In the row in front of them, Luigi Rivoli, Edouard Malvin, the Grasshopper, and Feodor Kyrilovitch. In the front row old Tant-de-Soif, Franz Josef Meyer, Tou-tou Boil-the-Cat, and Hans Djoolte. In front of them marched the four drummers. At the head of the Company rode Captain d'Armentières, beside whom walked Lieutenant Roberte.

Marching "at ease," the men discussed the probabilities and possibilities of the expedition. All the signs and tokens

---

[1] The postmaster.

to be read by experienced soldier-eyes, were those of a long march and active service.

"It'll be a case of 'best foot foremost' a few hours hence, Rupert, I fancy," remarked John Bull. "I shouldn't be surprised if we put up thirty miles on end, with no halt but the 'cigarette spaces.' "

"Sure thing," agreed the Bucking Bronco. "I got a hunch we're gwine ter throw our feet some, to-day."

Marching along the excellent sandy road through the cool of the night, under a glorious moon, with the blood of youth, and health, and strength coursing like fire through his veins, it was difficult for Rupert to realize that, within a few hours, he would be wearily dragging one foot after the other, his rifle weighing a hundred-weight, his pack weighing a ton, his mouth a lime-kiln, his body one awful ache. He had had some pretty grueling marches before, but this was the first time that the Battalion had gone out on a night-alarm with ball-cartridge, and every indication of it being the "real thing."

On tramped the Legion.

Anon there was a whistle, a cry of *Halt!* and there was a few minutes' rest. Men lit cigarettes; some sat down; several fumbled at straps and endeavoured to ease packs by shifting them. Malvin made his master lie down after removing his pack altogether. It is a pack well worth removing—that of the Legion—save when seconds are too precious to be thus spent, and you consider it the wiser plan to fall flat and lie from the word *"Halt!"* to the word *"Fall in!"* The knapsack of black canvas is heavy with two full uniforms, underclothing, cleaning materials and sundries. Weighty tent-canvas and bankets are rolled round it, tent-supports are fastened at the side, fire-wood, a cooking-pot, drinking-mug and spare boots go on top.

Attached to his belt the Legionary carries a sword-bayonet with a steel scabbard, four hundred rounds of ammunition in his cartridge-pouches, an entrenching tool, and his "sac." Add his rifle and water-bottle, and you have the most heavily laden soldier in the world. He does not carry his overcoat—he wears it, and is perhaps unique in considering a heavy overcoat to be correct desert wear. Under his overcoat he has only a canvas shirt and white linen trousers (when *en tennue de campagne d'Afrique*), tucked into leather gaiters. Round his waist, his blue sash —four yards of woollen cloth—acts as an excellent cholera-belt and body-support. The linen neckcloth, or *couvre-nuque,* buttoned on to the white cover of his képi, protects his neck and ears, and, to some extent, his face, and prevents sunstroke. . . .

The Battalion marched on through the glorious dawn, gaily singing *"Le sac, ma foi, toujours au dos,"* and the old favourite marching songs *"Brigadier," "L'Empereur de Danmark," "Père Bugeaud,"* and *"Tiens, voilà du boudin."* Occasionally a German would lift up his splendid voice and soon more than half the battalion would be singing—

> "Trinken wir noch ein Tröpfchen
> Aus dem kleinen Henkeltöpfchen."

or *Die Wacht am Rhein* or the pathetic *Morgenlied.*

At the second halt, when some eight miles had been covered, there were few signs of fatigue, and more men remained standing than sat down. As the long column wait-ed by the side of the road, a small cavalcade from the direc-tion of Sidi-bel-Abbès overtook it. At the head rode a white-haired, white-moustached officer on whose breast sparkled and shone that rare and glorious decoration, the Grand Cross of the Legion of Honour.

"That's the Commander-in-Chief in Algeria," said John Bull to Rupert. "That settles it: we're out for business this time, and I fancy you'll see some Arab-fighting before you are much older. . . . Feet going to be all right, do you think?"

"Fine," replied Rupert. "My boots are half full of tallow, and I've got a small bottle of bapédi in my sack. . . ."

On tramped the Legion.

The days grew hot and packs grew heavy. The Battalion undeniably and unashamedly slouched. Many men leant heavily forward against their straps, while some bent almost double, like coal-heavers carrying sacks of coal. Rifles changed frequently from right hand to left. There was no singing now. The only sound that came from dry-lipped, sticky mouth was an occasional bitter curse. Rupert began to wonder if his shoulder straps had not turned to wires. His arms felt numb, and the heavy weights, hung about his shoulders and waist, caused a feeling of constriction about the heart and lungs. He realized that he quite understood how people felt when they fainted. . . .

By the seventh halt, some forty kilometres, or twenty-seven miles lay behind the Battalion. At the word *Halt!* every man had thrown himself at full length on the sand, and very few wasted precious moments of the inexorably exact five minutes of the rest-period in removing knapsacks. Hardly a man spoke; none smoked.

On tramped the Legion.

Gone was all pretence of smartness and devil-may-care humour—that queer *macabre* and bitter humour of the Legion. Men slouched and staggered, and dragged their feet in utter hopeless weariness. Backs rounded more and more, heads sank lower, and those who limped almost outnumbered those who did not. A light push would have sent any man stumbling to the ground.

As the whistle blew for the next halt, the Legion sank to the ground with a groan as though it would never rise again. As the whistle blew for the advance the Legion staggered to its feet as one man. . . . Oh, the Legion march! Is not its motto, *"March or Die?"* The latter it may do, the former it must. The Legion has its orders and its destination, and it marches. If it did not reach its destination at the appointed time, it would be because it had died in getting there.

On tramped the Legion.

With horrible pains in its blistered shoulders, its raw-rubbed backs, its protesting, aching legs and blistered heels and toes, the Legion staggered on, a silent pitiable mass of suffering. Up and down the entire length of the Battalion rode its Colonel, "the Marching Pig." Every few yards he bawled with brazen throat and leathern lungs: "March or die, my children! March or die!" And the Legion clearly understood that it must march or it must die. To stagger from the ranks and fall was to die of thirst and starvation, or beneath the *flissa* of the Arab.

Legionary Rupert blessed those "Breakfasts of the Legion" and the hard training which achieved and maintained the hard condition of the Legionary. Sick, giddy and worn-out as he felt, he knew he could keep going at least as long as the average, and by the time the average man had reached the uttermost end of his tether, the end of their march must be reached. After all, though they were Legionaries whose motto was "March or Die," they were only human beings—and to all human effort and endeavour there is a limit. He glanced at his comrades. The Bucking Bronco swung along erect, his rifle held across his shoulder by the muzzle, and his belt, with all its impedimenta, swinging from his right hand. He stared straight ahead, and, with vacant mind and tireless iron body, "threw his feet."

Beside him, John Bull looked very white and worn and old. He leant heavily against the pull of his straps and marched with his chest bare. On Rupert's left, 'Erb, having unbuttoned and unbuckled everything unbuttonable and unbuckleable, slouched along, a picture of slack unsoldierliness and of dauntless dogged endurance. Suddenly throwing up his head he screamed from parched lips, "Aw we dahn 'earted?" and, having painfully swallowed, answered his own strident question with a long drawn, contemptuous "Ne—a—ow." Captain d'Armentiéres who knew England and the English, looked round with a smile. . . . "Bon garçon," he nodded.

On the right of the second row of fours marched Luigi Rivoli, in better case than most, as the bulk of his kit was now impartially distributed among Malvern, Meyer, Toutou and Tant-de-Soif. (The power of money in the Legion is utterly incredible.) Feodor Kyrilovitch was carrying the Grasshopper's rifle—and that made a mighty difference toward the end of a thirty-mile march.

At the end of the next halt, the Grasshopper declared that he could not get up. . . . At the command, "Fall in!" the unfortunate man did not stir.

"Kind God! What *shall* I do?" he groaned. It was his first failure as a soldier.

"Come on, my lad," said John Bull sharply. "Here, pull off his kit," he added and unfastened the Belgian's belt. Between them they pulled him to his feet and dragged him to his place in the ranks. John Bull took his pack, the Bucking Bronco his belt and its appurtenances, and Feodor his rifle. His eyes were closed and he sank to the ground.

"Here," said Rupert to 'Erb. "Get in his place and let him march in your beside me. We'll hold him up."

"Give us yer rifle, matey," replied 'Erb, and left Rupert with hands free to assist the Grasshopper.

With his right arm round the Belgian's waist, he helped him along, while John Bull insisted on having the poor fellow's right hand on his left shoulder.

On tramped the Legion.

Before long, almost the whole weight of the Grass-hopper's body was on Rupert's right arm and John Bull's left shoulder.

"Stick to it, my son," said the latter from time to time, "we are sure to stop at the fifty-kilometre stone."

The Belgian seemed to be semiconscious, and did not reply. His feet began to drag, and occasionally his two comrades bore his full weight for a few paces. Every few yards Feodor looked anxiously round. These four, in their anxiety for their weaker brother, forgot their own raw thighs, labouring lungs, inflamed eyes, numbed arms and agonizing feet.

Just as the Colonel rode by, the Grasshopper's feet ceased to move, and dragged lifeless along the ground.

Rupert stumbled and the three fell in a heap, beneath the Colonel's eye.

"Sacré Baptême!" he swore—the oath he only used when a Legionary fell out on the march—"March or die, accursed pigs."

Rupert and John Bull staggered to their feet, but the Grasshopper lay apparently lifeless. The Colonel swore again, and shouted an order. The Grasshopper was dragged to the side of the road, and a baggage-cart drove up. A tent-pole was thrust through its sides and tied securely. To this pole the Belgian was lashed, the pole passing across the upper part of his back and under his arms, which were pulled over it and tied together. If he could keep his feet, well and good. If he could not, he would hang from the pole by his arms (as an athlete hangs from a parallel-bar in a gymnasium, before revolving round and round it).

On tramped the Legion.

Before long the Grasshopper's feet dragged in the dust as he dropped inanimate, and then hung in the rope which lashed him to the pole.

At the fifty-fifth kilometre, thirty-five miles from Sidi-bel-Abbés the command to halt was followed by the thrice-blessed God-sent order:

"Campez!"

Almost before the words, *"Formez les faisceaux"* were out of the Company-Commanders' mouths, the men had piled arms. Nor was the order *"Sac à terre"* obeyed in any grudging spirit. In an incredibly short space of time the jointed tent-poles and canvas had been removed from the knapsacks. Corporals of sections had stepped forward, holding the tent-poles above their heads, marking each Company's tent-line, and a city of small white tents had come into being on the face of the desert. A few minutes later, cooking-trenches had been dug, camp fires lighted and water, containing meat and macaroni, put on to boil.

A busy and profitable hour followed for Madame la Cantiniére, who, even as her cart stopped, had set out her folding tables, benches and bar for the sale of her Algerian wine. Her first customer was the great Luigi, who, thanks to Carmelita's money, could sit and drink while his employees did his work. The fly in the worthy man's ointment was the fact that his Italian dinner and Italian wine were thirty-five miles behind him at Carmelita's café. Like ordinary men, he must, to-night and for many a night to come, content himself with the monotonous and meagre fare of common Legionaries. However—better half a sofa than no bed; and he was easily prime favourite with Madame. . . . This would be an excellent chance for consolidating his position with her, winning her for his bride, and apprising Carmelita, from afar, of the fact that he was now respectably settled in life. Thus would a disagreeable scene be avoided and, on the return of the Battalion to Sidi-bel-Abbés, he would give the Café de la Légion a wide berth. . . . Could he perhaps *sell* his rights and goodwill in the café and Carmelita to some Legionary of means? One or two of his own *chambrée* seemed to have money—the Englishman; the Russians. . . . Better still, sell out to Malvin, Tou-tou, Meyer, or some other penniless toady and *make him pay a weekly percentage* of what he screwed out of Carmelita. Excellent! And if the scoundrel did not get him enough, he would supplant him with a more competent lessee. . . . Meanwhile, to storm Madame's experienced and undecided heart. Anyhow, if she wouldn't have Luigi she shouldn't have anyone else. . . .

There was, that evening, exceeding little noise and movement, and "the stir and tread of armed camps." As soon as they had fed—and, in many cases, before they had fed—

the soldiers lay on their blankets, their heads on their knapsacks and their overcoats over their bodies.

Scarcely, as it seemed to Rupert, had they closed their eyes, when it was time to rise and resume their weary march. At one o'clock in the morning, the Battalion fell in, and each man got his two litres of water and strict orders to keep one quarter of it for to-morrow's cooking purposes. If he contributed no water to the cooking-cauldron he got no cooked food.

On tramped the Legion.

Day after day, day after day, it marched, and, on the twelfth day from Sidi-bel-Abbès, had covered nearly three hundred and fifty miles. Well might the Legion be known in the Nineteenth Division as the *Cavalerie à pied*.

2

Life for the Seventh Company of the First Battalion of the Legion in Aïnargoula was, as John Bull had promised Rupert, simply hell. Not even the relief of desert warfare had broken the cruel monotony of desert marches and life in desert stations—stations consisting of red-hot barracks, and the inevitable filthy and sordid *Village Nègre*. Men lived and sometimes died—in a state of unbearable irritation and morose savageness. Fights were frequent, suicide not infrequent, and murders not unknown. *Cafard* reigned supreme. The punishment-cells were overcrowded night and day, and abortive desertions occurred with extraordinary frequency.

The discontent and sense of wasted time, which had begun to oppress Rupert at Sidi-bel-Abbès, increased tenfold. To him and to the Bucking Bronco (who daily swore that he would desert that night, and tramp to Sidi-bel-Abbès to see Carmelita) John Bull proved a friend in need. Each afternoon, during that terrible time between eleven and three, when the incredible heat of the barrack-room made it impossible for any work to be done, and the men, by strict rule, were compelled to lie about on their cots, it was John Bull who found his friends something else to think about than their own sufferings and miseries.

A faithful coadjutor was 'Erb, who, with his mouth-organ and Jew's-harp, probably saved the reason, or the life, of more than one man. 'Erb seemed to feel the heat less than bigger men, and he would sit cross-legged upon his mattress, evoking tuneful strains from his beloved instruments when far stronger men could only lie panting like distressed dogs. Undoubtedly the three Englishmen and the American exercised a restraining and beneficial influence, inasmuch as they interfered as one man (following the lead of John Bull, the oldest soldier in the room) whenever a quarrel reached the point of blows, in their presence. . . . Under those conditions of life and temper a blow is commonly but the prelude to swift homicide.

One terrible afternoon, as the Legionaries lay on their beds, almost naked, in that stinking oven, the suddenness of these tragedies was manifested. It was too hot to play *bloquette* or *foutrou*, too hot to sing, too hot to smoke, too hot to do anything, and the hot bed positively burnt one's bare back. The Bucking Bronco lay gasping, his huge chest rising and falling with painful rapidity. John Bull was showing Rupert a wonderfully and beautifully Japanese-tattooed serpent which wound twice round his wrist and ran up the inner side of his right forearm, its head and expanded hood filling the hollow of his elbow. Rupert, who would have liked to copy it, was wondering how its brilliant colours had been achieved and had remained undimmed for over thirty-five years, as John Bull said was the case, it having been done at Nagasaki when he was a midshipman on the *Narcissus*. It was too hot even for 'Erb to make music and he lay fanning himself with an ancient copy of the *Echo d'Oron*. It was too hot to sleep, save in one or two cases, and these men groaned, moaned and rolled their heads as they snored. It was too hot to quarrel—almost. But not quite. Suddenly the swift *zweep* of a bayonet being snatched from its steel scabbard hissed through the room, and all eyes turned to where Legionary Franz Josef Meyer flashed his bayonet from his sheaf and, almost in the same movement, drove it up through the throat of the Greek, Dimitropoulos, and into his brain.

"Take that you scum of the Levant," he said, and then stared, wide-eyed and open-mouthed, at his handiwork. There had been bad blood between the men for some time, and for days the Austrian had accused the Greek

111

of stealing a piece of his wax. Some taunt of the dead man had completed the work of *le cafard*. . . .

That night Meyer escaped from the cells—and his body, three days later, was delivered up in return for the twenty-five francs paid for a live or dead deserter. It would perhaps be more accurate to say that parts of his body were brought in—sufficient, at any rate, for identification.

He had fallen into the hands of the Arabs.

To give the Arabs their due, however, they saved the situation. Just when Legionary John Bull had begun to give up hope, and nightly to dread what the morrow might bring forth for his friends and himself, the Arabs attacked the post. The strain on the over-stretched cord was released and men who, in another day would have been temporarily or permanently raving madmen, were saved.

The attack was easily beaten off and without loss to the Legionaries, firing from loopholes and behind stone walls.

On the morrow, a reconnaissance toward the nearest oasis discovered their camp and, on the next day, a tiny punitive column set forth from Aïnargoula—the Legionaries as happy, to use Rupert's too appropriate simile, as sand-boys. Like everybody else, he was in the highest spirits. Gone was the dark shadow of *le cafard* and the feeling that, unless something happened, he would become a homicidal maniac and run amuck.

Here was the "real thing." Here was that for which he had been so long and so drastically trained—desert warfare. He thrilled from head to foot with excitement, and wondered whether the day would bring forth one of the famous and terrible Arab cavalry charges, and whether he would have his first experience of taking part in the mad and fearful joy of a bayonet charge. Anyhow, there was a chance of either or both.

The Company marched on at its quickest, alternating five minutes of swift marching with five minutes of the *pas gymnastique,* the long, loping stride which is the "double" of the Legion.

Far ahead marched a small advance-guard; behind followed a rear-guard, and, well out on either side, marched the flankers. Where a sandy ridge ran parallel with the course of the Company, the flankers advanced along the crest of it, that they might watch the country which lay beyond. This did not avail them much, for, invariably, such a ridge was paralleled by a similar one at no great distance. To have rendered the little Company absolutely secure against sudden surprise-attack on either flank, would have necessitated sending out the majority of the force for miles on either side. Rupert, ever keen and deeply interested in military matters talked of this with John Bull, who agreed with him that, considerable as the danger of such an attack was, it could not be eliminated.

"Anyhow," concluded he, "we generally get something like at least five hundred yards' margin and if the Arabs can cut us up while we have that—they deserve so. Still, it's tricky country I admit, with all these *wadis* and folds in the ground, as well as rocks and ridges."

On marched the Company, and reached an area of rolling sand-hills, and loose heavy sand under foot.

The day grew terribly hot and the going terrible heavy. As usual, all pretences and semblance of smart marching had been abandoned, and the men marched in whatever posture, attitude or style seemed to them best. . . .

. . . . It came with the suddenness of a thunderclap on a fine day, at a moment when practically everything but the miseries of marching through loose sand in the hottest part of one of the hottest days of the year had faded from the minds of the straining, labouring men.

A sudden shout, followed by the firing of half a dozen shots brought the column automatically to a halt and drew all eyes to the right.

From a wide shallow *wadi,* or a fold in the ground, among the sand-hills a few hundred yards away, an avalanche of *haik* and *djellab*-clad men on swift horses suddenly materialized and swept down like a whirlwind on the little force. Behind them followed a far bigger mass of camel-riders howling *"Ul-Ul-Ullah-Akbar!"* as they came. Almost before the column had halted, a couple of barks from Lieutenant Roberte turned the Company to the right in two ranks, the front rank kneeling, the rear rank standing close up behind it, with bayonets fixed and magazines charged. . . . Having fired their warning shots, the flankers were running for their lives to join the main body. The Company watched and waited in grave silence. It was Lieutenant Roberte's intention that, when the Arabs

113

broke and fled before the Company's withering blast of lead, they should leave the maximum number of "souvenirs" behind them. His was the courage and nerve that is tempered and enhanced by imperturbable coolness. He would let the charging foe gallop to the very margin of safety for his Legionaries. To turn them back at fifty yards would be much more profitable than to do it at five hundred.

Trembling with excitement and the thrilling desire for violent action, Rupert knelt between John Bull and the Bucking Bronco, scarcely able to await the orders to fire and charge. Before any order came he saw a sight that for a moment sickened and shook him, a sight which remained before his eyes for many days. Corporal Auguste Gilles, who was commanding the flankers, either too weary or too ill to continue his sprint for comparative safety, turned and faced the thundering rush of the oncoming Arab *harka*, close behind him. Kneeling by a prickly pear or cactus bush he threw up his rifle and emptied his magazine into the swiftly rushing ranks that were almost upon him. As he fired his last shot, an Arab, riding ahead of the rest, lowered his lance and, with a cry of *"Kelb ibn kelb,"*[1] bent over towards him. Springing to his feet the Corporal gamely charged with his bayonet. There can be only one end to such a combat when the horseman knows his weapon. The Corporal was sent flying into the cactus, impaled upon the Arab's lance, and, as it was withdrawn as the horseman swept by, the horrified Rupert saw his comrade stagger to his feet and totter forward— tethered to the cactus by his own entrails. Happily, a second later, the sweep of an Arab *flissa* almost severed his head from his shoulders.

The Company stood firm and silent as a rock, the shining bayonets still and level. Just as it seemed to Rupert that it must be swept away and every man share the fate of that mangled lump of clay in front (for there is no more nerve-shaking spectacle than cavalry charging down upon you like a living avalanche or flood) one word rang out from Lieutenant Roberte.

When the crashing rattle (like mingled, tearing thunder and the wild hammer of hail upon a corrugated iron roof)

---

[1]Dog—and son of a dog.

ceased as magazines were emptied almost simultaneously, the Arabs were in flight at top speed, leaving two-thirds of their number on the plain; and upon the fleeing *harka* the Company made very pretty shooting—for the Legion shoots as well as it marches.

When the "Cease Fire" whistle had blown, Rupert remarked to John Bull—

"No chance for a bayonet charge, then?" to which the old soldier replied—

"No, my son, that is a pleasure to which the Arab does not treat us, unless we surprise his sleeping *douar* at dawn. . . ."

The Arabs having disappeared beyond the horizon, the Company camped and bivouacked on the battlefield, resuming its march at midnight. As Lieutenant Roberte feared and expected, the oasis which was surrounded and attacked at dawn, was found to be empty.

The Company marched back to Aïnargoula and, a few days later, returned to Sidi-bel-Abbés.

CHAPTER SEVEN

THE SHEEP IN WOLF'S CLOTHING

LEGIONNAIRE JOHN BULL sat on the edge of his cot at the hour of *astiquage*. Though his body was in the *chambrée* of the Seventh Company, his mind, as usual, was in England, and his thoughts, as usual, played around the woman whom he knew as Marquerite, and the world as Lady Huntingten.

What *could* he do next year when his third and last period of Legion service expired? Where could he possibly hide in such inviolable anonymity that there was no possible chance of any rumour arising that the dead Sir Montague Merline was in the land of the living? . . . How had it happened that he had survived the wounds and disease that he had suffered in Tonkin, Madagascar, Dahomey, and the Sahara—the stake-trap pit into which he had fallen at Nha-Nam—the bullet in his neck from the Malagasy rifle—the hack from the *coupe-coupe* which had split his collarbone in that ghastly West African jungle—the lance-thrust that had torn his arm from elbow to shoulder at Elsefra?

It was an absolute and undeniable fact that the man who desired to die in battle could never do it; while he who had everything to live for, was among the first to fall. If they went South again to-morrow and were cut up in a sudden Arab *razzia,* he would be the sole survivor. But if a letter arrived on the previous day, stating that Lady Huntingten had just heard of his survival and longed for his return—would he survive that fight? Most certainly not.

What to do at the end of the fifteenth year of his service? His face had been far too well known among the class of people who passed through Marseilles to India and elsewhere—who winter on the Riviera, who golf at Biarritz, who recuperate at Vichy or Aix, who go to Paris in the Spring; and who, in short, are to be found in various parts of France at various times of the year—for him to dream of using the Legion's free pass to any part of France. The risk might be infinitesimal, but it existed, and he would run no risk of ruining Marguerite's life, after more than twenty-five years.

She must be over forty-five now. . . . Had time dealt kindly to her? Was she as beautiful as ever? Sure to be. Marguerite was of the type that would ripen, mature, and improve until well on into middle life. Who was the eminent man who said that a woman was not interesting until she was forty? . . .

What would he not give for a sight of Marguerite? It would be easy enough, next year. Only next year—and it was a thousand to one, a million to one, against anyone recognizing him if he were well disguised and thoroughly careful. Just one sight of Marguerite—after more than twenty-five years! Had he not made sacrifices enough? Might he not take *that* much reward for half a lifetime of life in death—a lifetime in which his body dragged wretchedly and wearily along among the dregs of the earth, while his mind haunted the home of his wife, a home in which another man was lord and master. Was it much to ask—one glimpse of his wife after twenty-seven years of renunciation?

"Miserable, selfish cur!" he murmured aloud as he melted a piece of wax in the flame of a match. "You would risk the happiness of your wife, your old friend, and their children—all absolutely innocent of wrong—for the sake of a minute's self-indulgence. . . . Be ashamed of yourself, you whining weakling. . . ."

It had become a habit of Légionnaire John Bull to talk to himself aloud when alone—a habit he endeavoured to check as he had recently, on more than one occasion, found himself talking aloud in the company of others.

Having finished the polishing of his leather-work, he took his Lebel rifle from the rack and commenced to clean it. As he threw open the chamber, he paused, the bolt in his right hand, the rifle balanced in his left. Someone was running with great speed along the corridor towards the room. What was up? Was it a case of *Faites le sac*? Would the head of an excited and delighted Legionary be thrust in at the door with a yell of—"*Aux armes! Faites le sac*"?

The door burst open and in rushed Mikhail Kyrilovitch, bare-headed, coatless, with staring eyes and blanched cheeks.

"Save me, save me, Monsieur," he shrieked, rushing towards the old Legionary. "Save me—*I am a woman. . .*"

"Good God!" ejaculated Legionary John Bull, involuntarily glancing from the face to the flat chest of the speaker.

"I am a girl," sobbed the *soi-disant* Mikhail. . . . "I am a girl. . . . And that loathsome beast Luigi Rivoli has found me out. . . . He's coming. . . . He chased me . . . What shall I do? What *shall* I do? Poor Feodor . . . ."

As Légionnaire Luigi Rivoli entered the room, panting slightly with unwonted exertions, the girl crouched behind John Bull, her face in her hands, her body shaken by deep sobs. It had all happened so quickly that John Bull found himself standing with his gun balanced, still in the attitude into which he had frozen on hearing the running feet without.

So it had come, had it—and he was to try conclusions with Luigi Rivoli at last. Well, it should be no inconclusive rough-and-tumble. Perhaps this was the solution of his problem, and might settle once and for all the question of his future?

"Ho-ho! Ho-ho!" roared the Neapolitan, "she's your

117

girl, is she, you *aristocratico Inglese?* Ho-ho! You are *faisant Suisse* are you? Ho-ho! Your own private girl in the very *chambrée!* Corpor di Bacco! You shall learn the penalty for breaking the Legion's first law of share-and-share alike. Get out of my way, *cane Inglese."*

John Bull closed the breech of his rifle, and pointed the weapon at Rivoli's broad breast.

"Stand back," he said quietly. "Stand back, you foul-mouthed scum of Naples, or I'll blow your dirty little soul out of your greasy carcass." He raised his voice slightly. "Stand back, you dog, do you hear?" he added, advancing slightly towards his opponent.

Luigi Rivoli gave ground. The rifle might be loaded. You never knew with these cursed, quiet Northerners, with their cold, pale eyes. . . . The rifle might be loaded. . . . Rivoli was well aware that every Legionary makes it his business to steal a cartridge sooner or later, and keeps it by him for emergencies, be they of suicide, murder, self-defence, or desertion. . . . The Englishman had been standing in the attitude of one who loads a rifle at the moment of his entrance. Perhaps his girl had told him of the discovery and assault, and he had been loading the rifle to avenge her.

"Listen to me, Luigi Rivoli," said John Bull, still holding the rifle within a foot of the Italian's breast. "Listen, and I'll tell you what you are. Then I will tell the Section what you are, when they come in. . . . Then I will tell the whole Company. . . . Then I will stand on a table in the Canteen and shout it, night after night. . . . This is what you are. You are a coward. A *coward,* d'you hear? —a miserable, shrinking, frightened coward, who dare not fight. . . ."

"Fight! *Iddio! Fight!* Put down that rifle and I'll tear you limb from limb. Come down into the square and I will break your back. Come down now—and fight for the girl."

" . . . A trembling, frightened *coward* who dare not fight, and who calls punching and hugging and kicking 'fighting.' I challenge you to fight, Luigi Rivoli, with rifles —at one hundred yards and no cover; or with revolvers, at ten paces; or with swords of any sort or kind—if it's only sword-bayonets. Will you fight, or will you be known as *Rivoli the Coward* throughout both Battalions of the Legion?"

Rivoli half-crouched for a spring, and straightway the rifle sprang to the Englishman's shoulder, as his eyes blazed and his fingers fell round the trigger. Rivoli recoiled.

"I don't want to shoot you, unarmed, Coward," he said quietly. "I am going to shoot you, or stab you, or slash you, in fair fight or else you shall kneel and be christened *Rivoli the Coward* on the barrack square. . . . I've had enough of you, and so has everybody—unless it's your gang of pimps. . . . Now go. Go on—get out. . . Go on—before I lose patience. Clear out—and make up your mind whether you will fight or be christened."

"Oh, I'll fight you—you mangy old cur. You are brave enough with a loaded rifle, eh? Mother of Christ! I'll send you where the birds won't trouble you. . . . Shoot me in the back as I go, Brave Man with a Gun"—and Luigi Rivoli departed, in a state of horrid doubt and perturbation. . . . This cursed Englishman meant what he said. . . .

Legionary John Bull lowered his rifle with a laugh, and became aware of the fact that the Russian girl was hugging his leg in a way which would have effectually hampered him in the event of a struggle, and which made him feel supremely ridiculous.

"Get up, *petite,*" he said bending over her, as she lay moaning and weeping. "It's all right—he's gone. He won't trouble you again, for I am going to kill him. Come and lie on your bed and tell me all about it. . . . We must make up our minds as to what will be the best thing to do. . . . Rivoli will tell everybody."

He helped the girl to her feet partly led and partly carried her to her bed, and laid her on it.

Holding his lean brown hand between her little ones, in a voice broken and choked with sobs, she told him something of her story—a sad little story all too common.

The listener gathered that the two were children of a prominent revolutionary who had disappeared into Siberia, after what they considered a travesty of a trial. They had been students at the University of Moscow, and had followed in their father's political footsteps from the age of sixteen. Their youth and inexperience, their fanatical enthusiasm, and their unselfish courage had, in a few years, brought them to a point at which they must choose between death or the horrors of prison and Siberia on the other hand, and immediate flight, and most complete and utter evanishment on the other. When his beloved twin sister had been chosen by the Society as an "instrument," Feodor's heart had failed him. He had disobeyed the orders of the Central Committee; he had coerced the girl; he had made disclosures.

They had escaped to Paris. Before long it had been a question as to whether they were in more imminent and terrible danger from the secret agents of the Russian police or from those of the Nihilists. The sight of the notice, *"Bureau de recrutement. Engagements volontaires,"* over the door of a dirty little house in the Rue St. Dominique had suggested the Légion Estrangère, and a possible means of escape and five years' safety.

But the Medical Examination? . . .

Accompanied by a fellow-fugitive who was on his way to America, Feodor had gone to the Bureau and they had enlisted, passed the doctors, and received railway-passes to Marseilles, made out in the names of Feodor and Mikhail Kyrilovitch; sustenance money; and orders to proceed by the night train from the Gare de Lyons and report at Fort St. Jean in the morning, if not met at the station by a Sergeant of the Legion. Their compatriot had handed his travelling warrant to the girl (dressed in a suit of Feodor's) and had seen the twins off at the Gare de Lyons with his blessing. . . .

Monsieur Jean Boule knew the rest, and but for this hateful, bestial Luigi Rivoli, all might have been well, for she was very strong, and had meant to be very brave. Now, what should she do; what *should* she do? . . . And what would poor Feodor say when he came in from corvée and found that she had let herself get caught like this at last? . . . What could they do?

And indeed, Sir Montague Merline did not know what a lady could do when discovered in a *chambrée* of a *caserne* of the French Foreign Legion in Sidi-bel-Abbès. He did not know in the least. There was the first attitude of the authorities to consider, and then that of the men. Would a Court Martial hold that, having behaved as a man, she should be treated as one, and kept to her bargain, or sent to join the Zephyrs? Would they imprison her for fraud? Would they repatriate her? Would they communicate with the Russian police? Or would they just fling her out of the barracks-gate and let her go? There was probably no precedent, whatever, to go upon.

And supposing the matter were hushed up in the *chambrée,* and the authorities never knew—would life be livable for the girl? Could he, and Rupert, the Bucking Bronco, Herbert Higgins, Feodor, and perhaps one or two of the more decent foreigners, such as Hans Djoolte and old Tan-de-Soif, ensure her a decent life, free from molestation and annoyance. No, it couldn't be done. Life would be rendered utterly impossible for her by gross animals of the type of Rivoli, Malvin, the *Apache,* Hirsch, Bauer, Borges and the rest of Rivoli's sycophants. It was sufficiently ghastly, and almost unthinkable, to imagine a woman in that sink when nobody dreamed she was anything but what she seemed. How could one contemplate a woman, who was *known* to be a woman, living her life, waking and sleeping, in such a situation? The more devotedly her bodyguard shielded and protected her, the more venomously determined would the others be to annoy, insult and injure her in a thousand different ways. It would be insupportable, impossible. . . . But of course it could not be kept from the authorities for a week. What was to be done?

It was all very well to say that the three Englishmen and the American would protect her, that night, by forming a sentry-group and watching in turn—but how long could that go on? It would be all over the barracks to-morrow, and known to the authorities a few hours later. Oh, if he could only do her up in a parcel and post her to Marguerite with just a line, *"Please take care of this poor girl.—Monty."* Marguerite would keep her safe enough. . . . But thinking nonsense wasn't helping. He would load his rifle in earnest, and settle scores with Luigi Rivoli, once and for all, if he returned with a gang to back him. Incidentally, that would settle his own fate, for it would mean a Court Martial at Oran followed by a firing-party, or penal servitude in the Zephyrs, and, at his age, that would only be a slower death.

All very well for him and Rivoli, but what of the girl? . . . What ghastly danger it must have been that drove them to such a dreadful expedient. Truly the Legion was a net for queer fish. Poor, plucky little soul, what could he do for her?

Never since he wore the two stars[1] of a British Captain had he longed, as he did at that moment, for power and authority. If only he were a Captain again, Captain of the Seventh Company, the girl should go straight to his wife, or some other woman. Suddenly he rose to his feet, his face illuminated by the brilliance of the idea which had suddenly entered his mind.

"Carmelita!" he almost shouted to the empty room. He bent over the crying girl again, and shook her gently by the shoulder.

"I have it, little one," he said. "Thank God! Yes—it's a chance. I believe I have a plan. Carmelita! Let's get out of this at once, straight to the Café de la Légion. Carmelita has a heart of gold. . . ."

The girl half sat up. "She may be a kind girl—but she's Luigi Rivoli's mistress," she said. "She would do anything he ordered."

"Carmelita considers herself Rivoli's wife," replied the Englishman, "and so she would be, if he were not the biggest blackguard unhung. Very well, he can hardly go to the woman who is practically his wife and say, 'Hand over the woman you are hiding,'"

"When a woman loves a man she obeys him," said the girl, and added with innocent naïveté, "And I will obey you, Monsieur Jean Boule. . . . Anyhow, it *is* a hope— in a position which is hopeless."

"Get into walking-out kit quickly," urged the old soldier, "and see the Sergeant of the Guard has no excuse for turning you back. The sooner we're away the better. . . . I wish Rupert and the Bronco would roll up. . . . If you can get to Carmelita's unseen, and change back into a girl, you could either hide with Carmelita for a time, or simply desert in feminine apparel."

"And Feodor?" asked the Russian. "Will they shoot him? I can't leave. . . ."

"Bother Feodor," was the quick reply. "One soldier is

---

[1] Since increased to three, of course.

not responsible because another deserts. Let's get you safe to Carmelita's and then I'll find Feodor and tell him all about it."

Hiram Cyrus Milton, entering the room bare-footed and without noise, was not a little surprised to behold a young soldier fling his arms about the neck of the eminently staid and respectable Legionary John Bull with a cry of—

"Oh, may God reward you, kind good Monsieur."

"Change quickly, *petite*," said John Bull to the girl as he pushed her from him, and turned to the American.

"Come here, Buck," said he, taking the big man's arm and leading him to the window.

"Don't say as haow yure 'sins hev' come home to roost, John? Did yew reckernize the puling infant by the di'-mond coronite on the locket, or by the strawberry-mark in the middle of its back? Or was his name wrote on the tail of his little shirt? Put me next to it, John. Make me wise to the secret mystery of this 'ere drarmer."

The Bucking Bronco was getting more than a little jealous.

"I will, if you will give me chance," replied John Bull curtly. "Buck, that boy's a girl. Rivoli has found her out and acted as you might expect. I suppose he spotted her in the wash-house or somewhere. She rushed to me for protection, and the game's up. I am going to take her to Carmelita."

The big American stared at his friend with open mouth.

"Yew git me jingled, John," he said slowly. "Thet little looker a *gal*? Is this a story made out of whole cloth,[1] John?"

"Get hold of it, Buck, quickly," was the reply. "The two Russians are political refugees. Their number was up, in Russia, and they bolted to Paris. Same in Paris—and they made a dash for here. Out of the frying-pan into the fire. This one's a girl. Luigi Rivoli knows, and it will be all over the barracks before to-night. She rushed straight to me, and I am going to see her through. If you can think of anything better than taking her to Carmelita, say so."

"I'll swipe the head off'n Mister Lousy Loojey Rivoli," growled the American. "God smite me ef I don't. Thet's

---

[1] Untrue.

torn it, thet has. . . . The damned yaller-dog Dago. . . . Thet puts the lid on Mister Loojey Rivoli, thet does."

"*I'm* going to deal with Rivoli, Buck," said John Bull.

"He'd crush yew with a b'ars hug, sonny; he'd bust in yure ribs, an' break yure back an' then chuck yew down and dance on yew."

"He won't get the chance, Buck; it's not going to be a gutter-scrap. When he chased the girl in here I challenged him to fight with bullet or steel, and told him I'd brand him all over the shop till he was known as 'Rivoli the Coward,' or fought a fair and square duel. . . . Let's get the girl out of this, and then we'll put Master Luigi Rivoli in his place once and for all."

"Shake!" said the Bucking Bronco, extending a huge hand.

"Seen Rupert lately?" asked the Englishman.

"Yep," replied the other. "He's a-settin' on end a-rubberin' at his pants in the lavabo."

"Good! Go and fetch him quick, Buck."

The American sped from the room without glancing at the girl, returning a minute or two later with Rupert. The two men hurried to their respective cots and swiftly changed from fatigue-dress into blue and red.

"If Carmelita turns us down, let's all three desert and take the girl with us," said Rupert to John Bull. "I have plenty of money to buy mufti, disguises, and railway tickets. She would go as a woman of course. We could be a party of tourists. Yes, that's it, English tourists. Old Mendoza would fit us out—at a price."

"Thanks," was the reply. "We'll get her out somehow. . . . She'd stand a far better chance alone though, probably. If suspicion fell on one of us they'd arrest the lot."

"I am ready, Monsieur," said the girl Olga to John Bull. "But I do not want you, Monsieur, nor these other gentlemen, to make trouble for yourselves on my account. . . . I have brought this on myself, and there is no reason why you . . ."

"Oh, shucks! Come on, little gal," broke in the Bucking Bronco. "We'll see yew through. We ain't Loojeys. . . ."

"Of course we will. We shall be only too delighted," agreed Rupert. "Don't you worry."

"Pull yourself together and swagger all you can," advised

John Bull. "It might ruin everything if the Sergeant of the Guard took it into his head to turn you back. I wonder if we had better go through in a gang, or let you go first? If we are all together there is less likelihood of excessive scrutiny of any one of us, but on the other hand it may be remembered that you were last seen with us three, and that might hamper our future usefulness. . . . Just as well Feodor isn't here. . . . Tell you what, you and I will go out together, and I'll use my wits to divert attention from you if we are stopped. The others can come a few minutes later, or as soon as someone else has passed."

"That's it," agreed Rupert; "come on."

With beating hearts, the old soldier and the young girl approached the little side door by the huge barrack gates. Close by it stood the Sergeant of the Guard. Their anxiety increased as they realized that it was none other than Sergeant Legros, one of the most officious, domineering and brutal of the Legion's N.C.O.'s. Luck was against them. He would take a positive delight in standing by that door the whole evening and in turning back every single man whose appearance gave him the slightest opportunity for fault-finding, as well as a good many whose appearance did not.

As they drew near and saluted smartly, the little piggish eyes of Sergeant Legros took in every detail of their uniform. The girl felt the blood draining from her cheeks. What if they had made a mistake? What if red trousers and blue tunic should be wrong, and the *ordre du jour* should be white trousers and blue tunic or capote? What if she had a button undone or her bayonet on the wrong side? What if Sergeant Legros should see, or imagine a speck upon her tunic? . . . Had she been under his evil gaze for hours? Was the side of the Guard House miles in length? . . . Thank God, they were through the gate and free. Free for the moment, and if the good God was merciful she was free for ever from the horrors and fears of that terrible place. Could anything worse befall her? Yes, there were worse places for a girl than a barrack-room of the French Foreign Legion. There was a Russian prison—there was the dark prison van and warder—there was the journey to Siberia—there was Siberia itself. Yes, there were worse places than that she had just left—until her secret was discovered. A thousand times worse. And she thought of her friend, that poor girl who had been less fortunate than she. Poor, poor Marie! Would she herself be sent back to Russia to share Marie's fate, if these brave Englishmen and Carmelita failed to save her? What would become of Feodor? . . . Did this noble Englishman, with the gentle face, love this girl Carmelita? . . . Might not Carmelita's house be a very trap if the loathsome Italian brute owned its owner? . . .

"Let's stroll slowly now, my dear," said John Bull, "and let the others overtake us. The more the merrier, if we should run into Rivoli and his gang, or if he is already at Carmelita's. I don't think he will be. I fancy he puts in the first part of his evening with Madame la Cantinière, and goes down to Carmelita's later for his dinner. . . . If he should be there I don't quite see what line he can take in front of Carmelita. He could hardly molest you in front of the woman whom he pretends he is going to marry, and I don't see on what grounds he could raise any objection to her befriending you. . . . It's a deuced awkward position—for the fact that I intend to kill Rivoli, if I can, hardly gives me a claim on Carmelita. She loves the very ground the brute treads on, you know, and it would take me, or anybody else, a precious long time to persuade her that the man who rid the world of Luigi Rivoli would be her very best friend. . . . He's the most noxious and poisonous reptile I have ever come across, and I believe she is one of the best of good little women. . . . It *is* a hole we're in. We've got to see Carmelita swindled and then jilted and broken-hearted; or we've got to bring the blackest grief upon her by saving her from Rivoli."

"Do *you* love her too, Monsieur?" asked Olga.

"Good Heavens, no!" laughed the Englishman. "But I have a very great liking and regard for her, and so has my friend Rupert. It is poor old Buck who loves her, and I am really sorry for him. It's bad enough to love a woman and be unable to win her, but it must be awful to see her in the power of a man whom you know to be an utter blackguard. . . . Queer thing, Life. . . . I suppose there is some purpose in it. . . . Here they come," he added, looking round.

Le Café de la Légion was swept and garnished, and

126

Carmelita sat in her *sedia pieghevole*[1] behind her bar await-ing her evening guests.

It was a sadder-looking, thinner, somewhat older-look-ing Carmelita than she who had welcomed Rupert and his fellow *bleus* on the occasion of their first visit to her café. Carmelita's little doubt had grown, and worry was border-ing upon anxiety—for Luigi Rivoli was Carmelita's life, and Carmelita was not only a woman, but an Italian woman and a Neapolitan at that. Far better than life she loved Luigi Rivoli, and only next to him did she love her own self-respect and virtue. As has been said before, Carmelita considered herself a married woman. Partly owing to her equivocal position, partly to an innate purity of mind, Carmelita had a present passion for "respectability" such as had never troubled her before.

And Luigi was causing her grief and anxiety, doubt and care, and fear. For long she had fought it *off*, and had stoutly refused to confess it even to herself, but day by day and night by night, the persistent attack had worn down her defences of Hope and Faith until at length she stood face to face with the relentless and insidious assailant and recognized it for what it was—Fear. It had come to that, and Carmelita now frankly admitted to herself that she had fears for the faith, honesty and love of the man whom she regarded as her husband and knew to be the father of the so hoped-for *bambino*. . . .

Could it be possible that the man for whom she had lived, and for whom she would at any time have died, her own Luigi, who, but for her, would be in Marseilles grave-yard, her own husband—was laying siege to fat and ugly Madame la Cantinière, because her business was a more profitable one than Carmelita's? It could not be. Men were not devils. Men did not repay women like that. Not even ordinary men, far less her Luigi. Of course not—and besides, there was the Great Secret.

For the thousandth time Carmelita found reassurance, comfort and cheer in the thought of the Great Secret, and its inevitable effect upon Luigi when he knew it. What would he say when he realized that there might be another Luigi Rivoli, for, of course, it would be a boy—a boy who would grow up another giant among men, another Samson,

---

[1] Deck chair.

another Hercules, another winner of a World's Championship.

What would he do in the transports of his joy? How his face would shine. How heartily he would agree with her when she pointed out that it would be as well for them to marry now before the *bambino* came. No more procrastination now. What a wedding it should be, and what a feast they would give the brave *soldati!* Il Signor Jean Boule should have the seat of honour, and the Signor Americano should come, and Signor Rupert, and Signor 'Erbiggin, and the poor Grasshopper, and the two Russi (ah! what of that Russian girl, what would be her fate? It was wonderful how she kept up the deception. Poor, poor little soul, what a life—the constant fear, the watchfulness and anxiety. Fancy eating and drinking, walking, talking and working, dressing and undressing, waking and sleeping among those men—some of them such dreadful men). Yes, it should be a wedding to remember, without stint of food or drink—*un pranzo di tr e portate with maccheroni* and *la frittate d'uova* and the best of *couscous,* and there should be *vino Italiano*—they would welcome a change from the eternal *vino Algerino.* . . .

Four Legionaries entered, and Carmelita rose with a smile to greet them. There was no one she would sooner see than Il Signor Jean Boule and his friends—since it was not Luigi who entered.

"Che cosa posso offrirve?" she asked. (Although Carmelita spoke Legion-French fluently one noticed that she always welcomed one in Italian, and always counted in that language).

"I want a quiet talk with you, carissima Carmelita," said John Bull. "We are in great trouble, and we want your help."

"I am glad," replied Carmelita. "Not glad that you are in trouble, but glad you have come to me."

"It is about Mikhail Kyrilovitch," said the Englishman.

"I thought it was," said Carmelita.

"Don't think me mad, Carmelita," continued John Bull, "but listen. Mikhail Kyrilovitch is a *girl.*"

"Don't think me mad, Signor Jean Boule," mimicked Carmelita, "but listen. I have known Mikhail Kyrilovitch was a girl from the first evening that she came here."

The Englishman's blue eyes opened widely in surprise, as he stared at the girl. "How?" he asked.

"Oh, in a dozen ways," laughed Carmelita. "Hands, voice, manner. I stroked her cheek, it was as soft as my own, while her twin brother's was like sand-paper. When she went to catch a biscuit she made a 'lap,' as one does who wears a skirt, instead of bringing her knees together as a man does. . . . And what can I do for Mademoiselle Mikhail?"

"You can save her, Carmelita, from I don't know what dangers and horrors. She had been found out, and what her fate would be at the tender mercies of the authorities on the one hand, and of the men on the other, one does not like to think. The very least that could happen to her is to be turned into the streets of Sidi-bel-Abbès."

"Do the officers know yet?" asked Carmelita. "Who does know? Who found her out?"

"Luigi Rivoli found her out," replied John Bull.

"And sent her to me?" asked Carmelita. "I am glad he . . ."

"He did not send her to you," interrupted the Englishman gravely.

"What did he do?" asked Carmelita quickly.

"I will tell you what he did, Carmelita, as kindly as I can. . . . He forgot he was a soldier, Carmelita; he forgot he was an honest man; he forgot he was your—er—fidanzato, your sposo, Carmelita. . . ."

Carmelita went very white.

"Tell me, Signor," she said quickly. "Did you have to protect this Russian wretch from Luigi?"

"I did," was the reply. "Why do you speak contemptuously of the girl? She is as innocent as—as innocent as you are, Carmelita."

"I hate her," hissed Carmelita. . . . "Did Luigi kiss her? What happened? Did he . . .?"

The Englishman put his hand over Carmelita's little clenched fist as it lay on the bar.

"Listen, little one," he said. "You are one of the best, kindest and bravest women I have known. I am certain you are going to be worthy of yourself now. So is Rupert, so is Monsieur Bronco. He has been blaming us bitterly when we have even for a moment wondered whether you would save this girl. He is worth a thousand Rivolis, and loves you a thousand times better than Rivoli ever could. Don't disappoint him and us, Carmelita. Don't disappoint us *in yourself*, I mean. . . . What has the girl done that you should hate her?"

"Did Luigi kiss her?" again asked Carmelita.

"He did not," was the reply. "He behaved . . ."

"And he could not, of course, while she was with me, could he?" said Carmelita.

"Exactly," smiled the Englishman. "Take her in now, little woman, and lend her some clothes until we can get some things bought or made for her."

"Clothes cost francs, Signor Jean," was the practical reply of the girl, who had grown up in a hard school. "I can give her food and shelter, and I can lend her my things, but I have no francs for clothes."

"Rupert will find whatever is necessary for her clothes and board and lodging, and for her ticket too. She shan't be with you long, cara Carmelita, nor in Sidi-bel-Abbès."

Carmelita passed from behind the bar and went over to the table at which sat Rupert, the American, and the girl Olga. Putting her arm around the neck of the last, Carmelita kissed her on the cheek.

"Come, little one," she said. "Come to my bed and sleep. You shall be as safe as if in the Chapel of the Mother of God," and, as the girl burst into tears, led her away.

John Bull joined his friends as the two women disappeared through the door leading to Carmelita's room.

"Well, thank God for that," he said as he sat down, and wiped his forehead. "What's the next step?"

"Find the other little Roosian guy, and' put him wise to what's happened to sissy, guess," replied the American.

"Yes," agreed Rupert. "It's up to him to carry on now, with any sort or kind of help that we can give him. . . . Where did he go after parade, I wonder?"

"The gal got copped for a wheel-barrer corvèe—they was goin' scavengin' round the officers' houses and gardens I think—an' he took her place. . . . He'd be back by dark an' start washin' hisself," opined the American.

"I look in the *chambrèe*," said John Bull as they entered the barrack-square. "You go to the lavabo, Rupert, and you see if he is in the Canteen, Buck. Whoever finds him had better advise him to let Luigi Rivoli alone, and make his plans for going on pump. Tell him I think his best line would be to see Carmelita and arrange for him and his sister to get dresses alike, and clear out boldly by train to Oran, as girls. After that, they know their own business best, but I should recommend England as about the safest place for them."

"By jove! I could give him a letter to my mother," put in Rupert. "Good idea. My people would love to help them—especially as they could tell them all about me."

"Gee-whiz! Thet's a brainy notion," agreed the Bucking Bronco. "Let 'em skin out and make tracks for yure Old-Folk-at-Home. It's a cinch."

Legionary John Bull found Legionary Feodor Kyrilovitch sitting on his cot polishing "Rosalie," as the soldier of France terms his bayonet. Several other Legionaries were engaged in *astiquage* and accoutrement cleaning. For the thousandth time, the English gentleman realized that one of the most irksome and maddening of the hardships and disabilities of the common soldier's life is its utter lack of privacy.

"Bonsoir, cher Boule," remarked Kyrilovitch, looking up as the Englishman approached. "Have you seen my brother? He appears to have come in and changed and gone out without me."

Evidently the boy was anxious.

"Your brother is at Carmelita's," replied John Bull, and added: "Come over to my bed and sit beside me with your back to the room. I want to speak to you."

"Don't be alarmed," he continued as they seated themselves. "Your brother is absolutely all right."

The Russian gazed anxiously at the kindly face of the man whom he had instinctively liked and trusted from the first.

"Your brother is quite all right," continued the Englishman, "but I am afraid you will have to change your plans."

"Change our plans, Monsieur Boule?"

"Yes," replied the older man, as he laid his hand on Feodor's knee with a reassuring smile. "You will have to change your plans, for Mikhail can be Mikhail no longer."

The Russian bowed his head upon his hands with a groan.

"My poor little Olusha," he whispered.

"Courage, mon brave," said John Bull, patting him on the back. "We have a plan for you. As soon as your sister was discovered, we took her to Carmelita, with whom she will be quite safe for a while. Our idea is that she and Carmelita make and buy women's clothes for both of you, and that you escape as sisters. Since she made such a splendid boy, you ought to be able to become a fairly convincing girl. Légionnaire Mikhail Kyrilovitch will be looked for as a man—probably in uniform. By the time the hue and cry is over, and he is forgotten, everything will be ready for both of you, then one night you slip into Carmelita's café and, next day, two café-chantant girls who have been visiting Carmelita, walk coolly to the station and take train for Oran. . . Rivoli can't tell on them and still keep in with Carmelita. He'll have to help—or pretend to."

Feodor Kyrilovitch was himself again—a cool and level-headed conspirator, accustomed to weighing chances, taking risks and facing dangers.

"Thanks, mon ami," he said. "I believe I owe you my sister's salvation. . . . There will be difficulties, and there are risks—but it is a plan."

"Seems fairly hopeful," replied the other. "Anyhow, we could think of nothing better."

"We might get to Oran," mused Feodor; "but where can we go from there, God knows. We daren't go to Paris again, and I doubt if we have a hundred and fifty roubles between us. . . . And we dare not write to friends in Russia."

"We've thought of that too, my boy," interrupted the Englishman. "My friend Rupert has money in the Crédit Lyonnais, here in the town. He says he will be only too delighted to lend you enough to get to England, and write a letter for you to take to his people. He says his mother will welcome you with open arms as coming from him. . . . From what he has said to me about her at different times, I imagine her to be one of the best—and the best of Englishwomen are the best of women, let me tell you."

"And the best of Englishmen are the best of men," replied Feodor, seizing the old Legionary's hand and kissing it fervently—to the latter gentleman's consternation and utter discomfort.

"Don't be an ass," he replied in English. . . . "Clear out now, and go and have a talk with Carmelita. You can trust her absolutely. Give her what money you've got, and she'll poke round in the ghetto for clothes. She'll know lots of the Spanish Jew dealers and cheap *couturières*, if old Mendoza hasn't what she wants. Meanwhile, Rupert will draw some money from the *banque*.

The Russian rose to his feet.

"But how can I thank you, Monsieur? How can I repay Monsieur Rupert for his kindness?"

"Don't thank me, and repay Rupert by visiting his mother and waxing eloquent over his marvellous condition of health, happiness and prosperity. Tell her he is having a lovely time in a lovely place with lovely people."

"You joke, Monsieur, how *can* I repay you all?"

"Well, I'll tell you, my son—by getting your sister clear of this hell and safe into England."

The Russian struck himself violently on the forehead and turned away.

A minute later Rupert entered the *chambrèe*.

"He's not in the lavabo," he announced.

"No, it's all right. I found him here. He has just gone down to Carmelita's. . . . Let's go over to the Canteen, I want to meet the gentle Luigi Rivoli there."

On the stairs they encountered the Bucking Bronco, who was told that Feodor had been found and informed.

"Our Loojey's in the road-house," he announced, "layin' off ter Madam. . . . I wish she'd deliver the goods ef she's gwine ter. Then we could git next our Loojey without raisin' hell with Carmelita."

"Is the Canteen fairly full?" asked John Bull.

"Some!" replied the Bucking Bronco.

"Then I'm going over to seek sorrow," said the other.

"Yure not goin' to get fresh, an' slug the piker any, air yew, John?" enquired the American anxiously.

"No, Buck," was the reply. "I'm only going to make an interestin' announcement," and, turning to Rupert, he advised him not to identify himself with any proceedings which might ensue.

"You are hardly complimentary, Bull," commented Rupert resentfully. . . .

As the three entered the Canteen, which was rapidly filling up, they caught sight of Rivoli lolling against the bar in his accustomed corner, and whispering confidentially to Madame, during her intervals of leisure. Pushing his way through the throng John Bull, closely followed by his two friends, approached the Neapolitan. His back was towards them. The American, whose face wore an ugly look, touched Rivoli with his foot.

"Makin' yure sweet self agreeable as usual, Loojey, my dear? he enquired, and proceeded with the difficult task of making himself both sarcastic and intelligible in the French language. The Italian wheeled round with a scowl at the sound of the voice he hated.

John Bull stepped forward.

"I have come for your answer, Rivoli," he said quietly. "I wish to know when and with what weapons you would prefer to fight me. Personally, I don't care in the least what they are, so long as they're fatal."

A ring of interested listeners gathered round. The Neapolitan laughed contemptuously.

"Weapons!" he growled. "A *fico* for weapons. I'll twist your neck and break your back if you trouble me again."

"Very good," replied the Englishman. "Now listen, bully. We have had a little more than enough of you. You take advantage of your strength to terrorize men who are not street acrobats, and professional weight-lifters. Now *I* am going to take advantage of this, to terrorize *you*," and he produced a small revolver from his pocket. Now choose. Try your blackguard-rush games and get a bullet through your skull, or fight me like a man with any weapon you prefer."

An approving cheer broke from the quickly increasing audience. The Italian moistened his lips and glared round.

"Mais oui," observed Madame with cool impartiality, "but that is a fair offer."

As though stung by her remark, the Italian threw himself into wrestling attiture and extended his arms. John Bull moved only to extend his pistol-arm, and Luigi Rivoli recoiled. Strangling men who could not wrestle was one thing, being shot was quite another. The thrice-accursed

134

English dog had got him nicely cornered. To raise a hand to him was to die—better to face his enemy, himself armed than unarmed. Better still to catch him unarmed and stamp the life out of him. He must temporize.

"Ho-ho, Brave Little Man with a Pistol," he sneered. "Behold the English hero who fears the bare hands of no man—while he has a revolver in his own."

"You miss the point, Rivoli," was the reply. "I want nothing to do with you bare-handed. I want you to choose any weapon you like to name," and turning to the deeply interested crowd he raised his voice a little:

"Gentlemen of the Legion," he said, "I challenge le Légionnaire Luigi Rivoli of the Seventh Company of the First Battalion of La Légion Entrangère to fight me with whatever weapon he prefers. We can use our rifles; he can have the choice of the revolvers belonging to me and my friend Bouckaing Bronceau; we can use our sword-bayonets; we can get sabres from the Spahis; or it can be a rifle-and-bayonet fight. He can choose time, place, and weapon—and, if he will not fight, let him be known as *Rivoli the Coward* as long as he pollutes our glorious Regiment."

Ringing and repeated cheers greeted the longest public speech that Sir Montague Merline had ever made.

A bitter sneer was frozen on Rivoli's white face.

"Galamatias!" he laughed contemptuously, but the laugh rang a little uncertain.

Madame la Cantinière was charmed. She felt she was falling in love with ce brave Jean Boule *au grand galop*. This was a far finer man, and far more suitable husband for a hard-working Cantinière than that lump of a Rivoli, with his pockets always *pleine de vide* and his mouth always full of *langue vert*. A trifle on the elderly side perhaps, but aristocrat *au bout des ongles*. Yes, decidedly grey as to the hair, but then, how nice to be an old man's darling!—and Madame simpered, bridled and tried to blush.

"Speak up thou Rivoli," she cried sharply. "Do not stand there like a *blanc bec* before a Sergeant-Major. Speak, *bècasse*—or speak not again to me."

The Neapolitan darted a glance of hatred at her.

"Peace, fat sow," he hissed, and added unwisely—"You wag your beard too much."

In that moment vanished for ever all possibility of

135

Madame's trying an Italian husband. "Sow" may be a term of endearment, but no gentleman alludes to beards in the presence of a lady whose chin does not betray her sex.

Turning to his enemy, Rivoli struck an attitude and pointed to the door.

"Go, dig your grave *ci-devant*," he said portentously, "and I will kill you beside it, within the week."

"Thanks," replied the Englishman, and invited his friends to join him in a litre. . . .

The barracks of the First Battalion of the Foreign Legion hummed and buzzed that night, from end to end, in a ferment of excitement over the two tremendous items of most thrilling and exciting news, to wit, that there was among them a sheep in wolf's clothing—a girl in uniform —and, secondly, that there was a duel toward, a duel in which no less a person than the great Luigi Rivoli was involved.

Cherchez la femme was the game of the evening; and the catch-word of the wits on encountering any bearded and grisled *ancien* in corridor, *chambrée,* canteen, or staircase, was—

"Art *thou* the girl, petite?"

CHAPTER EIGHT

The Temptation of Sir Montague Merline

Il Signor Luigi Rivoli strode forth from the Canteen in an unpleasant frame of mind.

"Curse the Englishman," he growled. "Curse that hag behind the bar. Curse that Russian *ragazza.* Curse that thrice-damned American. . . ."

He turned into Carmelita's alley and entered the Café.

Carmelita, whose eyes had rarely left the door through out the evening, saw him as he entered, and her face lit up as does a lantern when the wick is kindled. Here was her noble and beautiful Luigi. Away with all wicked doubts and fears. Even the good Jean Boule was prejudiced against her Luigi. She would now hear his version of the discovery of the Russian girl. How amused he would be to know that she had guessed Mikhail's secret long ago.

Rivoli passed behind the bar. Carmelita held open the

door of her room, and having closed it behind him, turned and flung her arms round his neck.

"Marito amato!" she murmered as she kissed him again and again. How could she entertain these doubts of her Luigi in his absence? She was a wicked, wicked girl, and undeserving of her fortune in having so glorious a mate. She decided to utter no reproaches and ask no questions concerning the discovery of the Russian girl. She would just tell him that she had taken her in and that she counted on his help in keeping the girl's secret and getting her away.

"Beloved and beautiful Luigi of my heart," she said, as she placed a steaming dish of macaroni before him, "I want your help once more. That poor foolish, little Mikhail Kyrilovitch has come and told me he is in trouble, and begged my help. Fancy his thinking he could lead the life that my Luigi leads—that of a soldier of France's fiercest Regiment. Poor little fool. . . . Guess where he is at the moment, Luigi."

With his mouth full, the noble Luigi intimated that he knew not, cared not, and desired not to know.

"I will tell my lord," murmured Carmelita, bending over his lordship's huge and brawny shoulder, and kissing the tip of the ear into which she whispered, "He is in my bed."

Luigi had to think quickly. How much had the Russian girl told of what had happened in the wash-house? Nothing, or Carmelita would not be in this frame of mind. What did Carmelita know? Did she know that *he* knew? He sprang to his feet with an oath, and a well-assumed glare of ferocity. He raised his fist above his head, and by holding his breath, contrived to induce a dark flush and raise the veins upon his forehead.

"In your bed, *puttana?*" he hissed. (Carmelita was overjoyed, Luigi was angered and jealous. Where there is jealousy, there is love! Of course, Luigi loved her as he had always done. How dared she doubt it? Throwing her arms around his neck with a happy laugh, she reassured her ruffled mate until he permitted himself to calm down and resume his interrupted meal. Jean Boule had lied to her! Luigi knew nothing! . . .) She went to the bar.

Curse this Russian anarchist! But for her he would not have been in danger of losing Madame, nor of finding a violent death. Curse Carmelita, the stupid fool, for harbour-

137

ing her. What should he do? What could he say? If he thwarted Carmelita's plan, she would think he desired the Russian wench for himself, and fly into a rage. She would be a very fiend from hell if she were jealous! A pretty pass he would be brought to if both Canteen and Café were closed to him! He had better walk warily here, until he had ascertained the exact amount of damage he had done by his most unwise allusion to Madame's whiskers. He had an idea. . . . When Carmelita came into the room again from the bar, she should have the shock of her life, and the Russian *pottana*, another. Also the over-clever Jean Boule should learn that the race is not always to the slow, nor the battle to the weak. . . . Carmelita entered. Picking up his képi, he extended his arms, and with a smile of lofty sadness, bade her come and kiss him while she might. . . .

"While I may? Why do you say that, Luigi?" she asked in a dead voice.

The ruffian felt uncomfortable as he watched those great, black eyes blazing in the pinched, blanched face, and realized that there were depths in Carmelita that he had not sounded—and would be ill-advised to sound. What a devil she looked! Luigi Rivoli would do well to eat no food to which Carmelita had had access, when once she knew the truth. Luigi Rivoli would do well to watch warily, and move quickly, should Carmelita's hand go to the dagger in her garter when he told her that he was thinking of settling in life. In fact it was a question whether his life would be safe, so long as Carmelita was in Sidi-bel-Abbès, and he was husband of Madame! Another idea! *Madre de Dios!* A brilliant one. Denounce Carmelita for aiding and abbetting a deserter! Two birds with one stone—Carmelita jailed and deported, and the Russian recaptured—Luigi Rivoli rid of a danger from the one, and gratified by a vengeance on the other! As these thoughts flashed through the Italian's evil mind, he maintained his pose, and gently and sadly shook his head.

"While you may, indeed, my Carmelita," he murmured, and produced the first of his brilliant ideas. "While you may. Do not think I reproach you, Carmelita, for you have acted but in accordance with the dictates of your warm young heart in taking in this girl. How were *you* to know that this would involve me in a duel to the death with the

138

finest shot in the Nineteenth Division, the most famous marksman in the army of Africa?"

"What?" gasped Carmelita.

"What I say, my poor girl," was the reply, uttered with calm dignity. "Your English friend, this Jean Boule, who fears to meet me face to face, and man to man, with Nature's weapons, has forced a quarrel on me over this Russian girl. He challenged me in the Canteen this night, and I, who could break him like a dried stick, must stand up to be shot by him, like a dog. . . . I do not blame *you*, Carmelita. How were you to know? . . ."

Carmelita suddenly sat down.

"I do not understand," she whispered and sat agape.

"The Englishman owns this girl. . . ."

"He brought her here," Carmelita interrupted, nodding her head.

"Ha! I guessed it. . . . Yes, he owns her, and when I discovered the shameless *puttana's* sex he drew a pistol on *me*, an innocent, unarmed man. . . . Did he tell you it was I who found the shameful hussy out? What could I do against him empty-handed? And now I must fight him— and he can put a bullet where he will. . . . So kiss me, while you may, Carmelita."

With a low cry the girl sprang into his arms.

"My love! My love! My husband!" she wailed, and Luigi hoped that she would release her clasp from about his neck in time for him to avoid suffocation. . . . Curse all women—they were the cause of nine-tenths of the sorrows of mankind. But one could not do without them. . . . Suddenly Carmelita started back, and clapped her hands with a cry of glee. "The Holy Virgin be praised! I have it! I have it! Unless Légionnaire Jean Boule confesses his fault and begs my Luigi's pardon—out into the gutter goes his Russian mistress," and Carmelita pirouetted with joy. . . . Thank God! Thank God! Here was a solution, and she embraced her lover again and again. Luigi's face was wreathed in smiles. *Excellente!* That would do the trick admirably, and the thrice-accursed, and ten-times-too-clever English *aristocrato* should publicly apologize, if he wished to save his mistress. . . . Yes, that would be very much pleasanter than a mere stab-in-the-back revenge, as well as safer. There is always some slight risk, even in Sidi-bel-Abbès, about arranging a murder, and blackmail is always unpleasant—for the blackmailed.

Stroking her hair, he smiled superior upon Carmelita.

"A clever thought, my little one," he murmured, "and bravely meant, but your Luigi's days are numbered. Would that proud cold *aristocrato* eat the words he shouted before half the Company? No! He will leave the girl to shift for herself."

Carmelita's face fell.

"Do not say so," she begged. "No! No! He would not do that. You know how these English treat women. You know the sort of man this Jean Boule is," and for a moment, involuntarily, Carmelita contrasted her Luigi with Il Signor Jean Boule in the matter of their chivalry and honour, and ere she could thrust the thought from her mind, she had realized the comparison to be unfavourable to her lover.

"Luigi," she said, "I feel it in my heart that, since the Englishman has said that he will save his mistress, he will do it at any cost whatsoever to himself. . . . Go, dearest Luigi, go now, and I will send to him and say I must see him at once. He will surely come, thinking that I send on behalf of this Russian fool."

And with a last vehement embrace and burning kiss, she thrust him before her into the bar and watched him out of the Café.

Le Légionnaire Jean Boule was not among the score or so of Legionaries who sat drinking at the little tables, nor were either of his friends. Whom could she send? Was that funny English *ribaldo*, Légionnaire Erbiggin, there? . . . No. . . . Ah!—There sat the poor Grasshopper. He would do. She made her way with laugh and jest and badinage to where he sat, *faisant Suisse* as usual.

"Bonsoir, cher Monsieur Cigale," she said. "Would you do me a kindness?"

The Grasshopper rose, thrust his hands up the sleeves of his tunic as far as his elbows, bowed three times, and then knelt upon the ground and smote it thrice with his forehead. Rising he poured forth a torrent of some language entirely unknown to Carmelita.

"Speak French or Italian, cher Monsieur Cigale," she said.

"A thousand pardons, Signora," replied the Grasshopper. "But you will admit it is not usual for a Mandarin of the Highest Button to speak French. I was saying that the true kindness would be your allowing me to do you a kindness. May I doom your *wonk*[1] of an enemy to the death of a Thousand Cuts?"

"Not this evening, dear Mandarin, thank you," replied Carmelita; "but you can carry a message of the highest military importance. It is well known that you are a soldier of soldiers, and have never yet failed in any military duty."

The Mandarin bowed thrice.

"Will you go straight and find le Légionnaire Jean Boule of your Company, and tell him to come to me at once. Say Carmelita sent you and tell him you have the countersign: 'Our Ally, Russia, is in danger!' "

"I am honoured and I fly," was the reply.

Carmelita knew that John Bull would be with her that evening, and that the risk of eight days' *salle de police,* for being out after tattoo, would not deter him.

In a fever of anxiety, impatience, hope and fear, Carmelita paced up and down behind her bar, like a panther in its cage. One thought shone brightly on the troubled turmoil of her soul. Luigi loved her still; Luigi so loved her that he had been ready to strike her dead as the tide of jealousy surged in his soul. That was the sort of love that Carmelita understood. Let him take her by the throat until she choked—let him seize her by her hair and drag her round the room—let him stab her in the breast, so it be for jealousy. Better Luigi's knife in Carmelita's throat than Luigi's lips on Madame's face. Thank God! Luigi had suffered those pangs—on hearing of a Russian boy in her room—that she herself had suffered on hearing Malvin and the rest couple Luigi's name with Madame's. Thank God! that Luigi knew jealousy even as she did herself. Where there is jealousy, there is love. . . .

And then Carmelita struck her forehead with her clenched fists and laid her head upon her folded arms with a piteous groan. Luigi had been acting. Luigi had *pretended* that jealousy of the Russian. Luigi knew Mikhail Kyrilovitch was a girl—he had fooled her, and once again doubt raised its cruel head in Carmelita's poor distracted mind. "Oh,

---

[1] Chinese pariah dog.

141

Luigi! Luigi!" she sobbed beneath her breath. And then again a ray of comfort—the *bambino*. Merciful Mother of God grant that it might be true, and that her bright and golden hopes were based on more solid foundation than themselves. Why had she not told him that evening? But no, she was glad she hadn't. She would keep the wonderful secret until such moment as it really seemed to her that it should be produced as the gossamer fairy chain, weightless but unbreakable, that should bind them together, then and forever, in its indissoluble bonds. Yes, she must force herself to believe devoutly and implicitly in the glorious and beautiful secret, and she must treasure it up as long as possible and whisper it in Luigi's ear if it should ever seem that, for a moment, her Luigi strayed from the path of justice and honesty to his unwedded wife.

Faith again triumphed over Doubt.

These others were jealous of her Luigi, or mistook his natural and beautiful politeness to Madame, for overtures and love-making. Could not her Luigi converse with, and smile upon, Madame la Cantinière without setting all their idle and malicious tongues clacking and wagging? As for this Russian wretch, Luigi had given her no more thought than to the dust beneath his feet, and she should go forth into the gutter, in Carmelita's night-shift, before her protector should injure a hair of Luigi's head. She was surprised at Jean Boule, but there—men were all alike, all except her Luigi, that is. How deceived she had been in the kindly old Englishman! . . . Fancy coming to her with their cock-and-bull story. . . .

The voice of the man of whom she was thinking broke in upon her reverie.

"What is it, little one? Nothing wrong about Olga?"

"Come in here, Signor Jean Boule," said Carmelita, and led the way into her room.

The Englishman involuntarily glanced round the little sanctum into which no man save Luigi Rivoli had been known to penetrate, and noted the clean tablecloth, the vase with its bunch of krenfell and oleander flowers, the tiny, tidy dressing table, the dilapidated chest of drawers, bright oleographs, cheap rug, crucifix and plaster Madonna—a room still suggestive of Italy.

Turning, Carmelita faced the Englishman and pointed an

accusing finger at his face, her great black eyes staring hard and straight into the narrowest blue ones.

Signor Jean Boule," she said, "you have played a trick on me; you have deceived me; you have killed my faith in Englishmen—yes, in all men—except my Luigi. Why did you bring your mistress to me and beg my help whilst you knew you meant to kill my husband, because he had found you out? Oh, Monsieur Jean Boule—but you have hurt me so. And I had thought you like a father—so good a man, yes, like a holy padre, a *prête*. Oh, Signor Jean Boule, are you like those others, loving wickedly, killing wickedly? Are there *no* good honest men—except my Luigi? . . .

The Englishman shifted uncomfortably from foot to foot, twisting his képi in his fingers, a picture of embarrassment and misery. How could he persuade this girl that the man was a double-dealing, villainous blackguard? And if he could do so, why should he? Why destroy her faith and her happiness together? If this hound failed in his attempt upon the celibacy of Madame, he would very possibly marry the girl, and, in his own interests, treat her decently. Apparently he had kept her love for years—why should she not go on worshipping the man she believed her lover to be, until the end? But no, it was absurd. How should Luigi Rivoli ever treat a woman decently? Sooner or later he was certain to desert her. What would Carmelita's life be when Luigi Rivoli had the complete disposal of it? Sooner or later she must know what he was, and better sooner than later. A thousand times better that she should find him out now, while there was a risk of his marrying her. . . . It would be a really good deed to save Carmelita from the clutches of Luigi Rivoli. Stepping toward her, he laid his hands upon the girl's shoulders and gazed into her eyes with that look which he was wont to fasten upon the Grasshopper to soothe and influence him.

"Listen to me, Carmelita," he said, "and be perfectly sure that every word I say to you is absolutely true. . . . I did not know that Mikhail Kyrilovitch was a woman more than half an hour before you did. I only knew it when she rushed to me for protection from Luigi Rivoli, who had discovered her and behaved to her like the foul beast he is. I have challenged him to fight me in the only way in which it is possible for me to fight him, and I mean to kill him. I am going to kill him partly for your sake, partly for my own, and partly for that of every wretched recruit and decent man in the Company."

Carmelita drew back.

"Coward!" she hissed. "You only dare face my Luigi with a gun in your hand."

"I am not a coward, Carmelita. It is Rivoli who is the coward. He is by far the strongest man in the Regiment, and is a professional wrestler. He trades on this to bully and terrorize all who do not become his servants. He is a brutal ruffian, and he is a coward, for he would do anything rather than meet me in fair fight. He is only a *risquetout* where there are no weapons and the odds are a hundred to one in his favour. . . . If I hear one more word about my trading on my marksmanship, he shall fight me with revolvers across a handkerchief. Besides, I have told him he can choose any weapon in the world."

"And now hear *me*," replied Carmelita, "and I would say it if it were my last word. Either you take all that back and apologize to my Luigi, or out into the night goes this Russian girl," and she pointed with the dramatic gesture of the excited Southerner to the *bassourah*-cloth which screened off the little inner chamber which was just big enough to hold Carmelita's bed.

The Englishman started.

"You don't mean that, Carmelita!" he asked anxiously The girl laughed bitterly, cruelly.

"Do you think a thousand Russians would weigh with me against one hair of my husband's head?" she answered. "Give me your solemn promise now and here, or I will do more than throw her out, I will denounce her. I will give her to the Turcos and Spahis. I will have her dragged to the Village Négre."

"Hush! Carmelita. I am ashamed of you. Are you mad?" said John Bull sternly.

"I am sorry," was the reply. "Yes, I *am* mad, Signor Jean Boule. I am being driven mad by this horrible plot against my Luigi. Why are you all his enemies? It is because you are jealous of him and because you fear him—but you shall not hurt him. This, at least, I say and mean: Take the Russian girl away with you now, or promise me you will never fight my husband with lead or steel."

"I cannot promise it, Carmelita. I have challenged Rivoli publicly and must fight him. To draw out now would brand me as a coward, would make him twice the bully he is, and would be a cruelty to you. . . . You ask too much, you ask an impossibility. I must make some other plan for Olga Kyrilovitch."

Carmelita staggered, and stared open-mouthed. She could not believe her ears.

"What?" she gasped.

"The girl must go elsewhere," repeated the Englishman. Carmelita appeared to be about to faint. Could he mean it? Was it possible? Was her brilliant plan failing?

"Will you lend the girl some clothes?" asked John Bull.

"Most certainly I will not," she whispered.

"Then please go and tell her to dress again in uniform," was the answer, as he pointed to the uniform lying folded on a chair.

"And will you ruin her chance of escape, Signor Jean Boule?" asked Carmelita. "Is *that* how Englishmen treat women who throw themselves on their mercy? Do you put your own vengeance before her safety and honour and life?"

"No, Carmelita, I do not" answered the man. "I am in a terrible position, and am going to choose the lesser of two evils. It is better that I take the girl away and help her brother to desert with her, than let Rivoli wreck your life, break your heart, and doubly regain the bully's prestige and power to make weaker comrades' lives a misery and a burden. He, at any rate, shall be the cause of no more suicides."

Carmelita flung herself upon the hideous horsehair couch and burst into a torrent of hysterical tears. What could she say to this hard, cold man? What could she do? What *could* she do?

Carmelita sprang to her feet.

"I will denounce her," she cried. "I will throw open those shutters and scream and scream until there is a crowd, and they shall have her in her nightdress. *Now* will you spare my husband?"

"You'll do nothing of the kind," answered John Bull calmly. "You know you would regret it all the days of your life. Is this Italian hospitality, womanliness, and

145

honour? Be ashamed of yourself, to talk so. Be fair. Be just. Who needs protection most—your bully, or this wretched girl?" and here Legionary John Bull showed more than his wonted wisdom in dealing with women. Stepping up to Carmelita he seized her by the shoulders and shook her somewhat sharply, saying as he did so, "And understand once and for all, little fool, I keep my promise to Luigi Rivoli—whatever you do."

In return for her shaking, the surprising Carmelita smiled up into the old soldier's face and clasped her hands behind his head.

"Monsieur Jean Boule," she said, "I think I would have loved my father like I love you—but how you try to hide the soft, kind heart with the hard, cruel face!" and Carmelita gave John Bull the first kiss he had received for over a quarter of a century.

He pushed her from him roughly. Carmelita was glad. This was a thousand times better than that glacial immobility. This meant that he was moved.

"Save Olga's life, Babbo," she whispered coaxingly. "Save Olga and make me happy. Don't ruin two women for fear men should not think you brave. Who doubts the courage of the man who wears the *médaille?* The man who had the courage to challenge Luigi Rivoli can have the courage to withdraw it if it suits him."

"The man who killed Luigi Rivoli would be your best friend, Carmelita," was the reply, "and Olga Kyrilovitch must be saved in some other way. I must keep my word. It is due to others as well as to myself that I do so."

The two regarded each other without realizing that it was across an abyss of immeasurable width and unfathomable depth. He was a man, she was a woman; he a Northerner, she a Southerner. To him honour came first; and without love there could be, she thought, neither honour nor happiness nor life itself.

How should these two understand each other, these two whose souls spoke languages differing as widely as those spoken by their tongues? The woman understood and appreciated the rectitude and honour of the man as little as he realized and fathomed the depth and overwhelming intensity of her love and devotion.

Carmelita now made a great mistake and took a false

step—a mistake which turned to her advantage and a false step which led whither she so yearned to go. For Luigi's sake she played the temptress. In defence of her virtue let it be said that, as once before, she believed that her Luigi's life was actually at stake; in defence of her judgment, let it be remembered that she had grown up in a hard school, and had reason to believe that no man does something for nothing where a woman is concerned. She advanced with her bewitching smile, took the Englishman's face between her hands, drew his head down and kissed him upon the lips.

The Englishman blushed as he returned her kiss, and laughed to find himself blushing as the thought struck him that he might have had a daughter older than Carmelita. The girl misunderstood the kiss and smile. Alas! all men were alike in one thing and the best were like the worst. She put her lips to his ear and whispered. . . .

John Bull drew back. Placing his hands upon the girl's shoulders, he gazed into her eyes. Carmelita blushed painfully, and dropped her eyes before the man's searching stare. She heaved a sobbing sigh. Yes, all alike, all had their price—and any pretty woman could pay it. All alike—even grey-haired, kind old Babbo Jean Boule, who looked as though he might be her grandfather.

She felt his hand beneath her chin, raising her face to his. Again he gazed into her eyes and slowly shook his head.

"And is this what men and Life have taught you, Carmelita?" he said. . . .

A horrid fear gripped Carmelita's heart. Could she be wrong? Could she have offered herself in vain? Could this man's pride and hatred be so great that the bribe was not enough?

"And you would do this—*you*, Carmelita; for that filthy blackguard?"

"I would do *anything* for my Luigi. Sell me his life and I will pay you now, the highest price a woman can. Kiss me on the lips, dear Monsieur Jean, and I will trust you to keep your part of the bargain—never to fight nor attack my Luigi with a weapon in your hand. Kiss me! Kiss me!"

The Englishman drew the pleading girl to him and kissed her on the forehead. She flung her arms around his neck in a transport of joy and relief.

"You will sell me my Luigi's life?" she cried. "Oh, praise and thanks to the Mother of God. You *will*?"

"I will *give* you your Luigi's life," said Sir Montague Merline, and went out.

CHAPTER NINE

The Cafe and the Canteen

As THE DOOR CLOSED BEHIND the departing John Bull, the heavy *purdah* between the sitting-room and the tiny side-chamber or alcove in which was Carmelita's bed, was pushed aside, and Olga Kyrilovitch, barefooted and dressed in night attire belonging to Carmelita, entered the room. On the sofa lay Carmelita sobbing, her hands pressed over her eyes.

Looking more boy-like than ever, with her short hair, the Russian girl advanced noiselessly and shook Carmelita sharply by the shoulder.

"You fool," she hissed between clenched teeth. "You stupid fool. You blind, stubborn, hopeless *fool!*" Carmelita sat up. This was language she could understand, and a situation with which she could deal.

"Yes?" she replied without resentment, "and why?"

"Those two men. . . . Compare them. . . . I heard every word—I could not help it. I could not come out—I should not have been safe, even with you here, with that vile, filthy Italian in the room, nor could I come, for shame, like this, while the Englishman was here. . . . *Why did you let him say he does not love me?*" and the girl burst into tears. Carmelita stared.

"Oho! you love him, do you?" quoth she. . . .

"Then if you know what love is, why do you abuse the man I love?"

The girl raised her impassioned tear-stained face to Carmelita's.

"Will nothing persuade you, little fool," she cried, "that that Italian beast no more loves you than—than Jean Boule loves me—that he is playing with you, that he is battening on you, and that, the moment the fat Canteen woman accepts him, he will marry her and you will see him no more? Why should Jean Boule lie to you? Why should the American? Why should I?—Ask any Legionary in Sidi."

Carmelita clenched her little fist and appeared to be about to strike the Russian girl.

"Stop!" continued Olga, and pointed to the uniform which lay folded on the chair. "See! Prove your courage and prove us all liars if you can. Put on that uniform, disguise yourself, and go to the Canteen any night in the week. If your Rivoli is not there behind the bar, hand in-glove with Madame, turn me into the street—or leave me at the mercy of your Rivoli. There now. . . ."

"*I will,*" said Carmelita, and then screamed and laughed, laughed and screamed, as her overwrought nerves and brain gave way in a fit of hysterics.

When she recovered, Olga Kyrilovitch discovered that the seed which she had sown had taken root, and that it was Carmelita's unalterable intention to pay a visit to the Canteen on the very next evening.

"For my Luigi's own sake I will spy upon him," she said, "and to prove all his vile accusers wrong. When I have done it I will confess to him with tears and throw myself at his feet. He shall do as he likes with me... But he will understand that it was only to disprove these lies that I did it, and not because I for one moment doubted him."

At length came the relief of quiet weeping, and, having whispered to Olga her Great Secret, or rather her hopes of having one to tell, she sobbed herself to sleep on the girl's shoulder, to dream of the most wonderful of *bambinos*.

Meanwhile, John Bull spent one of the wretchedest evenings of a wretched life. Returning to his *chambrée* to find himself hailed and acclaimed "hero," he commenced at once, with his usual uncompromising directness and simplicity, to inform all and sundry, who mentioned the subject, that there would be no duel. It hurt him most of all to see the face of his friend Rupert fall and harden, as he informed him that he could not fight Rivoli after all. On his explaining the position to him, Reginald Rupert, decidedly shocked, remarked—

"*Your* business, of course," and privately wondered whether *les beaux yeux* of Carmelita, or of Olga, had shed the light in which his friend had come to see things so differently. Surely, Carmelita's best friend would be the person who saved her from Rivoli; and, if it were really Olga whom Bull were considering, there were more ways of killing a cat than choking it with melted butter. Anyhow, he didn't envy John Bull, nor yet the weaker vessel of the Seventh Company. What would John Bull do, if, on hearing of his change of mind, Rivoli simply took him and put him across his knee? Would his promise to Carmelita sustain him through that or similar indignities? After all, a challenge is a challenge; and some people would consider that the prior engagement to Rivoli could not in honour be cancelled afterwards by an engagement with Carmelita or anybody else.

"I say, look here, Bull, old chap," said he. "You'll of course do as you think best in the matter, and so shall I. I'm going to challenge Rivoli myself. I shall follow your admirable example and challenge him publicly, and I shall add point to it by wasting a litre of wine on his face, which I shall also smack with what violence I may. I am not Company Marksman like you, but, as Rivoli knows, I am a First Class shot. I shall say I have been brooding over his breaking my back, and now want to fight him on even terms."

A look of pain crossed the face of the old soldier.

"Rupert," he said, rising and laying his hand on his friend's shoulder, "you'll do nothing of the kind. . . . Not, that is, if you value my friendship in the least, or have the slightest regard for me. Do you not understand that I have given Carmelita my word that I will neither fight Rivoli with a weapon in my hand, nor attack him with one? Would she not instantly and naturally suppose that I had got you to do it for me? . . . Would anything persuade her to the contrary?"

"Is he to go unpunished then? Is he to ride roughshod over us all? He'll be ten times worse than before. You know he'll ascribe your withdrawal to cowardice—and so will everybody else," was the reply.

"They will," agreed John Bull.

"What's to be done then?"

"I don't know, but I'll tell you what is *not* to be done. No friend of mine is to challenge Rivoli to a duel."

The next day the news spread throughout the *caserne* of the First Battalion of the Legion that the promised treat was

150

off, the duel between the famous Luigi Rivoli and the Englishman, John Bull, would not take place, the latter, in spite of the publicity and virulence of his challenge, having apologized.

The news was ill received. In the first place the promise of a brilliant break in the monotony of the Depôt life was broken. In the second place, the undisputed reign of a despotic and brutal tyrant would continue and grow yet heavier and more insupportable; while in the third place, it was not in accordance with the traditions of the Legion that a man should fiercely challenge another in public, and afterwards apologize and withdraw.

That evening the Bucking Bronco, for the first time in his life, received a message from Carmelita, a message which raised him to the seventh heaven of expectation and hope, while the sanguine blood coursed merrily through his veins.

Carmelita wanted him. At five o'clock without fail, Carmelita would expect him at the Café. She needed his help and relied upon him for it. . . . *Gee*-whillikins! She should have it.

At half-past five that evening, the Bucking Bronco entered le Café de la Légion and stared in amazement at seeing a strange Legionary behind Carmelita's bar. He was a small, slight man in correct walking-out dress—a blue tunic red breeches and white spats. His képi was pulled well down over a small, intelligent face, the most marked feature of which were very broad black eyebrows, and a biggish dark moustache. The broad chin-strap of the képi was down, and pressed the man's chin up under the large moustache beneath which the strap passed. The soldier had a squint and the Bucking Bronco had always experienced a dislike and distrust of people so afflicted.

"An' what'n Hell are *yew* a-doin' thar, yew swivel-eyed tough?" he asked repeating his enquiry in Legion French.

The Legionary laughed—a ringing peal which was distinctly familiar.

"Don't yew git fresh with me, Bo, or I'll come roun' thar an' improve yure squint till you can see in each ear-'ole," said the American, trying to "place" the man.

Again the incongruous tinkling peal rang out and the Bucking Bronco received the shock of his life as Carmelita's voice issued through the big moustache. Words failed him as he devoured the girl with his eyes.

"Dear Monsieur Bouckaing Bronceau," said she. "Will you walk out to-night with the youngest recruit in the Legion?"

The Bronco still stared agape.

"I am in trouble," continued Carmelita, "and I turn to you for help."

The light of hope shone in the American's eyes.

"Holy Poker!" said he. "God bless yure sweet eyes, fer sayin' so, Carmelita. But why *me?* Have yew found yure Loojey out, at last? Why me?"

"I turn to you for help, Monsieur Bronco," said the girl, "because you have told me a hundred times that you love me. Love gives. It is not always asking, asking, asking. Now give me your help. I want to get at the truth. I want to clear a good and honest man from a web of lies. Take me to the Canteen with you to-night. They say my Luigi goes there to see Madame la Cantinière. They say he flirts and drinks with her, that he helps her there, and serves behind her bar. They even dare to say that he asks her to marry him. . . ."

"It's true," interrupted the Bucking Bronco.

"Very well—then take me there now. My Luigi has sworn to me a hundred times that he never sets foot in Madame's Canteen, that he would not touch her filthy Algerian wine—my Luigi who drinks only the best Chianti from Home. Take me there and prove your lies. Take me now, and either you and your friends, or else Luigi Rivoli, shall never cross my threshold again." Carmelita's voice was rising, tears were starting to her eyes, and her bosom rose and fell as no man's ever did.

"Easy honey," said the big American. "Ef yew're gwine ter carry on right here what'll you do in the Canteen when yew see yure Loojey right thar doin' bar-tender fer the woman he's a-doin' his damnedest to marry?"

"*Do?*" answered Carmelita in a low tense voice. "Do? I would be cold as ice. I would be still and hard as one of the statues in my own Naples. All Hell would be in my breast, but a Hell of frozen fire do you understand, and I would creep away. Like a silent spirit I would creep away —but I would be a spirit of vengeance. To Monsieur Jean Boule would I go and I would say, 'Kill him! Kill him!

152

for the love of God and the Holy Virgin and the Blessed Bambino, *kill* him—and let me come and stamp upon his face.' That is what I would say, Monsieur Bronco.''

The American covered the girl's small brown hand with his huge paw.

"Carmelita, honey," he whispered. "Don't go, little gel —don't go. May I be struck blind and balmy right hyar, right naow, ef I tell yew a word of a lie. Every night of his life he's thar, afore he comes down hyar with lies on his lips to yew. Don't go. Take my word fer it, an' John Bull's word, and young Rupert's word. They're White Men, honey, they wouldn't lie ter yew. Believe what we tell yew, and give ole John Bull back his promise, an' let him shoot-up this low-lifer rattlesnake. . . ."

"I will see with my own eyes," said Carmelita—adding with feminine logic, "and if he's not there to-night, I'll know that you have all lied to me, and that he never was there—and never, never, never again shall one of you enter my house, or my Legionaries shall nail you by the ears to the wall with their bayonets. . . . Shame on me, to doubt my Luigi for a moment."

The American gave way.

"Come on then, little gel," he said. P'raps it's fer the best."

2

Entering the Canteen that evening for his modest litre, 'Erb caught sight of his good friend, the Bucking Bronco, seated beside a Legionary whom 'Erb did not know. The American beckoned and 'Erb emitted a joyous sound to be heard more often in the Ratcliffe Highway than in the wilds of Algeria. Apparently his pal's companion was, or had been, in funds, for his head reposed upon his folded arms.

"Wotto, Bucko!" exclaimed the genial 'Erb. "We a goin' to ketch this pore bloke's complaint? Luvvus! Wish I got enuff to git as ill as wot 'e is."

"Sit down t'other side of him, 'Erb," responded the American. "We may hev' to help the gay-cat to bed. He's got a jag. Tight as a tick—an' lef' me in the lurch with two-francs' worth to drink up."

"Bless 'is 'eart," exclaimed 'Erb. "I dunno wevver 'e's a-drinkin' to drahn sorrer or wevver he's a-drinkin' to keep up 'is 'igh sperrits—but he shan't say as 'ow 'Erb 'Iggins didn't stand by im to the larst—the larst boll' I mean," and 'Erb filled the large glass which the American reached from the bar.

" 'Ere's 'ow, Cocky," he shouted in the ear of the apparently drunken man, giving him a sharp nudge in the ribs with his elbow.

The drunken man gasped at the blow, gave a realistic hiccough and murmured: "A votre santé, Monsieur."

"Carn't the pore feller swaller a little more, Buck?" enquired 'Erb with grave concern. "Fency two francs—an' he's 'ad ter give up! . . . Never mind, Ole Cock," he roared again the ear of the drunkard, "p'raps you be able ter go ahtside in a minnit an' git it orf yer chest. Then yer kin start afresh. See? . . . 'Ope hon, 'ope hever. . . . 'Sides," he added, as a cheering afterthought, "it'll tiste as good a-comin' up as wot it did a-goin' dahn." He then blew vinously into his mouth-organ and settled down for a really happy evening.

A knot of Legionaries, friends of Rivoli, stood at the bar talking with Madame.

"Here he comes," said one of them, leaning with his back against the bar. "Ask him."

Luigi Rivoli strode up, casting to right and left the proud glances of the consciously Great.

"Bonsoir, ma belle," quoth he to Madame. "And how is the Soul of the Soul of Luigi Rivoli?"

The drunken man, sitting between the Bucking Bronco and le Légionnaire 'Erbiggin, moved his head. He lay with the right side of it upon his folded arms and his flushed face toward the bar. His eyes were apparently closed in sottish slumber.

Madame la Cantinière fixed Rivoli with a cold and beady eye. (She "wagged her beard" too much, did she? Oho!)

"And since when have I been the Soul of the Soul of Luigi Rivoli?" she enquired.

"Can you ask it, My own?" was the reply. "Did not the virgin fortress of my heart capitulate to the trumpet of your voice when first its musical call rang o'er its unscaled walls?"

"Pouf!" replied Madame, bridling. . . . (What a way he had with him, and what a fine figure of a man he was, but "*beards*" quotha!) Raising the flap of the zinc-covered bar, Luigi, as usual, passed within and poured himself a bumper of wine. Raising the glass—

"To the brightest eyes and sweetest face that I ever looked upon," he toasted, and drank.

Madame simpered. Her wrath had, to some extent evaporated. . . . Not that she would ever *dream* of marrying him. No! that "beard" would be ever between them. No! No! He had dished himself finally. He had, as it were, hanged himself in that beard as did Absalom in the branches of a tree. The price he should pay for that insult was the value of her Canteen and income. There was balm and satisfaction in the thought. Still—until his successor were chosen, or rather, the successor of the late-lamented so cruelly, if skilfully, carved by those *sacrépans* and *galopins* of Arabs—the assistance of the big man as waiter and chucker-out should certainly not be refused. By no means.

"And what is this tale I hear of you and le Légionnaire Jean Boule?" enquired Madame. "They say that the Neapolitan trollop of Le Café de la Lègion (*sous ce nom-là!*) has begged your life of him."

The drunken man slowly opened his eyes and Rivoli put down his glass with a fierce frown.

"And who invented that paltry, silly lie?" he asked, and laughed scornfully. Madame pointed a fat forefinger at the Bucking Bronco who leant, head on fist, regarding Rivoli with a sardonic smile.

"Sure thing, Loojey. I'm spreadin' the glad joyous tidin's, as haow yure precious life has been saved, all over the whole caboodle," and proceeded to translate.

"Oh, is *that* the plot?" replied the Italian. "Is *that* the best lie the gang of you could hatch? Corpo di Bacco! It's a poor one. Couldn't the lot of you think of a likelier tale than that?"

The Bucking Bronco opined as haow thar was nuthin' like the trewth.

"Look you," said the Italian to Madame and the assembled loungers. This grey English cur—pot-valiant—comes yapping at me, being in his cups, and challenges

155

me, *me,* Luigi Rivoli to fight. I say: 'Go dig your grave, dog,' and he goes. I have not seen him since, but on all hands I hear that he has arranged with this strumpet of the Café to say that she has begged my life of him," and Luigi Rivoli roared with laughter at the idea. "Now listen you, and spread this truth abroad. . . . Madame will excuse me," and he turned with his stage bow to Madame. . . . "I am no plaster saint, I am a Légionnaire. Sometimes I go to this Café—I admit it," and again turning to Madame, he laid his hand upon his heart. "Madame," he appealed, "I have no home, no wife, no fireside to which to be faithful. . . . And as I honestly admit I visit this Café. The girl is glad of my custom and possibly a little honoured—of that I would say nothing. . . . Accidents will happen to the bravest and most skilful of men in duels. The girl begged me not to fight. "You are my best customer,' said she, 'and the handsomest of all my patrons,' and carried on as such wenches do, when trade is threatened. 'Peace, woman,' said I, 'trouble me not, or I go to Zuleika across the way.' . . . She then took another line. 'Look you, Signor,' said she, 'this old fool, Boule, comes to me when he has money; and he drinks here every night. Spare his miserable carcase for what I make out of it,' and with a laugh I gave the girl my franc and half-promise. . . . Still, what is one's word to a wanton? I may shoot the dog, yet, if he and his friends be not careful how they lie."

The drunken man had turned his face on to his arms. No one but the American and 'Erb noticed that his body was shaken convulsively. Perhaps with drunken laughter?

"Tole yer so, Cocky," bawled 'Erb in his ear. "You'll be sick as David's sow in a minnit, 'an' we'll all git blue-blind, paralytic drunk,' " and rising to his feet 'Erb lifted up his voice in song to the effect that—

"White wings they never grow whiskers,
    They kerry me cheerily over the sea
    To ye Banks and Braes o' Bonny Doon
    Where we drew 'is club money this mornin'.
    Witin' to 'ear the verdick on the boy in the prisoner's
        dock
    When Levi may I menshun drew my perlite attenshun
    To the tick of 'is grandfarver's clock.

Ninety years wivaht stumblin', Tick, Tick, Tick,—
Ninety years wivaht grumblin', gently does the trick,
When it stopped short, never to go agine
Till the ole man died.
An' ef yer wants ter know the time, git yer 'air cut."

For the moment 'Erb was the centre of interest, though not half a dozen men in the room understood the words of what the vast majority supposed to be a wild lament or dirge.

John Bull entered the Canteen, and 'Erb was forgotten. All near the counter, save the drunken man, watched his approach. He strode straight up to the bar, his eyes fixed on Rivoli.

"I wish to withdraw my challenge to you," he said in a clear voice. "I am not going to fight you after all."

"But, Mother of God, you are!" whispered the drunken man.

"Oho!" roared Rivoli. "Oho!" and exploded with laughter. "Sober to-night are you, English boaster? And how do you know that I will not fight you, *flaneur?"*

"That rests with you, of course," was the reply.

"Oho, it does, does it, Monsieur Coup Manqué? And suppose I decide *not* to fight you, but to punish you as little barking dogs should be punished? By the Wounds of God you shall learn a lesson, little cur. . . ."

The drunken man moved, as though to spring to his feet, but the big American's arm flung round him and pressed him down, as he lurched his huge body drunkenly against him, pinning him to the table.

" 'Ere," expostulated 'Erb. " 'E wants ter be sick, I tell yer. Free country ain't it, if 'e *is* a bloomin Legendary. . . . Might as well be a bleedn drummerdary if 'e carn't be sick w'en 'e wants to. . . . 'Ope 'e ain't got seven stummicks, eny'ow," he added as an afterthought, and again applied himself to the business of the evening.

John Bull turned, without a word, and left the Canteen. The knot about the bar broke up and Luigi was alone with Madame save for two drunken men and one who was doing his best to achieve that blissful state.

"Have you forgiven me, Beloved of my Soul?" asked

Rivoli of Madame, as she mopped the zinc surface of the bar.

"No," snapped Madame. "I have not."

"Then do it now, my Queen," he implored. "Forgive me, and then do one other thing."

"What is that?" enquired Madame.

"Marry me," replied Rivoli, seizing Madame's pudgy fist. The eyes of the drunken man were on him, and the American watching, thought of the eyes of the snake that lies with broken back watching its slayer. There was death and the hate of Hell in them, and while he shuddered, his heart sang with hope.

"Marry me, Véronique," he repeated. "Have pity on me and end this suspense. See you, I grow thin," and he raised his mighty arms in a pathetic gesture.

Madame glanced at the poor man's stomach. There was no noticeable *maigreur*.

"And what of the Neapolitan hussy and your goings on in the Café de la Légion?" she asked.

"To Hell with the *putain*," he almost shouted. "I am like other men—and I have been to her dive like the rest. Marry me and save me from this loose irregular soldier's life. Do you think I would stray from *thee*, Beloved, if thou wert mine?"

"Not twice," said Madame.

"Then away with this jealousy," replied the ardent Luigi. "Let me announce our nuptials here and now, and call upon my comrades-in-arms to drink long life and happiness to my beauteous bride — whom they all so chastely love and revere. Come, little Star of my Soul! Come, carissima, and I will most solemnly swear upon the Holy Cross that never, never, never again will I darken the doors of the *casse-croûte* of that girl of the Bazaar. I swear it, Véronique—so help me God and all the Holy Saints—your husband will die before he will set foot in Carmelita's brothel."

"Come," said the drunken man, with a little piteous moan. "Could you carry me out, Signor? I am going to faint."

The Bucking Bronco gathered Carmelita up in his arms and strode toward the door.

" 'Ere 'old on," ejaculated 'Erb. " 'Arf a mo'! I'll tike 'is 'oofs. . . ."

"Stay whar yew are, 'Erb," said the American sternly, over his shoulder.

"Right-o, ole bloke," agreed 'Erb, always willing to oblige. "Right-o! Shove 'im in 'is kip[1] while I 'soop 'is bare.' "[2]

Outside, the Bucking Bronco set Carmelita down upon a bench in a dark corner and chafed her hands as he peered anxiously into her face.

"Pull yureself together, honey," he urged. "Don't yew give way yit. Yaw've gotter walk past the Guard ef I carries yew all the rest of the way."

The broken-hearted girl could only moan. The American racked his brains for a solution of the difficulty and wished John Bull and Rupert were with him. It would be utterly hopeless to approach the gate with the girl in his arms. What would happen if he could not get her out that night? Suddenly the girl rose to her feet. Pride had come to her rescue.

"Come, Monsieur Bronco," she said in a dead emotionless voice. "Let me get home," and began to walk like an automaton. Slipping his arm through hers, the American guided and supported her, and in time, Carmelita awoke from a terrible dream to find herself at home. The Russian girl, in some clothing and a wrap of Carmelita's, admitted them at the back door.

"Get her some brandy," said the Bucking Bronco.

"Shall I open the Caffy and serve fer yew, Carmelita, ma gel?" he asked.

Before he could translate his question into Legion French, Carmelita had understood, partly from his gestures. She shook her head.

Olga Kyrilovitch looked a mute question at the American. He nodded slightly. Carmelita caught the unspoken communication between the two.

"Yes," she said turning to Olga, "you were right. . . . They were all right. And I was wrong. . . . He is the basest, meanest scoundrel who ever betrayed a woman. I do not realize it yet—I am stunned. . . . And I am punished too. I shall die or go mad when I understand.

---
* [1] Bed.
[2] Drink his beer.

. . . And I want to be alone. Go now, dear Signor Orso Americano, and take my love and this message to Signor Jean Boule. *I kiss his boots in humility and apology, and if he will kill this Rivoli for me I will be his slave for life.*"

"Let *me* kill him fer yew, Carmelita," begged the American as he turned to go, and then paused as his face lit up with the brightness of an idea. "No," he said. "Almighty God! I got another think come. I'll come an' see yew to-morrow, Carmelita—and make yew a *proposal* about Mounseer Loojey as'll do yew good." At the door he beckoned to the Russian girl.

"Look at hyar, Miss Mikhail," he whispered. "Stand by her like a man to-night. Nuss her, and coddle her and soothe her. You see she don't do herself no harm. Yew hev' her safe and in her right mind in the mornin'—an' we'll git yew and yure brother outer Sidi or my name ain't Hyram Cyrus Milton."

CHAPTER TEN

The Wages of Sin

IT WAS SOON EVIDENT that the word had been passed round that there would be "something doing" at the Café de la Légion that evening. Never before had its hospitable roof covered so large an assembly of guests. Though it was not exactly what could be called "a packed house," it was far from being a selected gathering of the special friends of Il Signor Luigi Rivoli. To Legionaries John Bull, Reginald Rupert and 'Erb 'Iggins it was obvious that the Bucking Bronco had been at some pains to arrange that the spectators of whatever might befall that evening, were men who would witness the undoing of Luigi Rivoli—should that occur—with considerable equanimity. Scarcely a man there but had felt at some time the weight of his brutal fist and the indignity of helpless obedience to his tyrannous behest. Of one thing they were sure—whatever they might, or might not behold, they would see a Homeric fight, a struggle that would become historic in the annals of la Légion. The atmosphere was electric with suppressed excitement and a sense of pleasurable expectation.

In a group by the bar, lounged the Bucking Bronco and

the three Englishmen with a few of their more immediate intimates, chiefly Frenchmen, and members of their *escouade*. Carmelita, a brilliant spot of colour glowing on either cheek, busied herself about her duties, flitting like a butterfly from table to table. Never had she appeared more light-hearted, gay, and *insouciante*. But to John Bull, who watched her anxiously, it was clear that her gaiety was feverish and hectic, her laughter forced and hysterical.

"Reckon 'e's got an earthly, matey?" asked 'Erb of Rupert. " 'e'll 'ave ter scrag an' kick, same as Rivoli, if 'e don't want ter be counted aht."

"I'd give a hundred pounds to see him win, anyhow," was the reply. "I expect he'll fight the brute with his own weapons. He'll go in for what he calls 'rough-housing' I hope. . . . No good following Amateur Boxing Association rules if you're fighting a bear, or a Zulu, or a Fuzzy-wuzzy, or Luigi Rivoli. . . ."

And that was precisely the intention of the American, whose fighting had been learnt in a very rough and varied school. When earning his living as a professional boxer, he had given referees no more than the average amount of trouble; and in the ring, against a clean fighter had put up a clean fight. A tricky opponent, resorting to fouls, had always found him able to respond with very satisfying tricks of his own—"and then some." But the Bucking Bronco had also done much mixed fighting as a hobo[1] with husky and adequate bulls[2] in many of the towns of the free and glorious United States of America, when guilty of having no visible means of support; with exasperated and homicidal shacks[3] on most of that proud country's railway's when "holding her down," and frustrating their endeavours to make him "hit the grit"; with terrible and dangerous lumber-jacks in timber camps when the rye whisky was in and all sense and decency were out; with cow-punchers and ranchers, with miners, with Bowery toughs, and assorted desperadoes.

Tonight, when he stood face to face with Luigi Rivoli, he intended to do precisely what his opponent would do, to use all Nature's weapons and every device, trick, shift

---

[1] Tramp, a rough.   [2] Policemen.   [3] Train conductors.

and artifice that his unusually wide experience had taught him.

He knew, and fully admitted, that, tremendously powerful and tough as he himself was, Rivoli was far stronger. Not only was the Italian a born Strong Man, but he had spent his life in developing his muscles, and it was probable that there were very few more finely developed athletes on the face of the earth. Moreover, he was a far younger man, far better fed (thanks to Carmelita), and a trained professional wrestler. Not only were his muscles of marvellous development, they were also trained and educated to an equally marvellous quickness, skill and poise. Add to this the fact that the man was no mean exponent of the arts of *la savate* and *la boxe,* utterly devoid of any scruples of honour and fair-play, and infused with a bitter hatred of the American—and small blame accrues to the latter for his determination to meet the Italian on his own ground.

As he stood leaning against the bar, his elbows on it and his face toward the big room, it would have required a very close observer to note any signs of the fact that he was about to fight for his life, and, far more important, for Carmelita, against an opponent in whose favor the odds were heavy. His hard strong face was calm, the eyes level and steady, and, more significant, the hands and fingers quiet and reposeful. Studying his friend, John Bull noticed the absence of any symptoms of excitement, nervousness, or anxiety. There was no moistening of lips, no working of jaw muscles, no change of posture, no quickening of speech. It was the same old Buck, large, lazy, and lethargic, with the same humorous eye, the same measured drawl, the same quaint turn of speech. In striking contrast with the immobility of the American, was the obvious excitement of the Cockney.

"It'll be an 'Ellova fight," he kept on saying. "Gawds-treuth, it'll be an 'Ellova fight," and bitterly regretted the self-denying ordinance which he had passed upon himself to the effect that no liquor should wet his lips till all was o'er. . . .

Luigi Rivoli, followed as usual by Malvin, Tou-tou Boil-the-Cat, Borges, Hirsch and Bauer, strode into the Café. He was accustomed to attracting attention and to the proud consciousness of nudges, glances and whisperings where-ever he went. Not for nothing is one the strongest and most dangerous man in the Foreign Legion. But tonight he was aware of more than usual interest as silence fell upon the abnormally large gathering in Carmelita's Café. He at once ascribed it to the widespread interest in the public challenge he had received from John Bull to a *duel à l'outrance* and the rumour that the Englishman had as publicly withdrawn it. He felt that fresh lustre had been added to his brilliant name. . . . Carmelita *had* been useful there, and had delivered him from a very real danger, positively from the fangs of a mad dog. Very useful. What a pity it was that he could not marry Madame, and run Carmelita. Might she not be brought to consent to some such arrangement? Not even when she found she could have him in no other way? . . . Never!

Absolutamente . . . Curse her. . . . Well, anyhow, there were a few more francs, dinners, and bottles of Chianti. One must take what one can, while one can— and after all the Canteen was worth ten Cafés. Madame had been very kind tonight and would give her final answer tomorrow. That had been a subtle idea of his, telling her that, unless she married him, she should marry no one, and remain a widow all the days of her life, for he'd break the back of any man who so much as looked at her. That had given the old sow something to think about. Ha! Ha! . . .

As he entered, John Bull was just saying to the Bucking Bronco, "Don't do it, Buck. I know all about that

'Thrice-armed is he who hath his quarrel just,
But four times is he who gets his blow in fust.'

But thrice is quite enough, believe me, old chap. You've no need to descend to such a trick as hitting him unawares, by way of starting the fight."

"Is this my night ter howl, John, or yourn? Whose funeral is it?"

"Fight him by his own methods if you like, Buck—but don't put yourself in the wrong for a start. . . . You'll win all right, or I shall cease to believe in Eternal Justice of Things."

Rivoli approached.

Ha! There was that cursed Englishman, was he? Well,

since he had given his promise to Carmelita and was debarred from a duel, he should repeat his apology of last night before this large assembly. Moreover, he would now be free to handle this English dog—to beat and torture and torment him like a new recruit. Bull's hands would be tied as far as weapons were concerned by his promise to Carmelita. . . . The dog was leaning against the flap of the bar which he would have to raise to pass through to his dinner. Should he take him by the ears and rub his face in the liquor-slops on the bar, or should he merely put him on the ground and wipe his feet on him? Better not perhaps, there was that thrice-accursed American *scelerato* and that indestructible young devil Rupert, who had smitten his jaw and ribs so vilely, and wanted to fight again directly he had left hospital and *salle de police*. The Devil smite all Englishmen. . . . His wrath boiled over, his arm shot out and he seized John Bull by the collar, shook him, and slung him from his path.

And then the Heavens fell.

With his open, horny palm, the Bucking Bronco smote the Italian as cruelly stinging a slap as ever human face received. But for his friend's recent behest, he would have struck with his closed fist, and the Italian would have entered the fight, if not with a broken jaw, at least with a very badly "rattled" head.

"Ponk!" observed 'Erb, dancing from foot to foot in excitement and glee.

"Ah—h—h!" breathed Carmelita.

The Italian recovered his balance and gathered himself for a spring.

"No you don't," shouted Rupert, and the three Englishmen simultaneously threw themselves in front of him, at the same time calling on the spectators to make a ring.

The scores and scores of willing hands assisting, the room was quickly cleared.

"This American would die, it appears, poor madman," observed M. Malvin ingratiatingly to Carmelita.

"I do not think he will die," replied the girl. "But I think that anyone who interferes with him will do so."

The eyes of the good M. Malvin narrowed. Lay the wind in that quarter? The excellent Luigi was found out, was he? Well, there might be a successor. . . .

Meantime the Italian had removed and methodically folded his tunic and canvas shirt. A broad belt sustained his baggy red breeches.

So it had come, had it? Well, so much the better. This American had been the fly in the ointment of his comfort too long. Why had he not strangled the insolent, or broken his back long ago? He would break him now, once and for all—maim him for life if he could; at least make a serious hospital case of him.

Bidding Malvin mount guard over his discarded garments, Rivoli stepped forth into the middle of the large cleared space, flexing and slapping his muscles. Having done so, he looked round the crowded sides of the room for the usual applause. To his surprise none followed. He gazed about him again. Was this a selected audience? It was certainly not the audience he would have selected for himself. It appeared to consist mostly of *miserabile* whom he had frequently had to punish for insubordination and defiance of his orders. They should have a demonstration, that evening, of the danger of defying Luigi Rivoli.

As the American stepped forward John Bull caught his sleeve. "Take off your tunic, Buck," he said in surprise.

"Take off nix," replied the American.

"But he'll get a better hold on you," remonstrated his friend.

"I should worry," was the cryptic reply, as the speaker unbuttoned the upper part of his tunic and pushed his collar well away from his neck at the back.

"'E'll cop 'old of 'im wiv that coller, an' bleed'n well strangle 'im," said 'Erb to Rupert.

"Fancy that now, sonny," said the Bucking Bronco, with an exaggerated air of surprise, and stepped into the arena.

Complete silence fell upon the room as the two antagonists faced each other.

Nom de nom de bon Dieu de Dieu! Why had not le Légionnaire Boucking Bronceau stripped? Was it sheer bravado? How could he, or any other living man, afford to add to the already overwhelming risks when fighting the great Luigi Rivoli? . . .

The Bucking Bronco got his "blow in fust" after all, and, as his friend had prophesied, was glad that it had not been a "foul poke"—taking his opponent unawares.

"Come hither, dog, and let me snap thy spine," growled the Italian as the Bucking Bronco faced him. As he spoke, he thrust his right hand forward, as though to seize the American in a wrestling-hold. With a swift snatch the latter grabbed the extended hand, gave a powerful jerking tug and released it before his enemy could free it and fasten upon him in turn. The violent pull upon his arm swung the Italian half left and before he could recover his balance and regain his position, the Bucking Bronco had let drive at the side of his face with all his weight and strength. It was a terrific blow and caught Rivoli on the right cheek-bone, laying the side of his face open.

Only those who have seen—or experienced—it, know the effect of skilled blows struck by hands unhampered by boxing gloves.

The Italian reeled and, like the skilled master of ring-craft that he was, the Bucking Bronco gave him no time in which to recover. With a leap he again put all his strength, weight, and skill behind a slashing right-hander on his enemy's face, and, as he raised his arms, a left-hander on his ribs. Had any of these three blows found the Italian's "point" or "mark," it is more than probable that the fight would have been decided. As it was, Rivoli was only shaken—and exasperated to the point of madness. . . .

Wait till he got his arms round the man! . . . Corpo di Bacco! But wait! Let him wait till he got his hands on that collar that the rash fool had left undone and sticking out so temptingly!

Ducking swiftly under a fourth blow, he assayed to fling his arms round the American's waist. As the mighty arms shot out for the deadly embrace, the Bucking Bronco's knee flew up with terrific force, to smash the face so temptingly passed above it. Like a flash the face swerved to the left, the knee missed it, and the American's leg was instantly seized as in a vice.

The spectators held their breath. Was this the end? Rivoli had him! Could there be any hope for him?

There could. This was "rough-housin'"—and at "rough-housin'" the Bucking Bronco had had few equals. He suddenly thought of one of *the* fights of his life—at 'Frisco, with the bucko mate of a hell-ship on which he had made a trip as fo'c's'le-hand, from the Klondyke. The mate had done his best to kill him at sea, and the Bucking Bronco had "laid for him" ashore as the mate quitted the ship. It had been "some" fight and the mate had collared his leg in just the same way. He would try the method that had then been successful. . . . He seized the Italian's neck with both huge hands, and, with all his strength, started to throttle him—his thumbs on the back of his opponent's neck, his fingers crushing relentlessly into his throat. Of course, Rivoli would throw him—that was to be expected—but that would not free Rivoli's throat. Not by any manner of means. With a fair and squarer two-handed hold on the skunk's throat, it would be no small thing to get that throat free again while there was any life left in its proprietor. . . .

With a heave and a thrust, the Italian threw the Bucking Bronco heavily and fell heavily upon him. The latter tightened his grip and saw his enemy going black in the face. . . . Swiftly Rivoli changed his hold. While keeping one arm round the American's leg, at the knee, he seized his foot with the other hand and pressed it backward with all his gigantic strength. As the leg bent back, he pressed his other arm more tightly into the back of the knee. In a moment the leg must snap like a carrot, and the American knew it—and also that he would be lame for life if his knee-joint were thus rent asunder. It was useless to hope that Rivoli would suffocate before the leg broke. . . . Nor would a dead Rivoli be a sufficient compensation for perpetual lameness. Never to walk nor ride nor fight. . . . A lame husband for Carmelita. . . . Loosing his hold on his antagonists throat, he punched him a paralyzing blow on the muscle of the arm that was bending his leg back, and then seized the same arm by the wrist with both hands and freed his foot. . . . A deadlock. . . . They glared into each other's eyes, mutually impotent, and then, by tacit mutual consent, released holds, rose, and confronted each other afresh.

So far, honours were decidedly with the American, and a loud spontaneous cheer arose from the spectators. "Vive le Boucking Bronceau!" was the general sentiment.

Carmelita sat like a statue on her high chair—lifeless save for terrible eyes. Though her lips did not move, she prayed with all the fervour of her ardent nature.

Breathing heavily, the antagonists faced each other like a pair of half-crouching tigers. . . . Suddenly Rivoli kicked.

167

Not the horizontal kick of *la savate* in which the leg is drawn up to the chest and the foot shot sideways and parallel with the floor, so that the sole strikes the object flatly—but in the ordinary manner, the foot rising from the ground, to strike with the toe. The Bucking Bronco raised his right foot and crossed his right leg over his left, so that the Italian's rising shin met his own while the rising foot met nothing at all. Had the kick been delivered fully, the leg would have broken as the shin was suddenly arrested while the foot met nothing. (This is the deadliest defence there is against a kicker, other than a savatist.) But so fine was the poise and skill of the professional acrobat, that, in full flight, he arrested the kick ere it struck the parrying leg with full violence. He did not escape scot-free from this venture, however, for, even as he raised his leg in defence, the Bucking Bronco shot forth his right hand with one of the terrible punches for which Rivoli was beginning to entertain a wholesome respect. He saved his leg, but received a blow on the right eye which he knew must, before long, cause it to close completely. He saw red, lost his temper and became as an infuriated bull. As he had done under like circumstances with the Légionnaire Rupert, he rushed at his opponent with a roar, casting aside wisdom and prudence in the madness of his desire to get his enemy in his arms. He expected to receive a blow in the face as he sprang, and was prepared to dodge it by averting his head. With an agility surprising in so big a man, the Bucking Bronco ducked below the Italian's outstretched arms and, covering his face with his bent left arm, drove at his antagonist's "mark" with a blow like the kick of a horse. The gasping groan with which the wind was driven out of Rivoli's body was music to the Bucking Bronco's ears. He knew that, for some seconds, his foe, be he the strongest man alive, was at his mercy. Springing erect he punched with left and right at his doubled-up and grasping enemy, his arms working like piston rods and his fists falling like sledge-hammers. The cheering became continuous as Rivoli shrank and staggered before that rain of terrific blows. Suddenly he recovered, drew a deep breath and flung his arms fairly round the Bucking Bronco's waist.

Corpo de Bacco! He had got him! . . .

Clasping his hands behind the American, he settled his

head comfortably down into that wily man's neck, and bided his time. He had got him. . . . He would rest and wait until his breathing was more normal. He would then tire the scelerato down . . . tire him down . . . and then . . .

This was his programme, but it was not that of the Bucking Bronco, or not in its entirety. He realized that "Loojey had the bulge on him." For the moment it was "Loojey's night ter howl." He would take a rest and permit Loojey to support him, also he would feign exhaustion and distress. It was a pity that it was his right arm that was imprisoned in the bear-hug of the wrestler. However, nothing much could happen so long as he kept his back convex.

Seconds, which seemed like long minutes, passed.

Suddenly the Italian made a powerful effort to draw him closer and decrease the convexity of his arched back. He resisted the constriction with all his strength, but realized that he had been drawn slightly inward.

Again a tremendous tensing of mighty muscles, again a tremendous heave in opposition, and again he was a little nearer.

The process was repeated. Soon the line of his back would be concave instead of convex. That would be the beginning of the end. Once he bent over backward there would be no hope; he would finally drop from the Italian's grasp with a sprained or broken back, to receive shattering kicks in the face, ribs and stomach, before Rivoli jumped upon him with both feet and twenty stone weight. For a moment he half regretted having so stringently prohibited any sort or kind of interference in the fight, whatever happened, short of Rivoli's producing a weapon. But only for a moment. He would not owe his life to the intervention of others, after having promised Carmelita to beat him up and bring him grovelling to her feet. He had been winning so far. . . . He *would* win. . . . As the Italian again put all his force into an inward-drawing hug, the American, for a fraction of a second, resisted with all his strength and then suddenly did precisely the opposite. Shooting his feet between the straddled legs of his adversary, he flung his left arm around his head, threw all his weight on to it and brought himself and Rivoli crashing to the ground. As the arms of the latter burst asunder, the Bucking Bronco had time to seize his head and bang it, violently, upon the floor. Both scrambled to their feet.

It had been a near thing. He must not get into that rib-crushing hug again, for the trick would not avail twice. Like a springing lion, Rivoli was on him. Ducking, he presented the top of his head to the charge and felt the Italian grip his collar. With an inarticulate cry of glee he braced his feet and with tremendous force and speed revolved his head and shoulders round and round in a small circle, the centre and axis of which was Rivoli's hand and forearm. The first lightning-like revolution entangled the tightly-gripping hand, the second twisted and wrenched the wrist and arm, the third completed the terrible work of mangling disintegration. In three seconds the bones, tendons, ligaments, and tissue of Rivoli's right hand and wrist were broken, wrenched and torn. The bones of the forearm were broken, the elbow and shoulder-joints were dislocated. Tearing himself free, the American sprang erect and struck the roaring, white-faced Italian between the eyes and then drove him before him, staggering backward under a ceaseless rain of violent punches. Drove him back and back, even as the bully put his uninjured left hand behind him for the dagger concealed in the hip pocket of his baggy trousers, and sent him reeling, stumbling and half-falling straight into the middle of his silent knot of jackals, Malvin, Borges, Hirsch, Bauer, and Tou-tou Boil-the-Cat. Against these he fell. Malvin was seen to put out his hands to stop him, Borges and Hirsch closed in on him to catch him, Bauer pressed against Malvin, Tou-tou Boil-the-Cat stooped with a swift movement. With a grunt Rivoli collapsed, his knees gave way and, in the middle of the dense throng, he slipped to the ground. As the Bucking Bronco thrust in, and the crowd pressed back, Rivoli lay on his face in the cleared space, a knife in his left hand, another in his back.

He never moved nor spoke again, but M. Tou-tou Boil-the-Cat did both.

As he left the Café he licked his lips, smiled and murmured: *"Je m'en ai souvenu."*

CHAPTER ELEVEN

Greater Love . . .

At the bottom of the alley, le bon Légionnaire Tou-tou Boil-the-Cat encountered Sergeant Legros. . . . A bright idea! . . . Stepping up to the worthy Sergeant, he saluted, and informed him that, passing the notorious Café de la Légion, a minute since, he had heard a terrible *tohuwabohu* and, looking in, had seen a crowd of excited Legionaries fighting with knives and side-arms. He had not entered, but from the door had seen at least one dead man upon the ground.

The worthy Sergeant's face lit up as he smacked his lips with joy. Ah, ha! here were punishments. . . . Here were crimes. . . . Here were victims for *salle de police* and *cellules*. . . . Fodder for the *peloton des hommes punis* and the Zephyrs. . . . Here was distinction for that keen disciplinarian, Sergeant Legros.

"V'la quelqu'un pour la boite," quoth he, and betook himself to the Café at the *pas gymnastique*.

2

At the sight of the knife buried in the naked back of the Italian, the silence of horror fell upon the stupefied crowd.

Nombril de Belzébuth! How had it happened?

Sacré nom de nom de bon Dieu de Dieu de Dieu de sort! Who had done it? Certainly not le Légionnaire Boucking Bronceau. Never for one second had the Légionnaire Rivoli's back been toward him. Never for one instant had there been a knife in the American's hand. Yet there lay the great Luigi Rivoli stabbed to the heart. There was a knife in his back. *Dame!*

Men's mouths hung open stupidly, as they stared wide-eyed. Gradually it grew clear and obvious. Of course—he had been knocked backwards into that group of his jackals, Malvin, Borges, Hirsch and Bauer, and one of them, who hated him, had been so excited and uplifted by the sight of his defeat that he had turned upon him. Yes, he had been stabbed by one of those four.

"Malvin did it. I saw him," ejaculated Tant-de-Soif. He

171

honestly thought he had—or thought he thought so. "God bless him," he added solemnly.

He had many a score to settle with M. Malvin, but he could afford to give him generous praise—since he was booked for the firing-party beside the open grave, or five years rabiau in Biribi. It is not every day that one's most hated enemies destroyed each other. . . .

"Wal! I allow that's torn it," opined the Bucking Bronco as he surveyed his dead enemy.

Carmelita came from behind the bar and down the room. What was happening? Why had the fight stopped. She saw the huddled heap that had been Rivoli. . . . She saw the knife—and thought she understood. This was as things should be. This was how justice and vengeance were executed in her own beloved Naples. Il Signor Americano was worthy to be a Neapolitan, worthy to inherit and transmit *vendetta.* How cruelly she had misjudged him in thinking him a barbarian. . . .

"*Payé,*" she cried, turning in disgust from the body, and threw her arms round the Bucking Bronco's neck, as the Sergeant burst in at the door. Sergeant Legros was in his element. Not only was there here a grand harvest of military criminals for his reaping, but here was vengeance—and vengeance and cruelty were the favourite food of the soul of Sergeant Legros. Here was a grand opportunity for vengeance on the Italian trollop who had, when he was a private Legionary, not only rejected his importunities with scorn, but had soundly smacked his face withal. Striding forward as soon as he had roared, "*Attention!*" he seized Carmelita roughly by the arm and shook her violently, with a shout of: "To your kennel, *prostituée.*" Whereupon the Bucking Bronco felled his superior officer to the ground with a smashing blow upon the jaw, thereby establishing an indisputable claim to life-servitude in the terrible Penal Battalions.

Among the vices of vile Sergeant Legros, physical cowardice found no place. Staggering to his feet, he spat out a tooth, wiped the blood from his face, drew his sword-bayonet, and rushed at the American intending to kill him forthwith, in "self-defence." At the best of times Sergeant Legros looked, and was, a dangerous person—but the blow had made him a savage, homicidal maniac. The Bucking

172

Bronco was dazed and astonished at what he had done. Circumstances had been too strong for him. He had naturally been in an abnormal state at the end of such a fight, and in no condition to think and act calmly when his adored Carmelita was insulted and assaulted. . . . What had he done? This meant death or penal servitude from the General Court Martial at Oran. He had lost her in the moment of winning her, and he dropped his hands as the Sergeant flew at him with the sword bayonet poised to strike. No—he would fight. . . . He would make his getaway. . . . He would skin out and Carmelita should join him. . . . He would fight. . . . Too late! . . . The bayonet was at his throat. . . . Crash! . . . Good old Johnny! That had been a near call. As the maddened Legros was in the act to thrust, Legionary John Bull had struck him on the side of the head with all his strength, sending him staggering, and had leapt upon him to secure the bayonet as they went crashing to the ground. As they struggled, Legionary Rupert set his foot heavily on the Sergeant's wrist and wrenched the bayonet from his hand.

The problem of Sir Montague Merline's future was settled and the hour of Reginald Rupert's desertion had struck.

An ominous growl had rumbled round the room at the brutal words and action of the detested Legros, and an audible grasp of consternation had followed the Bucking Bronco's blow. Sacré Dieu! Here were doings of which ignorance would be bliss—and there was a rush to the door, headed by Messieurs Malvin, Borges, Hirsch and Bauer.

Several Legionaries, as though rooted to the spot by a fearful fascination, or by the hope of seeing Legros share the fate of Rivoli, had stood their ground until John Bull struck him and Rupert snatched the bayonet as though to kill him. Then, with two exceptions, this remainder fled. These two were Tant-de-Soif and the Dutchman, Hans Djoolte; the former, absolutely unable to think of flight and the establishment of an *alibi* while the man who had made his life a hell was fighting for his own life; the latter, clear of conscience, honestly innocent and wholly unafraid. Staring round-eyed, they saw Sergeant Legros mightily heave his body upward, his head pinned to the ground by 'Erb 'Iggins, his throat clutched by Légionnaire Jean Boule,

173

his right hand held down by Légionnaire Rupert. Again he made a tremendous effort, emitted a hideous bellowing sound and then collapsed and lay curiously still. Meanwhile, Carmelita had closed and fastened the doors and shutters of the Café and was turning out the lamps. Within half a minute of the entrance of the Sergeant, the Café was closed and in semi-darkness.

"The bloomin' ol' fox is shammin' dead," panted 'Erb, and removed his own belt. " 'Eave 'im up and shove this rahnd 'is elbers while 'e's a-playin' 'possum. Shove yourn rahnd 'is legs, Buck," he added.

While still lying perfectly supine, the Sergeant was trussed like a fowl.

"Naow we gotter hit the high places. We gotter vamoose some," opined the Bucking Bronco, as the four arose, their task completed. They looked at each other in consternation. Circumstances had been too much for them. Fate and forces outside themselves had whirled them along in a spate of mischance, and cast them up, stranded and gasping. Entering the place with every innocent and praiseworthy intention they now stood under the shadow of the gallows and the gaol. With them in that room was a murdered man and an assaulted, battered and outraged superior. . . .

The crooaking voice of Tant-de-Soif broke the silence. *"Pour vous,"* quoth he, *"il n'y a plus que l'Enfer."*

"Shut up, you ugly old crow," replied Reginald Rupert, "and clear out. . . . Look here, what are you going to do about it? What are you going to say?"

"I?" enquired Tant-de-Soif. "Le Légionnaire Djoolte and I have seen each other in the Bar de Madagascar off the Rue de Daya the whole evening. We have been here *peau-dezébie.* It is not, my Djoolte. Eh, *mon salop?"*

But the sturdy Dutch boy was of a different moral fibre.

"I have not been in the Bar de Madagascar," replied he, in halting Legion French. "I have been in le Café de la Légion the whole evening and seen all that happened."

" 'E's a-seekin' sorrer. 'E wants a fick ear," put in 'Erb in his own vernacular.

"If my evidence is demanded, I saw a fair fight between the Légionnaire Boucking Bronceau and le Légionnaire Luigi Rivoli. I then saw le Légionnaire Luigi Rivoli fall dead, having been stabbed by either le Légionnaire Malvin or le Légionnaire Bauer, if it were not le Légionnaire Hirsch, or le Légionnaire Borges. I believe Malvin stabbed him while these three held him, but I do not know. I then saw le Sergeant Legros enter and assault and abuse Mam'zelle Carmelita. I then saw him fall as though some-one had struck him and he then attempted to murder le Légionnaire Bronco with his Rosalie. I then saw some Légionnaires tie him up. . . . That is the evidence that I shall give if I give any at all. I may refuse to answer, but I shall tell no lies."

"That is all right," said the Bucking Bronco. "Naow yew git up an' yew git—an' yew too, Tant-de Soif, and tell the b'ys ter help Carmelita any they can, ef Legros gits 'er inter trouble an' gits 'er Caffy shut. . . . An' when yew gits the Gospel truth orf yure chest, Fatty, yew kin say, honest Injun, as haow I tol' yew, thet me an' John Bull was a-goin' on pump ter Merocker, an Mounseers Rupert and 'Erb was a goin' fer ter do likewise ter Toonis. Naow git," and the two were hustled out of the Café.

"Now," said John Bull, taking command, "we've got to be quick, as it's just possible the news of what's happened may reach the picket and you may be looked for before you're missing. First thing is Carmelita, second thing's money, and third thing's plan of campaign. . . . Is Carmelita in any danger over this?"

"Don't see why she should be," said Rupert. "It's not her fault that there was a fight in her Café. It has never been in any sense a 'disorderly house,' and what happened, merely happened here."

"Yep," agreed the Bucking Bronco. "But I'm plum anxious. I'm sure telling yew, I don't like ter make my git-away an' leave her hyar. But we can't take a gal on pump."

"Arx the young lidy," suggested 'Erb, and with one con-sent they went to the bar, leaning on which Carmelita was sobbing painfully. The strain and agony of the last twenty-four hours had been too much and she had broken down. As they passed the two silent bodies, 'Erb stopped and bent over Sergeant Legros, remarking: "Knows 'ow ter lie doggo, don't 'e—the ol' cunnin' chops?" He fell silent a moment, and then in a very different voice ejaculated, "Gawds-treuth 'e's *mort*, 'e is. 'E's *tué*."

"Cerebral hæmorrhage," suggested John Bull. "I struck him on the side of the head."

" 'Eart failure," suggested 'Erb. "I set on 'is 'ead till 'is 'eart stopped, blimey!"

"Apple Plexy, I opine," put in the Bucking Bronco. "All comes o' gittin' excited, don't it?"

"He certainly made himself perfectly miserable when I took his bayonet away," admitted Legionary Rupert.

"Anyhow, it's a fair swingin' job nah, wotever it was afore," said 'Erb. Whatever the cause and whosoever the hand, Sergeant Legros was undoubtedly dead. They removed the belts, straightened his limbs, closed his eyes and 'Erb placed the dead man's képi over the face, bursting as he did so into semi-hysterical song—

"Ours is a 'appy little 'ome,
I wisht I was a kipper on the foam,
There's no carpet on the door,
There's no knocker on the floor,
Oo! Ours *is* a 'appy little 'ome."

"Shut that damned row," said Legionary Rupert.

"Carmelita, honey," said the Bucking Bronco, stroking the hair of the weeping girl. "Yew got the brains. Wot'll we do? Shall we stop an' look arter ye? Will yew come on pump with us? Will yew ketch the nine-fifteen ter Oran? Yew could light out fer the railroad *de*-pot right now—or will you stick it out here, an' see ef they takes away yure licence? They couldn't do nuthin' more. . . . Give it a name, little gal—we've gotter hike quick, ef we ain't a-goin' ter stay."

"You must all go at once," she said unhesitatingly. "Take Signor Rupert's money and make for Mendoza's in the Ghetto. He'll sell you mufti and food. Change, and then run, all night, along the railway. Lie up all day, and then run all night again. Then take different trains at different wayside stations, one by one, and avoid each other like poison in Oran; and leave by different boats on different days. I shall stay here. After trying for some hours to revive Legros, I shall send for the picket. You will be far from Sidi then. I shall give the Police all information as to the fight, and as to the murder of *that*, by Malvin;

and shall conceal nothing of Legros' murderous attempt upon the Légionnaire Bouckaing Bronceau and of his death by *apoplessia*. . . . They will see he has no wound. . . . This will give weight and truth to my evidence to the effect that it was a fair, clean fight and that no blame attaches to le Légionnaire Bouckaing Bronceau. . . . Where am I to blame? . . . No, you can leave me without fear. Also will I give evidence to having heard you plotting to make the promenade in different direction and to avoid the railway and Oran. . . ."

The Bucking Bronco was overcome with admiration.

"Ain't that horse-sense?" he ejaculated.

Laying her hands upon his shoulders, Carmelita looked him in the eyes.

"And when you write to me to join you also, dear Americano, I will come," she said. "I Carmelita, have said it. . . . Now that *that* is dead, I shall be able to save some money. Write to me when you are safe, and I will join you wherever you are—whether it be Napoli or Inghilterra or America."

"God bless ye, little gal," growled the American, folding her in his arms, and for the first time of his life being on the verge of an exhibition of weakness. "We'll make our gitaway all right, an' we couldn't be no use ter yew in prison hyar. . . . I'll earn or steal some money ter send yer, Carmelita, honey."

"I can help you there," put in Legionary Rupert.

"You and your loose cash are the *deus ex machina,* Rupert, my boy," said John Bull. . . . "But for you, the Russians would hardly have got away, and now a few pounds will make all the difference between life and death to Buck and Carmelita, not to mention yourself and 'Erb."

"I am very fortunate," said Rupert gracefully. "By the way, how much have we left Carmelita?" he added.

"Exactly seven hundred francs, Monsieur," she replied. "Monsieur drew one thousand, he will remember, and the Russians after all, needed only three hundred in addition to their own roubles."

"What are you going to do 'Erb?" asked John Bull. "You haven't committed yourself very deeply you know. Legros can't give evidence against you and I doubt whether Tan-de-Soif or Djoolte will. . . . I don't suppose any of the others noticed you, but there's a risk—and ten years of Dartmoor would be preferable to six months in the Penal Battalions. What shall you do?"

"Bung orf," replied 'Erb. "I'm fair fed full wiv Hafrica. Wot price the Ol' Kent Road on a Sat'day night!"

"Then seven hundred francs will be most ample for three of you, to get mufti, railway tickets and tramp-steamer passages from Oran to Hamburg."

"Why three?" asked Rupert.

"You, Buck and 'Erb," replied John Bull.

"Oh, I see. You have money for your own needs?" observed Rupert in some surprise.

"I'm not going," announced John Bull.

"What!" exclaimed four voices simultaneously, three in English and one in French.

"I'm not going," he reiterated, "for several reasons. . . . To begin with, I've nowhere to go. Secondly, I don't want to go. Thirdly, I did not kill Legros," and, as an inducement to the Bucking Bronco to agree with his wishes, he added, "and fourthly, I may be able to be of some service to Carmelita if only by supporting her testimony with my evidence at the trial—supposing that I am arrested."

"Come off it, old chap," said Rupert. "There are a hundred men whose testimony will support Carmelita's."

"Don't talk tosh, my dear chap, about having nowhere to go, please," said Rupert. "You're coming home with me of course. My mother will *love* to have you.."

"Thanks awfully, but I'm afraid I can't go to England," was the reply. "I must . . ."

John Bull and Reginald Rupert smiled at each other.

"Thanks, awfully, Rupert," said the former, "but I can't go to England. I'm staying here."

"Shucks," observed the American with an air of finality, and turning to Carmelita requested her to fetch the nuggets, the spondulicks, the dope—in short, the wad. Carmelita disappeared into her little room and returned in a few moments with a roll of notes.

"Well, good-bye, my dear old chap," said John Bull taking the American's hand. "You understand all I can't say, don't you? . . . Good-bye."

"Nothin' doin', John," was the answer.

"Hurry him off, Carmelita, we've wasted quite time

enough," said John Bull, turning to the girl. "If he doesn't go now and do his best for himself, he doesn't love you. Do clear him out. It's death or penal servitude if he's caught. He struck Legros before Legros even threatened him—and Legros is dead."

"You hear what Signor Jean Boule says. Are you going?" said Carmelita, turning to the American.

"No, my gal. I ain't," was the prompt reply. "How can I, Carmelita? . . . I'm his pal. . . . Hev' I got ter choose between yew and 'im?"

"Of course you have," put in John Bull. "Stay here and you will never see her again. It won't be a choice between me and her then; it'll be between death and penal servitude."

The Bucking Bronco took Carmelita's face between his hands.

"Little gal," he said, "I didn't reckon there was no such thing as 'love,' outside books, ontil I saw yew. Life wasn't worth a red cent ontil you came hyar. Then every time I gits inter my bunk, I thinks over agin every word I'd said ter yew thet night, an' every word yew'd said ter me. An' every mornin' when I gits up, I ses, 'I shall see Carmelita ter-night,' an' nuthin didn't jar me so long as that was all right. An' when I knowed yew wasn't fer mine, because yew loved Loojey Rivoli, then I ses 'Hell!' An' I didn't shoot him up because I see how much yew loved him. An' I put up with him when he uster git fresh, because ef I'd beat 'im up yew'd hev druv me away from the Caffy, an' life was jest Hell, 'cause I knowed 'e was a low-lifer reptile an' yew'd never believe it. . . . An' now yew've found him out, an' he's gorn, an' yew're *mine*—an' it's too late. . . . Will yew think I don't love yew, little gal? . . . Don't tell me to go or I might sneak off an leave John in the lurch."

"You can't help me, Buck," put in John Bull. "I shall be all right. Who'll you benefit by walking into gaol?"

The American looked appealingly at the girl, and his face was more haggard and anxious than when he was fighting for his life.

"This is my answer, Signor Bouckaing Bronceau," spake Carmelita. "Had you gone without Signor Jean Boule, I should not have followed you. Now I have heard you speak I trust you for ever. Had you deserted your friend in trouble, you would have deserted me in trouble. If Signor Jean Boule will not go, then you must stay, for he struck Legros to save your life, as you struck him to avenge me. Would *I* run away while you paid for that blow? . . ."

Carmelita then turned with feminine wiles upon John Bull.

"Since Signor Jean Boule will not go on pump," she continued, "you must stay and be shot, or sent to penal servitude, and I must be left to starve in the gutter."

Sir Montague Merline came to the conclusion that after all the problem of his immediate future was *not* settled.

"Very well," said he, "come on. We'll cut over to Mendoza's and go to earth. As soon as he has rigged us out, we'll get clear of Sidi."

(He could always give himself up when they had to separate and he could help them no more. Yes, that was it. He would pretend that he had changed his mind and when they had to separate he would pretend that he was going to continue his journey. He would return and give himself up. Having told the exact truth with regard to his share in the matter he would take his chance and face whatever followed.)

A *rivederci*, Carmelita," said he and kissed her.

"*Mille grazie*, Signor," replied Carmelita. "*Buon viaggio*," and wept afresh.

"So long, Miss," said 'Erb. "Are we dahn'arted, *Naow!*"

"We'd better go separately to Mendoza's," said John Bull. "Buck had better come last. I'll go first and bargain with the old devil. We shan't be missed until the morning, but we needn't exactly obtrude ourselves on people."

He went out, followed a few minutes later by Rupert and 'Erb.

Left alone with Carmelita, the Bucking Bronco picked her up in his arms and held her like a baby, as with haggard face and hoarse voice he tried to tell her of his love and of his misery in having to choose between losing her and leaving her. Having arranged with her that he should write to her in the name of Jules Lebrun from an address which would not be in France or any of her colonies, the Bucking Bronco allowed himself to be driven from the back door of the Café. Carmelita's last words were—

"Good-bye, *amato*. When you send for me I shall come, and you need not wait until you can send me money."

3

The good Monsieur Mendoza, discovered in a dirty unsavoury room, at the top of a broken winding staircase of a modestly unobtrusive, windowless house, in a dirty unsavoury slum of the Ghetto, was exceedingly surprised to learn that le Légionnaire Jean Boule had come to *him*, of all people in the world, for assistance in deserting.

The surprise of le bon Monsieur Mendoza was in itself surprising, in view of the fact that the facilitation of desertion was his profession. Still, there it was, manifest upon his expressive and filthy countenance, not to mention his expressive and filthy hands, which waggled, palms upward, beside his shrugged shoulders, as he gave vent to his pained astonishment, not to say indignation, at the Legionary's suggestion. . . . He was not that sort of man. . . . Besides, how did he know that Monsieur le Légionnaire had enough? . . .

John Bull explained patiently to le bon Monsieur Mendoza, of whose little ways he knew a good deal, that he had come to him because he was subterraneously famous in the Legion as the fairy god-papa who could, with a wave of his wand, convert a uniformed Légionnaire into a most convincing civilian. Further, that he was known to be wholly reliable and incorruptibly honest in his dealings with those who could afford to be his god-sons.

All of which was perfectly true.

(Monsieur Mendoza did not display a gilt-lettered board upon the wall of his house, bearing any such inscription as *"Haroun Mendoza, Desertion Agent. Costumier to Poumpistes and All who make the Promenade. Desertions arranged with promptitude and despatch. Perfect Disguises a Specialty. Foreign Money Changed. Healthy Itineraries mapped out. Second-hand Uniforms disposed of. H.M.'s Agents and Interpreters meet All Trains at Oran; and Best Berths secured on all Steamers. Convincing Labelled Luggage Supplied. Special Terms for Parties. . . ."* nor advertise in the *Echo d'Oran*, for it would have been as unnecessary as unwise. . . .)

All very well and all very interesting, parried Monsieur Mendoza, but while compliments garlic no *caldo,* shekels undoubtedly make the mule to go. Had le bon Légionnaire shekels?

No, he had not, but they would very shortly arrive.

"And how many shekels will arrive?" enquired the good Monsieur Mendoza.

"Sufficient unto the purpose," was the answer, and then the bargaining began. For the sum of fifty francs the Jew would provide one Legionary with a satisfactory suit of clothes. The hat, boots, linen and tie consistent with each particular suit would cost from thirty to forty francs extra. . . . Say, roughly, a hundred francs for food and complete outfit per individual. The attention of the worthy Israelite was here directed to the incontrovertible fact that he was dealing, not with the Rothschild brothers, but with four Legionaries of modest ambition and slender purse. To which M. Mendoza replied that he who supped with the Devil required not only a long, but a golden spoon. In the end, it was agreed that, for the sum of three hundred francs, four complete outfits should be provided.

The next thing was the production and exhibition of the promised disguises. Would M. Mendoza display them forthwith, that they might be selected by the time that the other clients arrived?

"*Si, si,*" said M. Mendoza. "*Ciertamente. Con placer.*" It was no desire of M. Mendoza that any client should be expected *comprar a ciegas*—to buy a pig in a poke. No, *de ningun modo.* . . .

Shuffling into an inner room, the old gentleman returned, a few minutes later, laden with a huge bundle of second-hand clothing.

"Will you travel as a party—say two tourists and their servants? Or as a party of bourgeoisie interested in the wine trade? Or—say worthy artisans or working men returning to Marseilles? . . . What do you say to some walnut-juice and haiks—wild men from the *Tanezrafet?* One of you a Negro, perhaps (pebbles in the nostrils), carrying an *angareb* and a bundle. I could let you have some *hashish.* . . . I could also arrange for camels—it's eighty miles to Oran, you know. . . Say, three francs a day, per camel, and *bakshish* for the men. . . . Not *meharis* of course, but you'll be relying more on disguise than speed, for your escape. . . ."

"No," interrupted John Bull. "It only means more trouble turning into Europeans again at Oran. We want to be four obvious civilians, of the sort who could, without exciting suspicion, take the train at a wayside station."

"What nationalities are you?" enquired the Jew.

"English," was the reply.

"Then take my advice and don't pretend to be French," said the other, and added, "Are any of the others gentlemen?"

Sir Montague Merline smiled.

"One," he said.

"Then you and that other had better go as what you are —English gentlemen. If you are questioned, do not speak too good French, but get red in the face and say, 'Goddam' . . . Yes, I think one of you might have a green veil around his hat . . . the others might be horsey or seamen. . . . Swiss waiters. . . .Music-hall artistes. . . . Or German touts, bagmen or spies. . . . Father Abraham! That's an idea! To get deported as a German spy! Ha, ha!" There was a knock at the door. . . .

"*Escuche!*" he whispered with an air of mystery, and added, "*Quien esta ahi?*"

"It's the Lord Mayor o' Lunnon, Ole Cock," announced 'Erb as he entered. "Come fer a new set of robes and' a pearly 'at."

"That one can go either as a dismissed groom, making his way back to England, or an out-of-work Swiss waiter," declared Mendoza, as his artist's eye and ear took in the details of 'Erb's personality.

The two Legionairies divested themselves of their uniforms and put on the clothes handed to them.

Another knock, and Rupert came in.

"Hallo, Willie Clarkson," said he to Mendoza, who courteously replied with a "*Buenos tardes, señor.*"

"That one will be an English caballero," he observed.

"Thought I should never get here," said Rupert. "Got into the wrong rabbit-warren," and took off his tunic.

The Jew did not "place" the Bucking Bronco immediately upon his entrance, but studied him carefully, for some minutes, before announcing that he had better shave off his moustache and be a Spanish fisherman, muleteer, or sailor. If questioned, he might tell some tale in execrable French, of a wife or daughter kidnapped at Barcelona and traced to a Tlemcen brothel. He should rave and be violent and more than a little drunk. . . .

And could the worthy M. Mendoza supply a couple of good revolvers with ammunition?

"*Si, si,*" said M. Mendoza. "*Ciertamente. Coplacer.* A most excellent one of very large calibre and with twenty-eight rounds of ammunition for forty francs, and another of smaller calibre and longer barrel, but with, unfortunately, only eleven rounds for thirty-five francs. . . ."

"Keep your right hand in your pocket, each of you," said M. Mendoza as they parted, "or you'll respectfully salute the first Sergeant you meet. . . ."

4

The two Englishmen, in light summer suits, one wearing white buckskin boots, the other light brown ones, both carrying gloves and light canes, attracted no second glance of attention as they strolled along the boulevard, nor would anyone have suspected the vehement beating of their hearts as they passed the Guard at the gate in the fortification walls.

Similarly innocent of appearance, was an ordinary-looking and humble little person who shuffled along, round-shouldered, shrilly whistling "Viens Poupoule, viens Poupoule, viens."

Nor more calculated to arouse suspicion in the breast of the most observant Guard, was the big, slouching, blue-jowled Spaniard, who rolled along with his *béret* over one eye, and his *cigarillo* pendent from the corner of his mouth. The distance separating these from the two English gentlemen lessened as the latter, leaving the main promenades, passed through a suburb and, turning to the right, followed a quiet country road, which led to a railway station.

Making a wide détour and avoiding the station the four marching parallel with the railway line, headed north for Oran.

So far, so good. They were clear of Sidi-bel-Abbès and they were free. Free, but in the greatest danger. The next

184

thing was to get clear of Africa and from beneath the shadow of the tri-couleur.

"*Free!*" said Rupert, as the other two joined him and John Bull, and drew a long, deep breath, as of relief.

"Not a bit of it, Rupert," said John Bull. "It's merely a case of a good beginning and a sporting chance."

"Anyhow, well begun's half done, Old Thing. I feel like a boy let out of school," and he began to sing—

> "Si tu veux
> Faire mon bonheur,
> Marguerite, Marguerite,
> Si tu veux
> Faire mon bonheur,
> Marguerite, donne-moi ton cœur.

You'll have to sing that, Buck, and put 'Carmelita' for 'Marguerite,' " he added.

"Business first," interrupted John Bull. "This is the programme. We'll go steady all night at the 'quick' and the 'double' alternately, and five minutes' rest to the hour. If we can't do thirty miles by daylight, we're no Legionaries. Sleep all day tomorrow, in the shadow of a boulder, or trees. . . . By the way, we mustn't fetch up too near Les Imberts or we might be seen by somebody while we're asleep. Les Imberts is about thirty miles from Sidi, I believe. Tomorrow night, we'll do another thirty miles and that'll bring us to Wady-el-hotoma. From there I vote we go independently by different trains. . . ."

"That's it," agreed Rupert. "United for defence— separated for concealment. We'd better hang together as far as Wady-what-is-it, in case a Goum patrol overtakes us."

"Why not bung orf from this 'ere Lace Imbear?" enquired 'Erb. "Better'n doin' a kip in the desert, and paddin' the 'oof another bloomin' night. I'm a bloomin' gennelman naow, Ole Cock. I ain't a lousy Legendary."

"Far too risky," replied John Bull. "We should look silly if Corporal Martel and a guard of men from our own *chambrée* were on the next train, shouldn't we? Which-ever of us went into the station would be pinched. The later we hit the line the better, though on the other hand we can't hang about too long. We're between the Devil and the Deep Sea—station-guards and mounted patrols."

It occurred to the Bucking Bronco that his own best "lay" would be an application of the art of "holding her down." In other words, waiting outside Sidi-bel-Abbès railway station until the night train pulled out, and jumping on to her in the darkness and "decking her"—in other words, climbing on to the roof and lying flat. As a past-master in "beating an overland," he could do this without the slightest difficulty, leaving the train as it slowed down into stations and making a détour to pick up again as it left. Before daylight he could leave the train altogether and book as a passenger from the next station (since John strongly advised against walking into Oran by road, as that was the way a penniless Legionary might be expected to arrive). By that means he would arrive at Oran before they were missed at roll-call in the morning. Should he, by any chance, be seen and "ditched" by what he called the "brakemen" and "train-crew," he would merely have "to hit the grit," and wait for the next train. Yes, that's what he would do if he were alone—but the four of them couldn't do it, even if they possessed the necessary nerve, skill and endurance—and he wasn't going to leave them.

"Come on, boys, *en avant, marche*," said John Bull, and they started on their thirty-mile run, keeping a sharp look-out for patrols, and halting for a second to listen for the sound of hoofs each time they changed from the *pas gym-nastique* to the quick march. Galloping hoofs would mean a patrol of Arab gens-d'armes, the natural enemies of the *poumpiste*, the villains who make a handsome bonus on their pay by hunting white men down like mad dogs and shooting them, as such, if they resist. (It is not for nothing that the twenty-five francs reward is paid for the return of a deserter *"dead* or alive.")

On through the night struggled the little band, keeping as far from the railway as was possible without losing its guidance. When a train rolled by in the distance, the dry mouth of the Bucking Bronco almost watered, as he imagined himself "holding her down," "decking her," "riding the blind," or perhaps doing the journey safely and comfortably in a "side-door Pullman" (or goods-waggon).

Before daylight, the utterly weary and footsore travellers threw themselves down to sleep in the middle of a collection of huge boulders that looked as though they had been emptied out upon the plain from a giant sack. During the night they had passed near many villages and had made many détours to avoid others which lay near the line, as well as farms and country houses, surrounded by their fig, orange and citron trees, their groves of date-palms, and their gardens. For miles they had travelled over sandy desert, and for miles through patches of cultivation, vineyards and well-tilled fields. They had met no one and had heard nothing more alarming than the barking of dogs. Now they had reached an utterly desert spot, and it had seemed to the leader of the party to be as safe a place as they would find in which to sleep away the day. It was not too near road, path, building, or cultivation, so far as he could tell, and about a mile from the railway.

The next trouble would be water. They'd probably want water pretty badly before they got it. Perhaps it would rain. That would give them water, but would hardly improve the chances of himself and Rupert as convincing tourists. Thank Heaven they had a spare clean collar each, anyhow. Good old Mendoza. What an artist he was! . . .

John Bull fell asleep.

5

"Look, my brothers! Behold!" cried "Goum" Hassan ibn Marbuk, an hour later, as he reined in his horse and pointed to where the footprints of four men left a track and turned off into the desert. "Franzwazi—they were boots. It is they. Allah be praised. A hundred francs for us, and death for four Roumis. Let us kill the dogs."

Turning his horse from the road, he cantered along the trail of the footsteps, followed by his two companions.

"Allah be praised!" he cried again. "But our Kismet is good. Had it been but five minutes earlier it would have been too dark to notice them."

"The footprints lead into that el Ahagger," he added later, pointing to the group of great boulders.

The three men drew their revolvers and rode in among the rocks. The leading Arab gave a cry of joy and covered Rupert, who was nearest to him. As the Arab shouted, John Bull awoke and, even as he opened his eyes, yelled "*Aux armes!*" at the top of his voice. (He had shouted those words and heard them shouted, off and on, for fifteen years.) As he cried out, Hassan ibn Marbuk changed his aim from Rupert to John Bull and fired. The report of the revolver was instantly followed by three others in the quickest succession. John Bull's cry had awakened the Bucking Bronco and that wary man had slept with his "gun" in his hand. A second after Hassan ibn Marbuk fired, the Bucking Bronco shot him through the head, and then with lightning rapidity and apparently without aim, fired at the other two "Goums" who were behind their leader. Not for nothing had the Bucking Bronco been, for a time, trick pistol-shot in a Wild West show. Hassan ibn Marbuk fell from his saddle, the second Arab hung over his horse's neck, and the third, after a convulsive start, drooped and slowly bent backward, until he lay over the high crupper of his saddle.

"Arabs ain't no derned good with guns," remarked the Bucking Bronco, as he rose to his feet, thought it must, in justice, be admitted that the leading Arab had decidedly screened the view, and hampered the activity of the other two as he emerged from the little gully between the two mighty rocks.

"Gawd luvvus," said 'Erb, sitting up and rubbing his eyes. "Done in three coppers in a bloomin' lump."

The Bucking Bronco secured the horses.

"I say," said Rupert, who was bending over Sir Montague Merlin. "Bull's badly hit."

"Ketch holt, quick," cried the Bucking Bronco, holding out to 'Erb the three reins which he had drawn over the horses' heads. He threw himself down beside his friend and swore softly, as his experienced eye recognized the unmistakable signs.

"Is he dying?" whispered Rupert.

"His number's up," groaned the American.

"Done in by a copper!" marvelled 'Erb, and, putting 'his arm across his face, he leaned against the nearest horse and sobbed. . . . He was a child-like person, and, without knowing it, had come to centre all his powers of affection on John Bull.

The dying man opened his eyes. "Got it where the chicken got the axe," he whispered. "Good-by, Buck.

. . . See you in the . . . Happy Hunting Grounds . . . I hope."

The Bucking Bronco looked at Rupert.

"Carmelita put thisyer brandy in my pocket, Rupert," he said, producing a medicine bottle. "Shall I dope him?"

He coughed and swallowed, his mouth and chin twitched and worked, and tears trickled down his face.

"Can't do much harm," said Rupert, and took the bottle from the American's shaking hand.

The brandy revived the mortally wounded man.

"Good-bye, Rupert," he said. "I advise you to go straight down to Les Imberts station . . . and take the next train. . . . There will be a patrol . . . after this patrol . . . before long. You can't lie up here for long now. . . . Buck might take a horse and gallop for it. . . . Lie up somewhere else. . . . And ride to Oran tonight. . . . 'Erb should go as Rupert's servant . . . or by a different train. . . . Remember Mendoza's tips."

The stertorous, wheezy breathing was painfully interrupted by a paroxysm of coughing.

"Much pain, old chap?" asked the white-faced Rupert, as he wiped the blood from his friend's lips.

"No," whispered Sir Montague Merlin. "I am dead . . . up to . . . the heart. . . . Expanding bullet. . . . Lungs . . . and spine . . . I . . . expect . . . Shan't be . . . long."

"Anything I can do—any message or anything?" asked Rupert.

The dying man closed his eyes.

The Bucking Bronco was frankly blubbering. Turning to the dead "Goum" who had shot his friend, he swore horribly, and deplored that the man was dead and beyond the reach of his further vengeance. He fell instantly silent as his stricken friend spoke again.

"If you . . . get . . . to Eng . . . land, Rupert . . . will . . . you go . . . to . . . my wife? She's Lady . . ." he whispered.

"Yes—Lady . . . *who?*" asked Rupert eagerly.

"NO," continued the dying man, in a stronger voice, as he opened his eyes. "I never . . . had . . . a . . . wife."

Silence again.

"Why *Marguerite* . . . My . . . darling . . . girl. *Darling* . . . at . . . last *Marguerite*"

Sir Montague Merline's problem was solved, and the last of his wages paid. . . .

6

The Honorable Reginald Rupert Huntingten never forgot the hour that followed. The three broken-hearted men buried their friend in a shallow, sandy grave and piled a cairn of rocks and stones above the spot. It gave them a feeling akin to pleasure to realize that every minute devoted to this labor of love, lessened their chance of escape.

Their task accomplished, they shook hands and parted— the Bucking Bronco incapable of speech. Before he rode away, Huntingten thrust a piece of paper into his hand, upon which he had scribbled: "*R. R. Huntingten, Elham Old Hall, Elham, Kent,*" and said, "Wire me there. Or —better still, come—and we'll arrange about Carmelita."

The Bucking Bronco rode away in the cool of the morning.

Having settled by the toss of a coin whether he or 'Erb should attempt the next train, he gave that grief-stricken warrior the same address and invitation.

With a crushing hand-clasp they parted, and Huntingten, with a light and jaunty step, and a sore and heavy heart, set forth for the station of Les Imberts to put his nerve and fortune to the test.

"WELL, GOOD NIGHT, my own darling Boy," said the beautiful Lady Huntingten, as she lit her candle from that of her son, by the table in the hall. "Don't keep Father up all night, if he and General Strong come to your bedroom."

"Good night, dearest," replied he, kissing her fondly.

Setting down her candlestick, she took him by the lapels of his coat as though loth to let him out of her sight and part with him, even for the night.

"O, but it is good to have you again, darling," she murmured, gazing long at his bronzed and weather-beaten face. "You won't go off again for a long, long time, will you? And we must keep your promise to that wholly delightful 'Erb, if it's humanly possible. But I really cannot picture him as a discreet and silent-footed valet. . . . I simply loved him and the Bucking Bronco. I don't know which is th more precious and priceless. . . . I do so wonder whether he'll be happy with his Carmelita. . . . I shall love seeing her."

"Yes, 'Erb and Buck are great birds," replied her son, "but poor old John Bull was the chap."

"Poor man, how awful—with freedom in sight. . . . You knew nothing of his story?" she asked.

"Absolutely nothing, dearest. All I know about him is that he was one the very best. Funny thing, y' know, Mother—I simply lived with that chap, night and day, for a year, and know no more about him than just that. That, and his marks—and by Jove, he'd got some. . . . Simply a mass of scars, beginning with the crown of his head, where was a hole you could have laid your thumb in. Been about a bit, too; fought in China, Madagascar, West Africa, the Sahara and Morocco, in the Legion. Certainly been in the British Army—in Africa, too. I fancy he'd been a sailor as well—anyhow he'd been in Japan and got the loveliest bit of tattooing I ever set eyes on. Wonderful colors—snake winding round his wrist and up his forearm. Thing looked alive though it had been done for over thirty years. Nagasaki, I think he said. . . ." He yawned hugely. "But here I am rambling on about a person you never saw, and keeping you up," he added. He bent to kiss his mother again.

"Mother!—*darling!* Don't you feel well? Here, I'll get you a little brandy."

Lady Huntingten was clutching at the edge of the table, and staring at her son, white-lipped. Her face looked drawn and suddenly old.

"No, no," she said. "Come back. I—sometimes—a little . . ." and she sat down on the oak settle beside the table.

"The heat . . ." she continued incoherently. "There I'm all right now. Tell me some more about this—John Bull. . . . He *is* dead? . . . You buried him yourself, you said."

"Yes, poor old chap, it was awful."

"And he gave you no messages for his people? He did not tell you his real name?"

"No. Nothing. He's taken his story with him. The last words he said were 'Will you go and tell my wife, Lady . . .' and there he pulled himself up, and said he never had a wife. But he had, I'm sure—and he called to her by her Christian name. As he died, he cried out, '*At last—my darling—*'"

"*Marguerite,*" whispered Lady Huntingten.